# King of Hearts
## *Book One*
## *The Giovanni*

# C.A. SZAREK

King of Hearts
C.A. Szarek
The Giovanni Book One



**Paper Dragon Publishing**
**North Richland Hills, TX**



eBook ISBN: 978-1-941151-39-6
Paperback ISBN: 978-1-941151-40-2

Published in the United States of America

First eBook Edition: October, 2019
First Print Edition: October, 2019

<u>Crossing Forces—Romantic Suspense—</u>
**<u>WHOLE SERIES ALSO IN AUDIO!</u>**

Collision Force (Book One)
Cole in Her Stocking (A Crossing Forces Christmas)—*FREE read!*
Chance Collision (Book Two)
Calculated Collision (Book Three)
Collision Control (Book Four)
Weekend Collision (A Crossing Forces HEA Story)—*FREE read!*
Superior Collision (Book Five)
Incendiary Collision (Book Six)—*Coming soon!*


<u>The King's Riders—Epic Fantasy Romance—</u>
**<u>WHOLE SERIES ALSO IN AUDIO!</u>**

Sword's Call (Book One)
Love's Call (Book Two)
Rogue's Call (Book Three)
Fate's Call (A Novella from the World of the

King's Riders)


<u>Highland Secrets—Historical Fantasy/ Time Travel</u>

The Tartan MP3 Player (Book One)
The Fae Ring (Book Two)
The Parchment Scroll (Book Three)
Highlander's Portrait (A Highland Secrets Story)—*Coming soon to Audio!*
Highland Valentine (A Highland Secrets Story)—*only .99*
The Princess and The Laird (A Highland Secrets Prequel)


<u>Highland Treasures—Historical Fantasy/ Time Travel</u>

Highland Oath (Book One)
Highland Essence (Book Two)—*Coming soon!*


<u>Anthologies</u>

Deep in the Hearts of Texas—*FREE read!*
    Story: Promise (A Crossing Forces Companion)

This book was a long time in coming. So, it's dedicated
to anyone who perseveres. Even when life is difficult,
you can still follow your dreams.

He dived for the cellphone vibrating across his coffee table, and knocked over an empty glass. Didn't stop to grab it, because there was probably only one more ring before voicemail kicked in, and Gio was on call.

The screen told him it was Elise.

His gaze shot to the clock above his flat-screen; 9:37. It was unusual for his sister to call him so late, even if she was working into the night at the casino. "Hey," was hurried, after the swipe of his thumb.

There was a pause, then a heavy sound, as if she sighed. "Nico."

He sat taller.

Like most people in his world, she never called him by his given name.

"Lise, what's wrong?" The cop in him wouldn't let him freak, but Gio swallowed when she failed, again, to answer before taking another breath.

"It's Dad."

He frowned. Instinct told him to bark that Antonio Giovanni could go to hell, but she'd only get more upset, and something was obviously wrong already.

She'd never been down with his ghosting routine on the fam.

He cleared his throat. "What happened?" he made himself ask.

His sister sniffled as if she was crying, or trying hard not to, and suddenly he wanted to shoot something.

"He collapsed in his office. We called 9-1-1, but—" Elise had to stop stifle a sob, and he cursed.

"But what?" Gio glanced at the police radio next to the glass he'd tipped over. The green light indicated it was on, but the volume was low. If he'd had it turned up, he might've heard the dispatcher sending the brigade to *The Giovanni*.

He must've dozed off on the couch after stuffing his face with pizza he'd have to run off in the morning.

"He was unconscious when the paramedics got here. We thought it was a heart attack or stroke, but it's not." Again, his younger sister pushed words through tears.

"What's wrong with him?" At least he'd managed to *sound* like he gave a shit.

He didn't—mostly.

Elise took a big gulp of air in his ear. "Pancreatic cancer. The doctor said he was diagnosed months ago. *Months* ago, Gio. Dad's been hiding it."

"Son of a bitch."

She was sobbing in earnest now, and he wanted to punch their old man for putting her through this.

His give-a-damn wasn't totally broken where their father was concerned, after all.

Most days, it was.

"He…he hasn't agreed to any treatment. He won't discuss it with me."

"Of course, he won't." Gio shook his head and rolled his eyes to his ceiling. His bastard of a father had to be a fucking tough guy.

Nothing could ever touch Big Tony Giovanni.

The old man certainly wasn't about to show weakness in front of his only daughter. His father believed girls shouldn't worry about things like that. They should get married, and let their husbands think for them, have a few babies dangling from arms and hips.

Elise complained about the diatribe all the time. She'd hit twenty-eight on her last birthday and hadn't done either yet. She'd excelled at numbers instead. Ran several departments at the casino, including the main accounting hub.

Ol' Pops bitched about it frequently, but for some reason he'd never stopped her. Maybe Big Tony wasn't completely stupid after all.

"Where are you now?" Gio asked, trying to sound as calm as he could.

"The hospital."

"Where're Dom and Sam?" Their brothers had better be there to support Elise, or he would kick their asses.

"Sam's in with him now. I stepped out to call you."

"Where's Dom?"

She sighed. "Not answering his phone."

Gio snorted.

*Not a shocker.*

The brother between Elise and Sam had middle-child syndrome, even at twenty-six.

"Hope he didn't get picked up."

"Me too, Dad doesn't need additional stress right now."

"Don't worry about it. If he did, I'll take care of it."

His sister didn't comment.

He'd had many phone calls from a street cop to save his brother's ass, and the last time, when Dom had been stopped for drunk driving, Gio had told the sergeant to arrest him. His brother was too old to be fucking up like he was, and needed a lesson.

Oddly enough, it was one thing their dad agreed with him on. But he'd still bailed his ne'er-do-well third child out of jail the next morning, and sic'd their vast legal team on Vegas PD.

Like the boys in blue had actually done anything wrong. He should've paid them to rough Dom up a bit. Maybe it'd be a deterrent to the back of another police car. Then again, maybe real time behind bars was the only thing that'd do the trick.

Dad would never let that happen. He'd bail Dom out no matter how many times it took.

That was the thing about Big Tony; he'd say one thing and do another.

*Hypocritical bastard.*

Dom had been pissed he hadn't rescued him, but Daddy had come galloping in on the white horse, and Gio would eventually work things out with his brother; always did. The guy was still a touch irked with him, no matter a few months had passed.

Things with Dad — not so much.

Guess being a womanizing drunk was okay, but being a cop landed one in black-sheep territory, and Big Tony didn't speak to *that* son.

But hey, at least their baggage was mutual.

"Gio."

He cringed. His nickname had been so serious, no trace of tears making it shake.

He wouldn't like whatever she was about to say, but he made himself ask anyway. "What?"

"I really need you to come home."

K<br>♥

Gian shuffled through the papers he found in every desk drawer, since the three filing cabinets had been a bust.

*Nothing.*

"Fuck."

Where could the old man have left it?

Would he even keep something like that here?

God knew Big Tony Giovanni wouldn't put any info on a computer hard drive or the cloud. He was famous for saying he didn't trust technology, so even a thumb-drive was out.

Gian had to search for good, old-fashioned sheets of dead trees, likely of the leather-bound variety. Besides, with something has aged as what he sought, it made sense it'd be old school, even considering the man's allergy to modern-day vices.

Elise nagged her father about working smart, not

hard, regarding technology all the time, but it wasn't like the man would let his daughter tell him what to do.

She was lucky he let her use whatever software she needed for her departments of the casino. All for the better, because it made it easier to cook the books through the computer—not that she knew what Gian had been up to.

The recent overhaul of the whole accounting department had been something he'd driven, and it was him who'd been at Elise's side to convince the old man it was time to step into the twenty-first century. Had Gian not been involved, the changes would've never happened.

It'd been pure luck that the codger had collapsed tonight, and his fiancée had rushed to the hospital with her youngest brother after the ambulance.

He'd finally had time to search the office without a chance of being caught.

The casino president and founder treated his office as an inner sanctum, and rarely let people in, let alone unattended. As close as he'd weaseled to Big Tony, he'd never been alone inside. That leeriness, along with the older man's conceit, led to Gian's belief that he'd keep the ledger close. It was an heirloom, a slice of history.

He *would* find it.

It had to be in *this* room.

Now, it'd been too long, and Elise had already called. Told him she was going to head back soon, since her father had been sedated and was resting comfortably.

There wasn't anything else she could do at the

hospital that night. She'd been trying hard not to sob through the whole short conversation.

It wasn't a heart attack or stroke.

Pancreatic cancer.

It was a stroke all right. A stroke of luck for Gian.

*Couldn't have planned it better myself.*

He could only hope schmoozing with the son of a bitch over the last nine months had gained what he'd sought—a starring role in Big Tony's will.

If he hadn't earned the right on his own, finding the ledger would do the trick. Nothing wrong with a little blackmail, after all.

Boning his hot daughter hadn't been a chore, but that was about the only thing that hadn't.

It'd taken months of sweeping her off her feet to slip a ring on her finger, and he had every intention of going through with the wedding.

Old School Italians like Big Tony wouldn't consider leaving him even a poker chip if he didn't buy the cow. Not that the old man knew Gian had very much sampled the milk.

Out of all the requirements of his mission as his alias, Marco Fratelli, he couldn't complain about Elise. He'd actually enjoyed his time with her. She was fiery, smart, gorgeous, and sweet. If he was a different man, he might've had a twinge of guilt over hoodwinking her.

She was good in the sack, too. Had kept his interest, so he'd not had to supplement fulfilling his needs with other females. Probably for the better, so he didn't have to hide cheating.

Her younger brothers were the overprotective sort, and even the made-of-trouble Dominic, who was usually mired in his own affairs, didn't care for him much, or the lightning fast closeness Gian had gained to their old man.

Salvatore, whom everyone called Sam, was young and naïve, so he wasn't an issue, yet. During the week, he wasn't around at the casino much, since he was still in college. He didn't have many responsibilities around the place, unlike Gian's fiancée, who ran the accounting departments and headed the middle-management staff over the cashiers.

Her sharpness and involvement had made getting his laundering business up and running a challenge, but he'd weaseled in with *her* as much as her father, of course.

She fancied herself in love with him, and had trusted him more and more in the numbers game, so he'd gained some control over the dough, too.

There was another brother, Elise's older sibling. Big Tony's firstborn, but according to his fiancée, the man and their father didn't jive.

All for the better, because the oldest Giovanni child was a police detective.

Gian wasn't afraid of cops, but he didn't need a dead one on his hands, either, if 'things' happened. With the risks he'd taken, something *could* happen. He was trying to fly under the radar, and murder wasn't on the menu unless it had to be.

Eventually the man would end up his brother-in-law down the road. Although, he wouldn't be an issue in Gian's eventual succession. According to Elise, her older brother had no interest in the casino.

Also in his favor; Big Tony *wouldn't* leave everything to his only daughter. He was really conservative, after all, and Elise might be a math genius, but she was still expected to marry and provide heirs that way, not be one herself.

He smiled. From his quick trip to Google, Gian had discovered there wasn't a high survival rate for pancreatic cancer.

This news was better than taking out a hit on the old man—which he'd considered. Gian's father might be pissed off, but in the long run, he'd been prepared for the fallout.

With Giovanni funds as his business base, he didn't need his father's money. Hadn't told his old man a thing yet, but the truth remained.

They hadn't spoken since he'd been kicked out of the family, of course, but this plan he'd concocted could—no, *would*—get him back into Luciano Falcone's good graces, as well as back into the family business.

He was going to prove himself with real numbers, real cash flow. Prove he could help clean the money from his father's doings, and they could stay *way* under the radar.

*The Giovanni* had been around for forty years, and one of the perks of Big Tony turning his back on the family and keeping his nose clean was all the federal agencies didn't pay him much attention. Gian could keep it that way long term, and show his father he sure as hell knew what he was doing.

The Falcone patriarch would be pleased Elise had accepted Gian's marriage proposal, so the man would forgive him, eventually. It would be a kick in the balls to Big Tony for the old feud. Maybe when the wedding invitation arrived, provided he could put his real name on it.

When his fiancée got back, he'd be appropriately affected by the horrible news. He'd hold her while she sobbed. Listen to her rant and rave about her stubborn father.

Then he'd kick his plan up a notch.

As soon as he found the damn ledger.

Noise at the double glass doors, the entrance to the executive suites, caught his attention, and he straightened from the desk, shutting the top drawer and securing it.

He'd picked his way through the lock, but he'd taken care not to break it. It'd been easy-peasy. Big Tony should do something about that. He was usually pretty security-conscious, but he'd probably thought no one would have the balls to break into his desk.

Gian narrowed his eyes and calculated a quick reason for his presence in the boss' office. Then he waited to see who was about to join him.

*I really need you to come home.*

Elise's words reverberated until his brain hurt.

He stared at the dark screen of his phone. The device sat on the table in front of him, taunting.

Gio had ended their call about ten minutes before, and he'd been sitting on the edge of his couch since, elbows on knees, rocking like a fucking psycho. Wished with all his might he could take back the promise she'd dragged out of him.

Unlike his father, *he* didn't break his word.

*Thank God for small favors.*

If he smoked, he would've lit up a bunch of the motherfuckers, imitating a smokestack. If he still drank, he would've downed a twelve — no, a twenty-four pack. Maybe a keg. Of course, he'd always liked the hard stuff better. Maybe two or three bottles of Lag?

*Home.*

Shouldn't be a volatile word, right?

His little sister hadn't meant the house the four of them had been raised in, in the suburbs of Sin City.

She'd meant the monstrosity on the Vegas strip.

The building his father cared about more than his damn family.

*The Giovanni.*

"Piece of shit." Gio couldn't confirm whether he meant the glowing lights of the huge edifice or the man it was named after.

He'd never wished for a murder case before, but right then, he would've taken a dozen bodies. A bloody messy massacre scene—a good dismemberment even, Dexter Morgan style. He'd rather that than get on his Ducati and take his ass to the casino.

Or the hospital.

Elise hadn't asked *that* of him. Maybe she knew he wouldn't, *couldn't,* look into the dark eyes that matched hers.

*Just get off your ass. You promised.*

The pep talk wasn't cutting it.

Gio dragged his hand down his face, then scratched the stubble on his cheek. He'd lose a damn bet at work if the phone didn't ring. The guys had wagered he'd go through his required on-call period without catching a case, and he never had before.

He'd slapped fifty bucks down, insisting he wasn't that lucky.

"First time for fucking everything."

He growled and knocked his fist into his forehead. Then did it a few more times. Could he knock his own brain loose until he passed out?

*Excuses, excuses.*

Elise rarely asked anything of him. However, this was too much. Even if he was grateful his sister had been the glue of their family after their mother had died, eight long years ago.

Same amount of time since he'd spoken to his father. At least a real conversation without shouting and cursing in Italian.

Gio spoke to his siblings regularly. Even Dom. Yet, he refused to be in the same room as Big Tony, and after tricking him one Christmas a few years ago, Elise had given up on chiding him about it, most of the time.

He wanted to puke, but managed to stand. He was no desire to experience pizza 2.0.

He made his muscles haul his ass off the couch. Stretched, but not because he needed to. He was stalling. Wanted to roll his eyes at himself, but that wouldn't help his stupid fucking promise, either.

She wanted him at the casino—said she'd meet him in their father's office. What else she'd expected of him, Elise hadn't said, but it didn't matter.

Going into that place was stepping into a past he didn't want anything to do with. He'd never gotten over the hurt and rejection from Big Tony, but there was more to it than that.

Inside *The Giovanni* was the last time he'd seen his mother alive.

Then, also inside that monstrosity was where he'd lost the other female who'd been most important to him—a US Marshal he never should've had in his bed.

The one who'd gotten away. Had never contacted him after a drunken night that'd ended with a huge fight and her fleeing.

It'd been his wake up call to quit drinking. It hadn't

brought her back.

He'd never had the balls to track her down, either.

Gio snatched his keys from the hook on the wall right inside his front door and growled.

*Let's get this the fuck over with.*

It was cool outside, but his forehead was like a faucet; sweat rolled down his temple even before he jogged up the ramp into his complex's parking garage. He probably should take his GTO instead of the bike, since he was so rattled, but it was the Ducati, his second pride and joy, he went to first.

Motorcycles were another thing Big Tony didn't approve of, so maybe that was the real reason he swung his leg over and planted his ass on his favorite toy.

The drive was agonizing even though it was short, and he parked on the private level of the garage for the casino higher-ups, half-shocked his fob still worked. Probably due to his sister.

Gio made his way inside, strolling through the bling, and the lights and the sounds, electronic beeps and bops, and even the occasional siren when someone hit it big.

He winced at the cigarette smoke clouding the atmosphere, scowled at the alcohol, and disregarded the little waitresses in their scant uniforms.

Eventually he went through hallways that weren't open to the public. His chest was tight, and breathing hurt. Like a vise was gripping his lungs. No shocker there.

This wasn't a puppies and rainbows homecoming.

The pressure was stifling, and his dad wasn't even

on the premises.

Dark walls surrounded him, a soft glow from dim sconces every few feet didn't offer more than the exact light needed to navigate the corridors. Why spend money on electricity here?

Only a fraction of the people coming into the place—employees—would see the back alleys of the huge place.

He started honest-to-God shaking before he made the turn that would take him to the executive offices.

*Fuck this.*

Gio couldn't leave. He'd promised his sister.

Hell, *The Giovanni* was still better than the hospital.

He missed the first time he reached for the ornate handle on the glass door leading to the lobby where his dad's receptionist would be sitting at the huge dark wood desk. The gigantic thing was curved and made whoever sat behind it seem like a hobbit, or a gnome. The computer monitor wasn't visible until one got closer.

He cleared his throat. Twice.

To the right there was a hallway that lead to a few back offices; Elise had one there, but hell if he knew who held the other casino execs were these days. To the left was a set of double glass doors that led to the throne room—his father's office.

Gio cursed some more and ordered his feet to take him to the left, as opposed to whirling him around and running.

He'd never been a coward. Had he?

Suddenly it was eight years ago, where the

argument of his life had occurred with Big Tony in that very office.

Then he'd gone down to the bar, where he'd had another fight.

A different fight that'd resulted in too many shots to count, a shattered heart and shrunken balls.

"Fuck. Me." He ran his hand through his hair. Still shaking his head, Gio tugged himself from the past and pushed his way toward his father's office.

Big Tony wasn't in there. He could go in and wait for Elise with no risk of adding to his already huge headfuck.

There was a dark-haired man in an expensive-looking dove gray suit slightly bent over the desk. He closed a drawer and straightened when Gio rested his hand on the handle and pushed.

Had the door not made a slight noise, he could've watched the stranger longer, because the dude hadn't spotted him.

"Who're you?" The demand fell out when he was only one or two steps inside. He held back his alarm, and bit back the instinct to insert '*the fuck*' in his inquiry. No need to be rude to a guy he didn't know. Maybe he had a reason to be in Big Tony's office.

Maybe things had changed since the time he'd been away; maybe his dad wasn't as protective of the place as he'd always been. The office was his private inner space at the casino.

Invite only.

He'd never even taken meetings in it; there was a private conference room for those.

"I could ask the same of you." The guy flashed a slimy smile that raised Gio's hackles.

Something was off about this man. He'd never seen him before, and he appeared to be around his age.

They sized each other up, but he didn't answer the dude's statement.

The suit was Armani, if he hadn't lost his eye for such things. Dark loafers were equally as expensive—looked like Ferragamos—and the glint from the gold watch-face shouted Rolex.

Gio couldn't name the cologne off hand, maybe the scent was *a la sleaze ball*?

With as expensive as the asshat looked, it was probably Clive No. 1.

Couldn't name a reason, but an instant dislike hit his tongue like he'd sucked on a lemon. Or, his cop-instinct was telling him to be wary.

*Who's this loser?*

The door opening again caught their collective attention, and the man looked away, his expression relaxing, but it went unreadable.

"Gio!"

His sister's pretty face was made of relief when their eyes met, and his peripherals caught the douche-canoe rounding the desk to come stand beside him.

"I'm so glad you're here."

"I said I'd come."

She wrapped her arms around him and her familiar scent of women's Dior wiggled its way over his senses, almost like coming home was the right thing to do after all.

He held her for as long as she allowed.

Gio had missed Elise. They'd always been close. Best friends in a lot of ways. Generally united in their mutual ire aimed at their father, among other things.

"I know," she whispered, and he heard the smile in her voice.

Their eyes met when he released her. She appeared tired, and he didn't like it. Her naturally blonde hair was shorter than when he'd last seen her, dancing over her shoulders, and she had dark circles under her deep brown eyes, but her face was still young and pretty, despite her obvious exhaustion. His sister had always been tall, slender and lovely.

He could do without the tight red dress she was wearing, but at least the little number went past her knees and he didn't have the insta-need to cover her up. Some of the getup in her wardrobe was in his *hell no* category. She was his younger sister, after all.

Big Tony agreed with him on that one, too.

*Naturally.*

"You've met Marco?" Her eyes lit up, wiping some of the fatigue away.

She moved to the douchebag's side, and the asshole threw his arm around her, pulling her tight to him.

*Much* too close to his Armani-covered ass.

He narrowed his eyes. "Marco?" Gio practically growled. Again, his logical side popped up that he had no reason to dislike this man.

"My fiancé."

His world spun and he had to remind himself he

could not shoot someone he didn't know, no matter how his trigger finger itched to grab the Sig at his waist. "Your what?" he blurted. He hollered at himself to not show his abject horror at her revelation. Just because the guy's clothes bled *yuppie* didn't mean he really was cocktwit.

*Right?*

His eyes landed the guy again. He couldn't form words right away.

Marco wasn't as tall as Gio, and he was definitely Italian. No doubt Big Tony was on board with that.

He looked back at Elise.

She gazed at her *fiancé* like this loser hung the moon.

"Marco Fratelli." Armani shoved his hand out for a shake. His smile was pleasant enough. "You must be the older brother. Nico, right?"

Gio frowned. How did this man know of *him*, but Elise had never said a word in reverse? Especially…engaged?

His eyes zoned in on Elise's left hand. Sure enough, that third finger sported a gleaming rock the size of Texas.

He shot a glance at his sister's face, and she shrugged. Offered a half-smile. She wasn't going to explain now.

Gio didn't like it. At. All.

His eyes landed back on Marco.

*Why don't I like him?*

He had no basis for his first impression, given the guy hadn't been anything but polite when he'd been—

admittedly—prickly.

Gio forced his arm to move, to meet the dude's gesture. He grunted when Armani returned quite a strong grip. Was stating he wasn't a pussy.

That was good, too, right?

"Fratelli, huh?" He told himself to be nice, congenial, and relax. Didn't bother confirming his identity. If Armani wasn't a fidiot, he'd assume he was correct.

He immediately preferred his own moniker for the douche.

The guy smiled wider, but something still wasn't right. "Yeah, I guess our dads were friends back in the day."

That was the second time something felt *off* about the guy.

His sister intended to marry *this* twatwaffle?

Gio narrowed his eyes, but failed to discern anything. He studied Elise again. In the almost ten years he'd been a cop, he'd learned not to question his kneejerk instincts. His gut was shouting there was something off…wrong…about Marco Fratelli.

He couldn't pin it down, and he couldn't put his 40 cal to the guy's head. Not only because the subject may or may not be banging his sister.

*Nope. Not going there.*

If he did, Armani would definitely have a messed up suit…not to mention a face to match the rips and holes in fine fabric.

"Gio…" Elise chewed on her bottom lip. "We have to talk about Dad."

THREE

Maddie sighed and glanced at her Fitbit for the current time, and dragged her feet to baggage claim.

She wasn't glad to be back in Sin City. Wasn't looking forward to checking in at the office. She *especially* wasn't happy to have to form a taskforce with Las Vegas Metro PD, even if it was one of the rare times she'd be in command.

*He* was still there.

She'd verified it.

Gio was a detective now, not the patrol cop she'd first met eight long years ago.

Eight years that felt like twenty; or maybe a lifetime ago.

At least she got a small reprieve, and didn't have to show up anywhere until the next day. Maddie already had the keys to her new place and she hoped they hadn't found her a dump. The apartment was ten minutes off the strip, so she had a tiny bit of hope.

She'd be staying in Vegas after the case was wrapped, even though it'd originated in Chicago. A new, *very* unwanted post.

Her cell went off, indicating her sister's specific ringtone. She hit the green circle and put it to her ear.

"Hi, Mommy!" Jacob's high voice made her smile genuinely.

"Hi, baby."

"Are you there yet?"

"Just landed. Gonna grab my stuff and head to our new place."

Jake buzzed like a motor in her ear. "How was the plane ride? I can't wait to go on the plane!"

She laughed. Her seven-year-old was airplane-obsessed. Maddie could picture him holding his arms out, running all over their soon-to-be old living room, as if he was flying. He did it multiple times a day.

He'd cried when they'd parted ways at O'Hare; more because he couldn't join her past security and see the plane than because he'd miss her, she suspected.

"Aunt Jamie will bring you down soon, sweets. I promise, just like we talked about."

"When? When do I get on the plane?" Sound went in and out and he panted, as if he was jumping up and down.

"Jake, *sit* on your bed while you talk to me." She'd told him a hundred times his mattress wasn't a trampoline.

Her son didn't answer. Then there were grappling sounds, as if he'd dropped the phone, or handed it over.

Jamie laughed in her ear. "He has his arms crossed, and he demanded to know how you knew," her sister said by way of greeting.

"Great, I have to yell at him, and he ditches me. Tell him I know everything 'cause I'm his mom." Maddie sighed, somehow deflated by her little boy's minor show of temper.

"Nah, I had to wrestle the phone from him."

She could hear her sister's grin.

"Liar."

Jamie laughed again. "You're right. And he rolled his eyes when I explained your omnipotence."

Maddie had to smile. Wished they'd done a video call so she could see his little face—even sporting a gold-medal pout. "He'll get used to it, he's only seven."

"Oh, I've already warned him how difficult you are when one is a teenager."

It was her turn to roll her eyes. "*You* were the difficult one, as I remember it."

"Hmmm, revisionist historian, I think."

Maddie chuckled. "I miss you guys already."

"I love you, Mommy!" Jake yelled in the background.

"Glad I'm so quickly forgiven." Her heart melted a little, and she couldn't wait to spread kisses all over her little guy's face again. Even if he complained and tried to push her away.

Her job often took her from her son's side, but this time, Jake and Jamie were joining her. Her sister lived with them in Chicago, and had agreed to come to Las Vegas. It shouldn't be more than a week or two, and they'd be together again as their familiar unit of three.

Jamie had already put her two weeks in at her job, and their stuff was already shipped, even though they didn't have to be out of the old place until the end of the month.

The live-in childcare was a bonus, but Maddie had raised Jamie on her own from age nineteen—to Jamie's tender age eight—and she couldn't imagine life without her close by. Even at twenty-four, Jamie was more like a daughter than sister.

Their parents had died in a car crash; hit by a drunk driver, which was part of the reason she'd gone into law enforcement.

Her sister laughed. "I told him to be nice."

"You're not supposed to ruin it."

Jamie giggled again, as unrepentant as always. Something Jake had picked up, too. Not always a positive thing, but Maddie still loved them.

"I'm glad you guys called, but I just got to baggage claim. Let me get settled, and I'll call you later. I'm eager to see the apartment. Hopefully I can get most of our stuff set up before you get down here."

They chatted for another minute, and she told them she loved them before ending the call.

Before they stepped one foot off the plane, she needed to decide what exactly to tell Gio.

Maddie cringed.

The blurted confession when he'd been too drunk to comprehend had crushed her, *and* pissed her off. Her lover hadn't retained a damn thing, and the hurt over that had only carried her justification so far.

Right?

Her reasons had been sound—eight years ago.

The more time that'd passed, the more her baby

grew, the weaker they'd gotten, sounding more like poor excuses as the years flew by.

Jake wasn't a baby anymore. He was a sturdy, smart-as-a-whip kid, and he would only get older, ask more questions.

If Gio never forgave her, she wouldn't blame him.

Now that they'd be living in the same city, Maddie couldn't keep silent anymore. Not that geography should've made a difference; it only made more guilt swirl in her gut.

She wasn't looking forward to seeing him again. Since she had to work with his police department, she'd eventually have to face him. Not to mention how her case was interwoven with his family. Avoiding him would be impossible.

Maddie closed her eyes and took a breath. Grounding herself was going to have to be a part of her new routine.

K
♥

Gio shoved his heel into the kickstand on his bike. He sighed as he tucked his helmet under his arm and dismounted. Sometimes he left his headgear with the Ducati, but today he'd leave it on his desk.

He loved his job, but for some reason his feet fought his intent to enter Las Vegas Metro PD.

What'd happened last night churned in his head as much as his gut. Like a movie stuck on a loop, but all the worst parts — when the villain was on screen — were on slow-mo. Haunting him.

His dad. His sister. That cockwaffle, Marco.

The way Elise had regarded her *fiancé*, like the ass was her salvation, left more than a bad taste in his mouth. Not because she'd finally settled on a spouse, but because his instant disdain for the guy shouted something was *wrong*.

*Fiancé? Jesus.*

He'd have to figure it out, since Armani would be family soon. He was still a little more than bothered that his sister, as close as they were, had neglected to tell him about Marco, no matter how much of a douche the guy was.

Gio snorted. Well, it wasn't like he wasn't used to ignoring family, but he couldn't do that to her. Wouldn't put that added stress on her.

So he'd have to figure out just what it was about her man and get over it. Or convince Elise she'd picked the wrong dude.

*That* sounded like a plan.

His sister had been upset when Gio wouldn't agree to go to the hospital. The casino was one thing; he couldn't bring himself to look Big Tony in the eye. Didn't know when he could.

If he could. Ever.

She'd guilted him.

Their father could be...dying.

His youngest brother, Sam, had found them, and his youthful face had worn such grim turmoil, it'd made Gio want to puke all over again.

Elise had said she needed his help. *They* needed it. They'd freaking double-teamed him.

She and Sam wanted the four of them; provided

they could find their brother Dom — to approach their dad at the hospital and convince him to start treatment for the cancer. A controlled environment, his sister had said.

Gio couldn't do it.

The disappointment on Elise's face, as well as reflected in Sam's eyes had slayed him. Like a gut shot in an unfair fight.

Dom was another story. As of when he'd left *The Giovanni*, the guy was still unaccounted for. Not answering calls or texts from any of his siblings, and no one at the casino had seen him.

He was probably holed up with some chick, and Gio had left that for Elise to clean up, too, but he'd told her to call when their dickhead little bro finally showed.

He'd try to have a heart-to-heart with him so she wouldn't have to.

"Fuck my life," Gio whispered as he fobbed into the back door of the PD.

He'd just wrapped up a double homicide, so he didn't have work to distract him, provided the murder board in Robbery/Homicide was empty. Well, it'd never be empty, but he couldn't remember the detective order; wasn't sure who was up next.

No matter how he tried to push it to the back of his mind, he couldn't banish the desperation on his siblings' expressions from the previous night.

What Gio didn't want to face teetered between the idea of losing his father, and things he didn't want to reconcile.

Was he being selfish?

Of course he was.

Self-preservation, at least mentally, had kept him away from *The Giovanni*. His father had never threatened him physically, but nothing crushed him like a fight with Big Tony, or memories of his mother and the last time he'd seen her. So happy. So pretty in the silver dress at the gala.

Could he live with himself if his father died without things being right between them?

Could he get over Elise and his brothers looking at him with pain in their eyes all the time? Or worse, pity?

The guilt would eat him alive.

Gio shook himself and made is feet work.

One good thing about work; no one knew his business. That wasn't about to change.

He made his way to Robbery/Homicide with his head down, and trying to project broodiness, so everyone would leave him alone.

He wasn't next in line on the murder board after all, so even three cups of coffee later, it was apparent it'd be a looooooong day. It was only 8:42.

Gio needed to finish up his final reports on the double homicide. The captain had approved his sequence of events, but Chief Patton had had additional questions, and he needed to close out their side of things and wait for whoever the District Attorney's Office assigned to the case.

*Fun times.*

He had some vacation hours built up. Olinsky was always telling him, while his dedication was appreciated, he pushed too hard.

Maybe, considering what was going on with his father, he could take a week or two off. Didn't have to explain why if he didn't want.

He'd *never* want.

Elise might appreciate it. He could even end his ghosting on the fam thing, but...

Gio sighed. Not working would make things worse. He didn't need or want more time to *think*.

Although, he had promised his sister he'd consider going to the hospital. Help the cause on the united sibling front. Provided Dom—

He dug his phone from his pocket and fired off a quick text to his brother.

*Hey, dude. Need to talk to you. Call me or Lise. Important.*

He shoved his device away, doubting his brother would answer him any time soon. If Dom was on a bender, he was allergic to mornings.

Elise had explained the likely reason for Dom's scattering. Their father had removed him from being *The Giovanni's* head of security a few days ago, a job he was in no way ready for, and their brother hadn't taken it well. Big Tony hadn't fired him, just demoted Dom for being irresponsible, which was an understatement, but the guy was having an issue coping.

*Like fucking always.*

The problem was being a Giovanni meant Dom couldn't get permanently fired, so when he showed back up, their father would give him his job back. If it wasn't the same position—hopefully it wouldn't be—he'd put the guy in middle-management, like always. It was an annoying game they played, and one of the reasons Dominic had no reason to grow up.

Gio rolled his eyes. Even Sam was more grown up at twenty-two.

He fired up his PC and logged on, then adjusted the volume on the handheld radio he kept on his desk. He clicked on the icon for his email. Notifications told him there were a dozen or so.

"Listen up." Captain Olinsky caught his attention and he peered up from staring off into space, more than reading the emails he should've been addressing.

He whirled his chair to face his immediate supervisor, and noticed all his squadmates do some version of the same when the captain stopped in the middle of the bullpen.

"The US Marshals will be teaming up with us to form a taskforce. Details to follow, but I need three or four of you. Anyone game?"

Hector Garcia, his longtime friend and fellow detective leaned on Gio's desk and threw him a wink. "Nothing like a good man hunt. How about we dive in, *amigo*?"

He nodded and threw his hand up when Olinsky glanced his way. "Me and Gar are there, Cap."

Hector flashed a grin and echoed his nod.

"Excellent," the captain said.

"Count me in," Ollie Navarro said.

"If you need four, I'll do it," Mary Foster, one of the two female detectives on their squad offered.

"Sounds good. The marshals should be here for briefing shortly. I'll give y'all a holler when they arrive."

Gio went back to his computer when his boss left the room, and Hector headed to his own cubicle. Thank God the guy sensed he didn't want to chat; dude could be like a teenage girl when he wanted to talk.

Maybe working something new, different, would help him deal with his...*everything.*

Couldn't get any worse, could it?

The sense of dread only grew every step Maddie took farther down the hallway; farther *into* Las Vegas Metropolitan Police Department.

One glance at her Fitbit told her she wasn't late; the meeting was at ten, and she had fifteen minutes to spare. Bonus, she already had over 5k steps for the day.

*Happy Monday and all that shit, right?*

Except, wasn't it...

It *was.*

Wednesday.

How had she really lost track like that?

It only *felt* more like the first day of the week instead of three days away from her first weekend in her new place.

Alone. After the longest week of her life.

She couldn't blame it on the time change, Vegas was only two hours behind Chicago. Maybe the flight, the move, and getting her crap dropped off had scrambled her brains. She hadn't made it very far with the unpacking, but was trying to give herself a break.

Maddie needed to get a heads-up on it before Jamie and Jake came, though. She didn't have that much time, and wanted things to feel homey for them.

Before she'd arrived at the PD, she'd stopped in at the Marshals Office in the US District Court building on the other side of downtown, only to discover her colleagues, Roger Griggs and April Bailey, hadn't arrived yet. They were supposed to act as her second and third in command for their operation.

She assumed if they needed an office, they'd go back and forth from the courthouse and the PD. Most of the time when she'd worked with the local police in Chicago, her last posting, she'd stuck close to the police department. She had a government issued laptop for everything she needed federal-related.

The local personnel had been welcoming enough, but she hadn't stuck around to get really settled. Just checked in with her new boss, Doug Randall. She'd acquiesced at the clerk's urging, and had let the woman, Melissa Pearson, show her to her permanent office, and give her a brief tour of the building as well as the rest of the dedicated Marshals' space.

At LMVPD this morning, Maddie had to see the deputy chief and captain they'd been assigned to on her own to get the taskforce under way.

Her new boss had assured her Griggs and Bailey would join her soon enough. She left her cell number so someone could give her a call if they showed today, but it wasn't likely.

She didn't know either marshal inspector well. Griggs was from the Chicago office and they'd worked together a few times, but Bailey was new, in from El Paso temporarily.

Maddie wasn't leery of new coworkers, as long as they respected her lead. However, her tummy threated to eject her meager breakfast of coffee and a protein shake.

Her imminent meeting wasn't the cause of her nerves.

*He's here.*

She was bound to run into Nico Giovanni.

Maybe she should've stayed at the office. Waited for Griggs and Bailey. Chatted her new coworkers and boss up; Melissa was a talker. Set up her office. Hell, running errands or making copies held more appeal.

Her gut somersaulted; her palms were clammy. Opening and closing her hands didn't help worth a shit.

Somehow, instinct told her Gio was actually *in* the building, not out on a case, out sick, or hell, out to breakfast.

*He's here.*

Maddie tried to prevent the words from becoming a chant, a mantra in her head, but had little luck.

She was going to puke.

She fought nausea as best she could; ordered her feet to keep moving. Looked straight ahead, refusing to peer into any open doors she passed. Just wanted to get to Deputy Chief Patton's office.

Maddie had scanned the vast parking lot when she'd pulled her rental in. Her new boss had told her she'd get her assigned government unit in the next few days.

Her former lover had had a motorcycle back in the day, and there were a few in the lot. Her eyes had zoned in on a black Ducati that'd practically screamed Gio. She couldn't put her finger on how she'd known. She just *did*.

*Breathe, just breathe.*

Seeing the man she'd slept with didn't have to result in chaos. It wasn't like he could merely see her and find out about Jake. Not like she was going to blurt, *'hey, I had your baby. He's seven now, and a great kid. Wanna meet him?'*

Maddie snorted, but the shakes overtook her body, starting in her hands and arms, working their way down her spine and into her legs until her knees wobbled.

Her stomach flip-flopped again and she wanted to flee the police department.

The desk sergeant had given her directions to find the deputy chief's office, and she only had one more turn; one more corridor. Needed to concentrate on that.

*Not* Nico Giovanni.

"Marshal Granger?"

She jumped, then cursed herself to hell and back. Turned to meet a pair of hazel eyes.

The man was pleasant-looking, with light hair on the prematurely-thinning side, because he couldn't be much older than forty-five. He had a red-blond mustache, and wore a smile.

He wasn't in uniform, but was dressed in dark slacks and a white button down, also sporting a shoulder holster. His badge winked from his belt in the fluorescent light. He had a seaming Styrofoam cup in hand, as if one of those rooms she'd just passed was a breakroom, and the reason for him running into her in the corridor.

"It's actually Senior Inspector." She smiled. Not many knew the correct title for marshals assigned to the Organized Crime Drug Enforcement Department, but it wasn't like she wasn't used to gently correcting. Hopefully, the guy didn't take offense. "Deputy Chief Patton, I assume?"

The man shook his head. "Captain Roman Olinsky. Sorry about that, Inspector. I'll be working with your team, leading the PD side." He threw his hand out for a shake and she accepted.

His skin was rough, but not offensive. However, she had to tug free, as if he was reluctant to let her go.

"No worries. Nice to meet you."

"Likewise." He smiled.

The lack of a uniform meant she couldn't spot captain epaulets that would be on a Class A collar.

"How'd you know who I am?" She fought a cringe; there was probably a bad detective joke in there somewhere. Even so, Maddie had her gun at her waist, and her badge around her neck on a chain, but she wasn't labeled. She was dressed casually, in dark jeans and a plain maroon button-down.

"I've seen your picture, and let me say, it didn't do you justice." Olinsky smiled again, and gave her an obvious onceover. Appreciation shone in his eyes, and she wanted to roll hers.

He wasn't bad-looking, and he didn't wear a wedding ring, but she'd learned her lesson regarding sleeping with coworkers; even if she had been interested, which she *wasn't.*

She'd never have another Gio.

Not that the man before her could hold a candle to Nico Giovanni.

Maddie had always been a sucker for blue eyes, and Gio's might as well have been sapphires. He was much taller than the blond man, too, this guy had to be close to her own five feet six inches.

Her former lover's muscles certainly hadn't hurt her original attraction to him, either. He had dark hair and a sculpted face right out of *GQ*, of course.

Too bad her heart had gotten itself involved and mucked up a perfectly good fuck-buddy situation back then.

*Stop. Thinking. Of. Him.*

It was bad enough she could run into him at any moment.

Olinsky was talking, and her cheeks heated up to her ears, because she'd totally blocked him out and had no idea what the man had said.

"I'm sorry, what was that?"

He cocked his head to one side, making his hair shift. Pretty soon he'd need a comb-over.

"If you come with me, I'll take you to Deputy Chief Patton. Her meeting should be brief, then we can get started. Are you alone?"

"For now. Marshal Inspectors Griggs and Bailey should be joining us in a day or two. They were delayed due to some red tape at the office."

"Alrighty then." Another smile stretched across his mustached mouth. "I look forward to working with you. My squad does, too."

*As long as I don't see Gio, I'm good.*

She let Olinsky lead her around the corner, answering when required, but not offering much conversation otherwise. She was on edge; just wanted to get inside an office so she wouldn't chance running into Gio.

As if thought conjured him, her eyes collided with a very blue pair.

His went wide, as if he couldn't believe what he was seeing, and his step faltered. He was coming toward her and the captain down the hall, about ten feet away. He had a file folder in hand, and his brisk stride, despite the pause, suggested he was in a hurry.

*Of. Fucking. Course.*

It didn't matter how far away he was.

Maddie could see, sense — remember — every inch of his body, from the dark jeans, the blue polo that brought out the hue of those eyes, and the gun holstered at his waist; the badge pinned next to it on his belt. Even the black shitkickers he always wore, same as back then.

His hair was shorter, less messy-looking. Still just as dark. Sable locks that needed her fingertips in them.

Nico Giovanni was just as delicious as he'd been at twenty-three.

"Ah, here's one of my guys now. Gio, come meet the leader of the marshal taskforce." The captain gestured, and her former lover slowed.

The distance disappeared much too soon.

She flushed to her toes. Her gut churned and her

heart thundered, unable to decide between hot and cold.

Maybe she really was going to puke.

Recognition flared in those gorgeous eyes, and it took all she was made of not to flee like a felon running from a warrant being served.

Gio gave her a onceover, as if she was a gallon of water and he was stranded in a desert.

Maddie squirmed.

Captain Olinsky was oblivious. "Senior Inspector Madison Granger, this is one of my lead detectives, Nico Giovanni, but we all call him 'Gio' 'round here. He's going to be on the taskforce."

*Oh. Shit. Of course he is.*

She swallowed. Like a hundred times.

Vomit was only seconds away.

Maddie shoved her hand out. "N-n-n-ice to meet you, Detective." She'd stuttered, but at least her voice had come out.

He stared at her extended offer before those eyes landed on her face again. This time, narrowed. '*This is how you want to play it?*' his gaze asked.

Gio glanced back at his captain before taking her fingers in his.

Awareness zapped down her spine and she squared her shoulders. Wanted to yank away and scream for him not to touch her.

Even if polite and expected, the handshake had been a horrible, *horrible* idea.

She wanted to cut her hand off.

Just one brush of his fingers against hers. His palm

against hers.

The past sucked her into a black hole and Maddie was suddenly standing in the private bar area of the casino, tears running down her cheeks when the man before her spliced her heart into shards.

She blinked, but the vision was only replaced with Gio touching her in a different way.

Cupping her breasts, kissing her mouth, her neck, moving in and out of her…

*Stop. It!*

Maddie jolted back to the present and pulled back, damn-it-all if it seemed abrupt.

Gio released her, but his broad shoulders were stiff, and his stare was still pointed *at* her.

A *far* from professional stare. *Far* from appropriate for meeting a new coworker.

Captain Olinsky appraised them, but said nothing.

The silence lasted seconds too long, until Gio cleared his throat. "Nice to meet you, Senior Inspector Granger."

She should be grateful he was cooperating, but his gaze smoldered with promises that made her fidget all over again.

Maddie cleared her throat, too. "For sure."

Now his eyes were barely slits. "I'm sure you and I will talk later."

*Nod, just nod.*

Her spine flushed with heat and ice that made her shoulders and arms ache.

He'd made a vow.

She read it in his expression, and it scared the shit

out of her. Gio would have her babbling about Jake in two seconds flat.

"Briefing should be soon regarding the marshals' case," Olinsky said.

He spared his captain a glance and nodded. "Roger." Gio pinned Maddie with one last look. "See you there."

She wrestled the tremors in her limbs as she and Olinsky continued on to Deputy Chief Patton's office. Cursed herself to hell and back.

Her physical reaction to Nico Giovanni was just as potent as it had been eight years ago.

He was going to be on her taskforce?

*Fuck. My. Life.*

K<br>♥

Gio fought the urge to rub his eyes.

*Maddie's here?*

Or had he just dreamt the exchange in the hallway?

Had he really *'met'* the best lover he'd ever had? At work? Walking with his captain?

He'd been asking himself the same questions, over and over again since he'd returned to his cubicle from the records room.

Gio had touched her hand with what should've been an innocent greeting; except, touching her now had sent his brain to *back then* in two seconds flat. Had his mind in all the places he'd convinced himself he'd forgotten, or gotten over.

When Olinsky had asked if he'd wanted to be on US Marshal's taskforce that morning, he'd jumped on it. Hadn't really needed Hector's urging. Throwing himself into a new case would help with his headfuck over his family for sure, since his last investigation was over.

*Maddie* was heading it?

Sure, he'd known she was still with the Marshals' Service.

The woman who'd broken his heart was based out of Chicago for the last few years — not that he'd checked up on her or anything after she'd left him.

What the hell was she doing in Vegas?

They'd met years ago…

*Eight to be exact.*

Gio could try to kid himself and pretend he didn't know how long it'd been, but that was all bullshit.

Damn, she was still gorgeous. Petite and curvy in all the right places. Wavy shoulder-length blonde hair, but it had a honey-gold hue. It was longer now than when he'd known her. Huge hazel eyes, complete with gold flecks.

Maddie's eyes always looked like burnt amber when she was aroused.

God, the way she'd screamed when she came…

*Fuck. Stop.*

He didn't need a boner at work.

"What the fuck's up with you?"

A hard hand landed on his shoulder, and jolted him.

Gio met a pair of midnight eyes. "Jesus, you scared the shit out of me, Garcia."

Hector arched a dark eyebrow. "What'd I tell you

about calling me Jesus? It's not my fault it's my middle name. You look like you're daydreaming, dude. Same as this morning, but you looked like you wanted to be left alone, so I didn't say anything."

*Exactly. Same for right now.*

"Blow me." He shifted away from his buddy's grip, spinning his computer chair around to face him.

The short, stocky detective smirked and perched on the edge of his desk beside him, like he'd done that morning. "How many times I gotta tell you I'm not into dong? Gonna think you're after my *cojones* for sure, *amigo*."

Gio flashed a grin. "If I *was* gay, I wouldn't be into your ugly mug."

"Aww shucks, you're gonna hurt my one remaining feeling."

He snorted.

"In other news, did you see the US Marshal heading that taskforce? She's in Patton's office right now. I had to invent a few reasons to walk by. What a HPOA."

He arched an eyebrow. Had to ask, even if he wouldn't like he answer. "What the fuck is a HPOA?"

Hector winked, a gleam in his dark eyes. "Hot piece of ass."

He was up and out of the chair before he could take a breath, pushing his face in his friend's. "Don't fucking talk about her like that." He made a fist, in lieu of grabbing the guy. By the throat.

The detective's eyes widened. "Easy, *hombre*." Hector threw his palms up. Took a step back when Gio towered over him.

He shook himself, made his hands loosen. "Sorry," he muttered but didn't retake his seat. He had no right to…what? Defend Maddie's honor?

"You know this fed *chica* or somethin'?" Hector's nonchalant curiosity snagged his attention, but his buddy's gaze was shrewd, studying him.

He cleared his throat before he could answer. "Yeah. You could say that." He tried to deliver the words with the same ease, but failed miserably.

"Ah, *si, si*. History."

Gio wanted to deny it, but he'd already admitted he knew Maddie, and hell, *'history'* felt like too weak a word to describe his past with Madison Granger.

The other option was to tell Hector to go to hell, but that would just seal the smugness his friend already regarded him with.

"Wait. This is the one that fucked you up when you were a rook, huh?" One dark eyebrow shot up. It was more a statement than question.

"I'm gonna fuck you up," he grumbled. The dude knew too much about him. One drunken night rearing its ugly head at the last moment he needed it to. He'd gotten too honest, too friendly, with the guy when he'd first made detective.

*Figures.*

That eyebrow went higher. Hector opened his mouth, but Olinsky popped his head in the room.

"Gio, Garcia, Navarro, Foster, briefing room. Marshal Granger is ready for us."

*Thank God.*

They filed into the briefing room in an orderly manner, like good little boys and girls.

Maddie stood with a white board to her left and a projector to her right. On the cart next to the projector was an open laptop, but the hanging projector screen behind her was blank.

Her gaze appeared to sweep over them, but pointedly avoided *him.*

Gio narrowed his eyes and willed her to look his way, but she didn't. Like she wouldn't.

On purpose.

She introduced herself and talked about what she did for the Marshal's Service.

"So, not a fugitive hunt," Hector whispered from beside him, elbowing him in the side.

Gio tore his eyes from his former lover and glanced at his fellow detective. "Guess not."

"Did you know?"

He shook his head.

"We can thank the FBI for this case, people. It was a joint effort, but now it's all ours." Maddie flashed a smile that was somewhere between feral and proud. "Let's dive in."

She bent over and clicked on a few things at the computer. Images popped up on the big screen.

A few shots of paperwork he quickly discerned as someone's financials, and a photograph of an older man, with thick salt and pepper hair, olive skin and brown eyes.

Confusion swirled in his gut when he took in the last picture. It was a picture of *The Giovanni.*

The building he'd known all is life was unmistakable, with the ornate water fountain in front of it, and the attached hotel tower soaring into the Sin City skyline behind it.

The shot had been snapped in the daytime, so none of the bright colored night lights were visible.

Maddie's words didn't compute any more than the photos she'd called up from the laptop, and the projector's screen spotlighted.

All the crap from the previous night was shoved to the wayside.

The US Marshals and the FBI thought his father's casino was a front? Money laundering? For the mob? In Chicago?

*What. The. Actual. Fuck.*

No fucking wonder she wouldn't look at him.

Gio fidgeted on his seat, his stomach twisting itself further into knots the more she spoke.

Hector kept shooting him *'what the hell?'* looks, but he couldn't tear his eyes from his former lover. Maddie, the marshals, hell, the FBI was all *wrong*.

*So wrong. None of it's true.*

The old guy on the screen was Cesare Fratelli, the CEO of a huge accounting firm, and recently apprehended for a massive money laundering ring tied to the Falcone Syndicate—old school, old Chicago Italian mobsters that were as relevant today as they'd been in the fifties and sixties. A crime family.

According to Maddie, the FBI was still trying to get the Falcones behind bars, but intel from Fratelli indicated there was the same kind of activity at *The*

*Giovanni.*

Worse than that, Fratelli claimed his father's casino had been started with mob money over forty years ago.

*No. Fucking. Way.*

Sure, his father had grown up in Chicago, but he'd moved to Vegas and built the casino from the ground up before he'd met and married Gio's mother.

History and stereotypes alike proved Sin City had been shaped and grown by old mobsters, but his father had never been involved in organized crime. He'd never caved into pressures, even if he'd been susceptible.

"This shit is crazy," he murmured.

"I know, right? Nothing changes about ol' Vegas." Hector winked.

He didn't correct his buddy, let alone spare him a glance. His head was still spinning.

How could they suspect this shit about his family's casino?

He'd never heard of Fratelli's firm, and besides, his sister handled everything accounting-numbers-money related, and she sure-as-hell would *never* have anything to do with organized crime.

*Wait a minute…Elise.*

Elise's fiancé.

Gio straightened in the chair, then leaned forward, his stare boring a hole in the picture of old man Fratelli.

*Marco fucking Fratelli.*

He didn't believe in coincidences.

"I need to talk to you," Gio muttered in her ear.

"I don't have anything to say to you."

His large hand clamped on her wrist. Maddie tugged away, but he tightened the hold.

Her eyes darted around the corridor. There was no one around, but anyone could come at any moment. The ready-room door was ajar. It would likely empty momentarily.

The briefing had gone well, but she'd fled the room first, before any of the LVMPD detectives or Captain Olinsky.

She'd thanked them for their time and attention, answered questions as fast as lightning, then told them she'd check in soon.

Maddie hadn't had a direction or destination. She was supposed to stay there, work with them, but she'd copped out. Stated her colleagues from the Marshals would meet up with them soon and they'd proceed.

She'd just needed to get out of there.

Get away from *him*.

Even if she'd never given him the barest

acknowledgment during her talk of the case. Her reason for being in Vegas. With his father's casino at the center of things.

She hadn't spared him one glimpse.

Now, her eyes shot to his face, and she couldn't turn away. "N-n-not here." The stutter made her cringe, but Gio gave the barest nod and dragged her down the hallway.

He pushed open the nearest door and shoved her inside, slapping the light on and yanking the thick panel shut, just short of a slam.

The *click* of the lock resounded in her temples.

The contents of room told her it was an office supply hub, from the neatly organized stacks copy paper cases against one wall, to the shelves lining all the rest.

Post-it notes were next to boxes of pens, bundles of notebooks, highlighters, and multiple toner refills. File folders, and banker boxes galore. The scent of paper and cellophane tickled her nose.

She'd always loved going to the office supply store. New supplies made her want to do her job. She'd never been afraid of the paperwork side, what most cops dreaded. Maddie thrived on the investigation, being sharper than coworkers, researching and catching the little things others missed. She was detail-oriented, and good. She deserved this case, this command.

Her former lover whirled and stalked toward her, towering over her with his six-foot-four frame.

She refused to shrink way, but Maddie retreated

until her shoulders and upper back hit the edge of the far shelf. There was nowhere else to go. The contents shook and she waited for something to fall and smack her head, but it didn't happen.

Gio's sapphire eyes flashed with anger and he slammed his palm on the edge of the shelf right above her left ear.

She winced.

"Are you five?"

"Excuse me?" She met that gaze dead-on, not wanting to give in to her confusion. Whatever she'd contemplated he might open with, it wasn't that.

"Ignoring me. Pretending you don't *know* me. Leading the whole fucking briefing, avoiding even one glance in my direction? Real cute, Senior Inspector Granger, with the United States Marshals Service." He spat her title, last name and agency.

"I was trying to maintain professionalism." Her tone sounded defensive to her ears and she fought another wince.

He threw his head back and laughed. "Bullshit."

Maddie shuddered and wanted to rub her arm, but couldn't move when he looked at her like that.

Gio was right, of course, but she'd cut her tongue off before she admitted *that*.

"It doesn't matter how many years passed. You can't pretend *we* didn't exist."

"Why not?" she snapped. "None of it matters. We have a case, and you happen to be on my taskforce. We have to work together. So, let's just keep it professional. A work thing."

"Hell no."

His vehemence made her startle, and she reared back, knocking her head into the shelf.

"Shit." Maddie rubbed the throbbing spot.

Gio's expression lost some of its harshness. "You okay?"

He must not have been overly concerned, because her former lover still hovered too close for comfort. The heat coming off him warmed her, and her traitorous body only wanted him closer.

She needed a freaking distraction, stat. "Speaking of my case, how did you even get a spot on my taskforce? Olinsky doesn't know your family owns the casino?"

He jolted. Averted his eyes, and jammed his hand through his dark hair. His shoulders quaked, more than the barest denial of his headshake.

Surprise washed over Maddie.

Gio's hesitation shouted he hadn't wanted to admit that truth, and perhaps he *shouldn't* have. With one word to his captain, she could have him removed from her taskforce.

Probably should.

"It's not a conflict of interest," he said, as if he'd read her mind.

"How could he not know?" she demanded.

"I'm a private person," he said on an exhale, like he needed a second to gather himself.

"Gio—"

"My dad isn't laundering money!" His shout had her freezing. He rubbed the back of his neck, and again, avoided looking her way. "He has cancer. He's in the hospital."

Maddie blinked. "I'm sorry." The words were automatic, but no less sincere.

That intense gaze swung back to her face and he seemed like he wanted to say something, but nothing came out.

He'd always had tension with his father, but as someone who'd lost her parents, she sympathized. He might not always get along with his dad, but Antonio Giovanni was still his father.

If Gio dipped only a few inches toward her face, he could kiss her.

Maddie didn't want that.

At. All.

Cursed herself for the mere idea.

She cleared her throat. "I'm sorry about your dad," she repeated. "But it doesn't change the status of my case. We have to carry on the investigation, there are some serious accusations there, and it looks bad, as you know from briefing."

"My dad's never been involved with organized crime."

"Gio—"

"I'll prove it."

That gave her pause. "If Olinsky knew—"

"You'd do that to me? Fuck me over with my captain so you don't have to work with me?"

She ignored how her heart skipped. "Gio—"

His eyes flashed. For the third time he didn't let her get out more than his name. He hung closer, invading her bubble.

His mouth so close to hers.

"Let me stay on the taskforce, and I'll prove my dad has nothing to do with this. I deserve that much from you."

Maddie didn't have anywhere else to retreat to, so she stared into those glowing sapphires. She should be insulted but the way he'd said, *'from you'* like that.

Like *she* owed *him* something.

That was bullshit, wasn't it?

"Okay." The word of acquiescence fell out, even though she shouldn't have agreed. There was so much more to say, but she couldn't form anything coherent. Couldn't look away from his eyes.

He nodded.

She tried not to breathe him in. He smelled the same. His aftershave wrapped around her, making her dizzy. "Move. We're done now." She should push him away, but touching him was a bad idea.

"No. *We're* far from done."

Suddenly, he wasn't talking about the case or the taskforce.

She tried to ignore how her heart skipped into overdrive. "Yes we are, Gio. *We've* been done for eight years. It's been a long time. Things have changed."

Gio narrowed his eyes. "It was never *my* choice. You disappeared."

Maddie fought the urge to rear back again—didn't need a bruise on her head. "You could've found me. If you really wanted to." She frowned at the accusation in her statements. She was long over being crushed he hadn't come after her, wasn't she?

Why had this conversation taken such a turn?

It should be about him, the case, his dad.

"You're so full of shit, *you* don't even buy it." He shook his head and took a step back, running a hand through hair that short hair again.

The cut made him edgier, sexier.

She *hated* that she'd noticed.

"Look, it's bad enough we have to work together—"

"Is it?" Gio barked.

"I got over you a long time ago, Nico Giovanni," Maddie blurted the lie and squirmed as his gorgeous eyes appraised her all over again.

"I'll prove that's utter shit. Right. Now."

"No, you won't." Her protest came out as a squeak as he crowded her against the shelf again.

He bumped her breasts and it took all she was made of not to arch into him. Not to slip her arms around his neck. Not to rock her hips into his like she had so many times to see how fast she could get him hard.

*Push him away.*

Gio dipped down and took her mouth, absorbing her gasp. He coaxed her to open with a mere press of his tongue against her lips.

Maddie let him in, thrusting hers against his as he plastered her to his chest and slanted to deepen the kiss.

She didn't resist him. She *couldn't*.

It'd always been this way with Gio.

She was a puddle with the tiniest brush of his

mouth over hers.

His big hands claimed the small of her back and her ass, flattening her breasts into him and urging her hips flush to his.

She was grateful he was holding her up, because she would've been on her ass on the storage room floor otherwise.

He kissed her expertly, deeply, like no time had passed.

Desire shot low and hot, and her sex was pulsing for him, begging for what she hadn't had in more years than she could count.

Maddie had had a few lovers since Gio, but none that'd ever come close to making her feel like *he* did, and her body remembered. Wanted. Seared for more.

"Oh God, Maddie," he breathed against her mouth, then kissed her again, this time softer, tenderly and it made her tummy flip-flop.

It also snapped her back into her own skin. She couldn't deal with the appearance of emotion from him.

He didn't *really* give a shit about her.

She shoved him away, and raised her arm for a slap.

Gio caught her wrist when her palm was less than an inch from his too-handsome-for-his-own-good face. He smirked.

She'd expected shock, or anger that she'd been about to hit him, but the humor on that kiss-swollen mouth made Maddie want to shoot him, or at least glue her knee to his balls.

He was so damn sexy.

Even when she wanted to maim him, she could see it.

She wanted him.

*Dammit.*

"You still want me, Madison Granger. Deny it all you want with words, but your body screams louder."

He still held her wrist in a tight grip, but Gio wasn't hurting her. He panted as hard as she did. She cursed him to hell and back, but she couldn't say it aloud.

"Let me go," she was finally able to growl, but her chest heaved as she fought for normal respiration. "Or I'll kick your favorite body part."

He chuckled, and damn if his grin didn't make her burn for him even more. "If I recall, it's *your* favorite body part, too." He had the nerve to lift his hips and bring attention to the obvious tent in his jeans.

*Damn him.*

Heat rushed Maddie's face, wrapping around the back of her neck and scorching up to her ears. "Go to hell."

Gio's face lost his amusement and he sobered. He dropped her hand, but his eyes never left hers. "Been there, done that. It was bad after you left."

She stilled. "Not my problem."

Something akin to hurt flashed across his gaze and regret hit her gut.

Her need to throw up a line of self-defense controlled her next statement. "Forget what you think is between us, or I'll go have a talk with Captain Olinsky."

Shock, and perhaps fury, reflected from his expression. "Wow. That's low, even for you."

The burn of embarrassment flushed away her arousal, and she looked away. He was right, but she wouldn't admit it. Maddie fought the need to close her eyes.

Hurting him on purpose was beneath her, wasn't it?

It'd been bad—*really* bad—for her for a while too, after they'd ended. She'd had a baby all alone, with only her then-teen sister to help. As much as she loved Jamie, her sibling was no replacement for the man she'd been missing so much she'd been destroyed inside.

The man before her now.

The man she couldn't go down that path with again.

There was more than just her now.

She had Jake to think about.

Gio stepped back, no longer blocking her way to the only exit of the small room. He suddenly wouldn't spare her even a glimpse, and Maddie was hit with a second round of guilt.

She wouldn't apologize.

Not after he'd kissed her against her will.

She ignored the tremors that shot down her spine *and* the voice that accused her of protesting too hard.

Squaring her shoulders, she strolled out of the office supply room and tried not to slam the door.

Ignored the rush of disappointment when he didn't come after her.

*Again.*

G ian tried not to glance over his shoulder and betray the paranoia eating through his gut as he shoved cash onto a cart destined for one of the many counting rooms. He emptied three duffel bags that carried two hundred thousand dollars, and needed to get it done so he could disappear from an area of the casino he shouldn't be. Damn place had cameras everywhere.

He'd already had to steal into the main security central and delete footage a few times; a feat not easily accomplished, since the place was occupied by security officers twenty-four/seven. Like most high-dollar successful casinos, the security staff was vast, made up of plain-clothed, suited, and uniformed officers alike. Until a few weeks ago, security had been headed by Dominic, his fiancée's middle brother, but the younger man had ticked off Daddy Dearest and gotten himself removed from the position.

Unfortunately, Big Tony would likely give him back the job if the idiot groveled. No doubt it'd happen sooner or later. Although, Gian could benefit from that, because the man who'd taken Dom's place was doing a fine job—something the ne'er do well Giovanni couldn't manage.

If security was lacking, Gian could get his job done better, of course. He'd have to whisper in the boss' ear when the senior Giovanni was back at work, or maybe even at a hospital visit. *He'd* no doubt have to put in an appearance sooner or later, supportive fiancé and all that shit.

He'd rave about what a great job Dom had done, and how he was missed, especially since Big Tony was down for the count. Maybe it would help endear him to the little fucker, who didn't like him anyway.

Meeting the eldest son—the cop—hadn't gone well, either. The conceited ass didn't like him any more than Dom or Sam. Either Elise's brothers were just that protective of her, or they had great instincts. Neither scenario was fantastic for him.

He could only concentrate on the fact that the patriarch loved him. It was all that mattered, but if the man never came back to work, he'd really have to watch his ass, especially if Elise's older brother was going to be around more.

In the president's office, she'd begged him to come back into the family fold, with their younger brother cosigning everything she'd said. It hadn't gone stellar, but if he knew anything about Italian women, guilt was her weapon of choice. Step aside persuasion, pleading, tears. Enough guilt to make a guy's gut rot was an Italian woman's way.

Gian could totally relate. His mother could always

freeze him with the barest tremor of her bottom lip. Sometimes even with a smile and no sarcastic inflection.

Of course, the Giovanni children were all half Greek, but what a way to tap into one's heritage.

He snorted.

The tight stack of bills brought his attention back to his task. Uncle Dino was probably going to call to confirm he'd gotten the money delivery. He had to be done by then and get his ass out of the hallway.

The money cart had been left unattended, and when it was discovered, whoever had left it would get an ass-chewing by the nearest manager for sure. The cart's attached folder for the paperwork regarding the cash was also gone.

That gave him an idea. Perhaps he could stand by it and wait. Watch for the meandering idiot from security personnel who'd abandoned their duty to take a shit or bang a waitress in the closest bathroom.

He could demand, threaten, act like he'd come upon it by accident instead of having trolled the cameras on the app he'd had a hacker put on his phone so he could prey upon this very opportunity, this careless disregard of rules and regulations; a testament to why Dominic Giovanni had been removed from his position.

Gian always watched the cameras at the casino. Although, it wasn't *always* this easy to integrate the money his father's brother sent in weekly deliveries to be cleaned.

His burner cellphone rang. He jumped and cursed

simultaneously. They always scheduled their calls on disposable phones so their conversations would remain untraceable.

Uncle Dino, right on time, if his Rolex knew anything.

He locked the roller door on the money cart and put the phone to his ear.

"Hey, kid." His uncle's gravelly voice splashed over his senses, even though it was only two words. He was suddenly homesick for Chicago, even seeing the older man's beady dark eyes and pock-marked cheeks.

Gian didn't miss arguments with his father, but he did miss how his uncle had always taken him out for a drink while he smoked cigars and agreed what a dick the leader of the Falcone family could be.

"It's done." The confirmation came out on a croak, so he cleared his throat.

"Good." A pause. "You all good?" The Chicago accent was present in the question, and he was able to smile.

"Yeah. Of course. Have you told him, yet?"

A few heartbeats passed before the man spoke, which gave him the answer he didn't want to hear.

"It hasn't been enough time for you to prove yourself. Trust me, *paisan*."

"A year isn't enough time?" he hissed a whisper, in case the recalcitrant security officers came back for the cart.

"Patience. Trust me, *nipote*."

Gian growled, but inhaled so he could talk with some semblance of calm. "I want him to know *I'm* the one handling this operation. It was my idea, my undertaking. I've taken all the risk, here. I've been doing it. We've cleaned a substantial amount, with more to come. It hasn't been easy, but I'm established. The system is flawless."

"Yeah, about that..."

He stilled, and gripped the throwaway phone tighter. "What?"

"Other than me, have you had any contact with Chicago?"

Gian frowned. "No. Why?"

"We need to lay low for a while, and now, it's even more for your benefit if your father doesn't hear your name, no matter your recent success in cleaning our dough."

"Why?" he repeated, this time a harsh bark.

"Cesare Fratelli has disappeared. No one can find him, and no one offed him."

"So..."

"Intel from the cops we have on the payroll say the FBI got him."

"Motherfucker."

A humorless chuckle sounded in his ear. "Yeah, *nipote*. I'll halt deliveries for a few weeks, maybe a month. I think it's the smart thing to do. We watch and wait. When we confirm what happened to Fratelli, we can reassess."

"No. Keep the money coming. There's no way the old fart would roll on Dad, even if he's in an eight-by-ten. They go back too far."

His uncle was silent for a few beats again.

"The smart thing—"

"No." Gian entered demand-territory again. "I *will* prove myself. I can do this, and the feds don't have any ties to me and Fratelli. I've been away from Chicago for a year, remember?"

"Don't be a little fool. Your alias—"

"Is a non-issue. Not even Giovanni batted an eye."

"He's an idiot. Always was—"

"Follow our schedule. Another two hundred next week." With his final command, he ended the call, ignoring the flip-flop in his stomach.

If the leader of his father's CPA firm, which was on the up-and-up, as much as it played with the mob, really had been arrested by the FBI, the guys they had on the inside would find out. A hit would be taken out on the old man, no matter how loyal he had been to the Falcone family.

Gian believed Fratelli wouldn't talk—the dude was his father's ride-or-die, but if there was any doubt, the organization would have him killed. Even in prison, guards could be bought and sold like traded cigarettes.

Fratelli and Falcone went back generations. Their many shared skeletons were stuffed in closets, built into walls and drowned at the bottom of local rivers and lakes. If Fratelli decided to be a think-for-himselfer, the issue would be resolved. He might be taken care of no matter what, anyway. His father could be a ruthless bastard.

Maybe this didn't complicate things for him. He could keep things going, even if Uncle Dino screamed caution. He *would* show his father he was worthy no matter what, *and* take down an old enemy, to boot.

With Fratelli no longer in the picture, the Falcone patriarch would be even more grateful to his ostracized son.

Gian would totally do this.

No. Matter. What.

K ♥

Gio spent the next day observing, more than communicating with the taskforce about Maddie's case. He'd been the quiet guy in the back of the room, listening to the rest of the team talk, strategize, and go over financials that just couldn't be right.

She hadn't said much to *him*, nor did she spare him much attention; like she approved of his minimal involvement. It was probably part acceptance of his disbelief over his father's guilt, and part because of that kiss.

That *perfect* kiss he couldn't quite get out of his mind, despite the shit about his dad and the casino.

He watched her like some stalker, staring at how her body moved in the simple dark jeans and tucked-in black button-down, her gun and badge on her belt just like his.

She was so damn appealing, even with her glorious honey waves gathered in a ponytail, but he drew the line on the memories of her in his bed. Otherwise, he'd be in boner at work territory. Again.

Maddie had been animated with his fellow detectives, and in the short time, showed him how good of an investigator she was. Back when they'd met eight years ago, she'd been in town on a fugitive retrieval mission, and he'd been a uniformed rookie cop.

They hadn't worked together, not like they were now.

Well, she was working. He was voyeur-ing.

He'd finally excused himself late afternoon, lying to her about having to complete a few things from his last homicide case. He'd even assured her after he was finished, he was all hers.

Maddie had arched an eyebrow at his wording and Gio had dared her to verbally deny him, and added a wink for good measure. She hadn't, of course, but her pink cheeks were adorable.

Thank God Captain Olinsky had been in a meeting, and not present in the conference room the taskforce had taken over. His boss would've called him on his bullshit about the closed case, and he would've been stuck there.

His task was complete in no time, because it'd only taken about ten minutes to do a cursory background check on Marco Fratelli.

The dude had no paper trail in Sin City, until about nine months ago when he'd started working at *The Giovanni*. No history on the social security number, or proof that he'd ever had a job before arriving in Las Vegas.

*What the fuck?*

His father had created a position for the prick. He was part liaison, part VP, part casino sales, and obviously a general gigantic kiss-ass to Big Tony. Probably had his lips glued to Gio's father's cornhole.

The cockstain worked in the accounting department with Elise, too. If that wasn't a red flag, he didn't know what was.

He dug deeper, going back to Chicago, starting with some background on the old man who'd rolled over for the FBI and the Marshals Service, Cesare Fratelli. The man was around Big Tony's age and married.

His father had been born and raised in Chicago in a tightknit Italian-only community, so maybe what his sister's soon-to-be ex-fiancé had said about their fathers being friends was true. Big Tony didn't really discuss his childhood any the time before he'd moved to Vegas.

He'd married a Greek, instead of an Italian, and had always alluded that their extended family had an issue with Gio's mother's ethnicity. As they'd never had much contact with any Chicago family, it'd be hard to confirm.

Gio had copies of Maddie's case files, so building on her information about Fratelli wasn't difficult. The former CEO had a few kids, and among them, a son, Marco.

His heartrate had kicked up the more he read.

The boy had been born thirty-two years ago, so the age was about right, but there were no photos, no other pertinents. Like his birth had been recorded, and nothing else. No school records, and the social security number he'd managed to locate didn't match the one his sister's fiancé had on file at the casino.

The more he uncovered, the more he hung on the edge of his chair.

The kicker made him curse.

According to a death certificate from Cook County Records, Marco Alberto Marino Fratelli had died at age five.

He'd had a short, tragic life. Born with a congenital defect in his little heart, and he'd passed before he could receive a transplant.

So, who the fuck was engaged to his sister?

Gio was sure as hell going to find out.

He pushed his chair into his desk and cursed some more. Shoved his arms into his leather jacket and grabbed his helmet. His brooding face didn't get far; since LVMPD was fond of glass walls and doors, and he had to walk past the conference room the taskforce was working in.

The door was open, and his team was in various stages of investigating. Hector jotted notes on the whiteboard from a paper in his hand, Navarro stared at a computer screen.

The captain was still gone, but he didn't expect Olinsky to remain hands-on over the course of the investigation.

"Gio? What're you doing?" Maddie asked, peering up from some paperwork with Mary Foster at her side.

Both women had yellow highlighters in hand, and sat across from each other, stacks of bound papers on the table in front of them.

More fucking financials that couldn't be right.

He gritted his teeth. Thrust away his curiosity. He could go over their evidence later, when he was done with his own quest.

Gio couldn't share with the class just yet. Needed to figure out who the hell his sister's *'Marco Fratelli'* really was.

Then maybe he could clue Maddie and the team in.

He looked at his watch. "It's ten to five. Sorry, but I have to call it a day."

Maddie exchanged a glance with Foster, and he didn't miss that Hector was subtly watching over his shoulder.

Navarro generally didn't miss much, but the guy didn't look up from whatever he was doing on the computer.

Gio was going to have to lie.

Maddie hated liars.

His former lover pushed her chair back and joined him in the hallway.

He took a few steps away from the door; didn't need an audience from nosey coworkers.

"Gio?" A frown marred Maddie's pretty face. She'd followed his feet, and stood too close for comfort.

Her familiar scent of fresh-cut flowers tickled his nose and he really wanted to grab her up. Couldn't help but watch her mouth and again remember that kiss yesterday in the supply room. Like he hadn't been obsessing about it all day.

She'd stated she'd moved on long ago. Declared she didn't want him, but that was all bullshit.

Maddie had kissed him back. Fervently. Hungrily. Her body had melted against his, like it always had.

God, his blood had boiled. No other woman could make him so hard so fast. He'd had to stay in that little room until he'd gotten his shit under control.

He'd wanted to strip her and take her against the shelves that held more office supplies than *Staples*. If she hadn't pushed him away, he would have. Been inside her in two seconds flat.

Gio wanted to knock his head against the wall.

How the fuck had they gotten here?

He wanted her back; wanted another chance with her, but *everything* was an obstacle.

Maddie had shoved him away and rejected him.

Her case made it look like his dad and his whole family were a bunch of criminals. Even if he could prove otherwise, how could they make things work?

She was likely leaving when the case was over, too. Could he let her walk away again? He'd barely survived the first time.

He'd have to convince her to give him another shot, first.

The idea straightened his shoulders. Convincing her could be fun. A challenge.

"Gio?" she prompted again, irritation lacing his nickname, and she crossed her arms over her breasts.

Bad idea to call his attention there.

He cleared his throat. "Uh, sorry. I know you're not done for the day, but my sister called. I need to head to the hospital."

Her expression softened and she dropped her arms. Maddie reached for him, but stopped short of touching him.

That was probably for the best.

Her genuine concern churned guilt low in his gut,

but she'd promised to let him prove his father was innocent, and that was what he was doing.

He just couldn't tell her yet.

"How's Elise? How're your brothers coping?"

Gio bit his bottom lip to hide his surprise.

Right, Maddie and Elise had made fast friends back in the day. His sister had been in college, and in her rookie year of officially working at *The Giovanni*.

Genius that she was, his sister had graduated high school at sixteen and wrapped up her double-bachelor's in accounting and business in three years.

Their father had only let her do so because she was so good with numbers, and as far as the family business was concerned, Elise was a benefit. Big Tony could look past conservative presumptions for a fatter bottom line.

One more reason to growl at his hypocrisy.

His brothers had been kids back then, Dom barely eighteen, and Sam only fourteen. Dom had already been on the path he was currently embracing, but Sam had been much like he was now, sweet; shy and quiet. His baby brother had really connected with Maddie, who'd been raising her younger sister.

He'd never met Jamie, since Maddie had been in Vegas temporarily on a man hunt, but she was around Sam's age, if memory served.

Gio and Maddie had had an incendiary affair lasting eight weeks that felt like years.

She'd marked him.

Ruined him for other women.

He'd never been the same, and hadn't told her how he'd felt. Regret and pain had driven him for a long time.

Breast cancer had taken his mother only a few weeks after he'd met the US Marshal who'd shattered his heart, so the Giovanni family had been in a rough place.

Mix in the shit with Big Tony, and he'd been a fucking mess.

For a long time.

Maybe he still was.

"Gio, are you okay?"

Now her worry made his chest hurt. It was so honest.

So Maddie…his Mads.

The nickname he'd given her all those years ago made it hard to breathe.

"I…know what it's like to lose your parents, and your dad's all you have. This must be hard…"

Gio didn't correct her. She couldn't know how badly things between him and his father had deteriorated after she'd left. Didn't know he hadn't talked to the man in years.

He couldn't tell her now. Big Tony needed to be his cover.

He averted his gaze, and it was an urge he didn't have to fake. "I need to go."

Her hand landed on his, and he almost jumped. It was warm, and welcome, but more than that, *familiar*, like no time had passed.

Tempting. The barest touch, and it made him crave more.

He looked there before he met those beautiful

hazel eyes.

Mixed emotions churned in his already roiling gut. How could she look at him like that when she thought his father was a criminal?

How could she give a shit?

Gio scanned her face, and all he could read was real worry. One hundred percent sincere.

*For me.*

"I'll see you tomorrow." He severed their physical contact, tightened his grip on his helmet and left.

By the time he parked his Ducati in the casino parking garage, rage surged in Gio's stomach; fury guided every beat of his heart.

Maddie. His father. His siblings.

The case.

Fucking Marco Fratelli.

It was a mishmash he couldn't make sense of, and it was so loud in his head he wanted to scream.

Maybe Dom had it right.

Gio didn't drink anymore, he'd had to quit when his sister had accused him of being an alcoholic. He'd never caved and gone to AA—he wasn't a pussy, but he'd seen her point—and wanted her to shut up about it. Besides, he'd wanted to be an example for Dominic.

Fucking failure there, but right then his brother's wayward habits weren't such a bad idea. Maybe it could quiet his headfuck.

He stalked into the casino, and jogged down the stairs in lieu of waiting on the escalator or the elevator. The security office was probably the fastest way to find the piece of shit he sought, so he headed to the private employees-only elevator that required a fob to operate.

It went to floors that weren't patron-public.

Getting to the top floor only took a few moments, but it felt like hours, and he tapped his foot as he waited for the elevator doors to retract.

This corridor was more lit than the one that lead to the executive suites a few floors down, and all the doors on both sides were sealed shut, as if forbidden.

The beige walls contrasted with the deep red carpet with swirled designs inside the black borders. Instead of sconces, the place was lit by fluorescents in the drop-ceiling that highlighted a lack of art on the walls, as in other casino hallways.

He tried not to stomp his way down, but he made it to the nondescript door with only a few strides. Scanning his fob on the black box next to the door resulted in a green light, but the door swung open and someone met him before he could set one foot inside the large security office.

"Uh, how can I help you, Mr. Giovanni?" The security officer game him a onceover, and slunk back a bit from Gio's obvious anger. He was dressed sharply, in a dark suit and wore a clear spiral-corded radio earpiece Secret Service-style, because it'd always been important that everything related to *The Giovanni* appear expensive and high-class.

They had uniformed security officers too, of course, but they were on all the floors, to be visible to the public. They were armed, like cops.

The Secret Service lookalike team watched from the shadows and handled real problems with stealth and discretion.

Gio didn't know the kid, but it wasn't unusual that *he'd* be known to all the casino staff. He straightened his shoulders.

*Don't be a dick*, needed to be his current mantra.

Like Maddie and his taskforce teammates, he didn't need anyone at the casino to know anything was amiss.

"I'm looking for Marco Fratelli. Have you seen him?" Over the guy's shoulder, his eyes scanned the curved wall of computer monitors stacked upon computer monitors.

The main security office had three huge banks on three separate enormous desks. Three full-time officers in the room at all times, manning each one, in addition to their teammates that roved the casino floors. It was a twenty-four/seven operation, and because his father had always been security-minded, the department was vast; one of the biggest percentage of employees at *The Giovanni.*

Had things not gone south with Daddy Dearest, Gio wouldn't have minded running it. Something Dom could never handle, yet he'd been given the task.

He'd wanted to be a cop more, always a point of contention with Big Tony, even before his mom had died. Partly, because of the choice of profession, and partly because his father had accused him of turning his back on his family.

Gio paused. His father had never wanted him to become a cop. Could there be more to that other than him not wanting to follow in casino-rooted footsteps?

*No, Dad's not a criminal.*

"Mr. Fratelli is likely with Ms. Giovanni, getting ready for the gala. It starts at seven."

The officer's voice yanked him back to the present.

"Ah, the gala." He pretended he knew what the fuck the guy was talking about. "So, the banquet center? What ballroom?"

The officer nodded. "Yes. It's in Sicily, A through D."

Damn, that meant it was going to be a giant thing. All of the ballrooms were named after Italian cities, and with its ability to be broken into four separate rooms, Sicily had the largest capacity.

"Thank you, I'll head over there."

"It's black tie." The guy flashed a small smile, like he was trying to be helpful.

"I don't think I'll be staying," Gio grunted and whirled at the officer's nod, striding back to the elevator before he even heard the door close.

He was going to have to find the fucker alone. Couldn't confront him with Elise around.

A glance at his watch told him it was five to five, so he had time to have a chat with the fuckwad and get gone.

His next move would be guided by what he discovered.

Luck was on his side, and when he got to the vast conference and banquet wing of the casino, cockstain number one was alone in the corridor, chatting on his phone, outside the farthest restrooms from the largest ballroom.

Like the bastard needed privacy.

Well, that was fine with Gio.

Marco's back was facing him, so he did a cursory search of the bathrooms to make sure they were really alone, then he approached from behind.

Guy still hadn't noticed him.

He slammed the shorter man against the wall.

The cellphone clattered to the carpet.

Marco, or whatever the fuck his real name was, at least had the decency to pale out. Dark eyes went wide, but he sensed it was out of surprise more than fear. Recognition was there, too, of course.

Instinct whispered the guy was a good actor.

"Sorry you didn't get to finish your call," Gio drawled.

"What the heck?" Marco sputtered. He was kitted out in another super expensive selection, but this time a black tux. Shocker, it was another Armani.

Looked like the shithead was a loyal wardrobe kinda guy.

"Who the fuck are you?" He slammed him again, to punctuate his demand, laying his forearm against the asshole's throat and giving him a little gas.

Again, surprise registered in his expression.

*Why?*

Because he'd been discovered, or because he really thought he *was* Marco Fratelli?

Assumed he'd never get caught?

"Wh-what? What're you talking about?"

"Marco Fratelli died when he was five years old from a genetic heart defect. Tragic, yeah, but *you* ain't him, true."

"*I am* Marco Fratelli." Armani didn't miss a beat; even seemed sincere. He pushed at him, but Gio tightened his hold, leaned harder.

The guy wasn't a pussy, had some good muscle to his frame, but Gio was a few inches taller, and had more mass.

"Bullshit."

Marco opened his mouth, but didn't get a chance to speak.

"Gio! What the *hell* are you doing?" Elise marched down the hall in five inch heels that sparkled in the dim light, perching her fists on both hips and glaring harder than he'd ever seen pointed in his direction.

He straightened and released her loser soon-to-be *ex*-fiancé. Gio hauled the cockwaffle away from the wall and brushed off his shoulders. "Nothing. Me and Armani just needed to have a little chat."

His sister frowned. "Armani?"

He smirked. "Just a little term of endearment I have for my soon-to-be brother-in-law, isn't that right, Armani?"

*Over my dead body.*

He couldn't clue her in. Yet.

This case was making her and their father look guilty as fuck. He had to make it right before he could let anyone know what he was doing.

Armani cleared his throat and forced a small laugh. "Nickname. Right. All in good fun. No worries, *tesoro.*"

'*Treasure*' in Italian. Gio sucked back a growl. The fucker had no right to call her that.

Elise's body loosened a little, but her eyes trailed her fiancé's frame slowly, like she was making sure he was in one piece.

He was.

*For now.*

Gio forced a smile and his sister narrowed her eyes.

"I know you still haven't mastered 'manners' yet, but don't practice on Marco." She cocked her head to one side, her long blonde locks shifting, brushing the shoulder left revealed by the design of the fancy platinum dress. Like her shoes, it glimmered in the available light, as if she was wearing a diamond.

The fabric dipped lower on one side, but covered her other shoulder and lead to a long sleeve where, like the shoulder, the other arm was bare. The bodice revealed more than he'd like to see his sister showing, but he didn't have time to holler at her. Besides, Elise Giovanni was a beautiful woman. Looked just like their mother.

The gala was likely some fancy party for high-rollers, so his sister and the douche-caboose were both dressed to the nines.

Black tie, like the security officer had mentioned.

Sam, also in a tux, hovered in the open ballroom doorway, silently watching the exchange, but he stayed where he was, about fifty feet away.

Well, Gio wouldn't take time to converse with baby bro. His mission with this asshole was far from done. Too bad his sister had found them together.

Not only did he have no answers, he hadn't been

able to blacken the fucking liar's eye. Or both of them. His two balls could use some damage, too.

"What's really going on here?" Elise's dark eyes were narrowed, and her hands were back on her hips.

"You know, I had to do my big brotherly duty and warn him to treat my sister well, and all that." Gio forced a smile, and Marco let out a nervous laugh.

"You don't have to worry about that," the fucker said, taking a step away, and pulling Elise to his side, much like he'd done last night in their father's office.

*You're right, 'cause there's no fucking way you're marrying her.*

His sister's expression softened when she looked up at her liar-fiancé. She wove her arm around his waist and moved closer. Then she put her eyes back at Gio. "Did you come for the gala?" She arched an eyebrow, like she already knew the answer to her own question.

"I came to make sure you were okay."

Elise offered a small smile. "We're…coping. Dom should be here soon. You should stay and talk to him. He's taking Dad's situation really hard. He went to the hospital this morning."

Gio fought the urge to swallow as his mouth went dry. "I can't tonight. But tell him to call me." Damn, he really wanted a drink now. His throat was a desert, begging for some scotch.

Her brows knitted, and he couldn't stand it.

He shot forward and tugged her away from Armani, urging her into an embrace. He glared at the fucker over her head. "You look great, Lise," he whispered and dropped a kiss on her neatly coiffed head.

"Thanks." When she pulled back, her dark eyes were misty. "I wish you'd stay. We can get you a tux or something."

"You know I'm not good at that shit."

She gave the barest nod and he wanted to shoot himself at the disappointment in her expression.

They just looked at each other for a moment that felt like an hour. After a mutual breath, they spoke at the same time.

"Did you think about going to the hospital?"

"I should head out."

Elise closed her eyes.

Gio sure as hell wanted to do the same.

G io stared at the white nondescript door. Little gold numbers formed 472 nailed to the front, which was the only thing differentiating it from the others lining both sides of the hallway.

The building was six floors of nice; not too ritzy and not too rundown, with shiny elevators and corridor decorations, at both ends of the hallway, with a floral display on a table by the elevators. It was bright, with welcoming golden light, and the blue carpet smelled new.

He tried to gather the balls to knock.

Why Gio had come, he couldn't figure, but after the latest disaster at *The Giovanni,* he'd gone back to the PD only to discover the taskforce had called it a night.

He needed to see Maddie. Couldn't explain why. Something drove him toward her.

She'd been the only person on his mind.

Maybe she was the only one who would keep him from breaking out the scotch.

It'd only taken the work of a few minutes to get the address of the place she was staying, and he'd been surprised to discover it was an apartment, instead of a hotel.

His curiosity about that equaled the total cluelessness of him standing at her door.

*If you knock, maybe you could ask.*

But really, why was he there?

It wasn't like he was about to tell her what he'd discovered about his sister's so-called fiancé, or what'd happened at the casino with said fucker.

*Or lack thereof.*

He should've pounded the guy's face into his ass, despite Elise and Sam's presence.

It wouldn't have helped his family sitch—his sister would've had an added reason to be displeased with him, but it would've made him feel a hell of a lot better.

He'd figure out who the turd was soon enough, then go from there.

Gio and Maddie had nothing to discuss about the case. If he opened his mouth, they'd argue, because her evidence pointed to something only his gut said was untrue. He had nothing concrete to exonerate his father, and *her* proof only crucified him. Or worse, implicated his sister, since she was in charge of everything money at *The Giovanni.*

Even if he *had* figured out Marco-the-cockstain, he wouldn't have been able to bring Maddie in on it yet.

"Fuck. Me."

*Fuck—fucking.*

That was a good idea.

Maybe he and Maddie—

He snorted. She'd denied him. Rejected him

yesterday.

That just heaped on another dose of crazy, since he was still standing at her door.

Is sex what he'd expected from coming here?

Gio only wanted everything in his head to stop. He made a fist and gave a quick double knock.

Then waited.

Waited some more.

So much time passed, he was about to give up and go, when Maddie finally wrenched the door open.

She was adorably disheveled. Her hair was damp and mussed, making the golden waves darker in color, and her pretty face was pink, as if she'd just gotten out of the shower.

Somehow, the idea revved up his resolve.

The scent of fresh soap swirled around him, mixed with something that was just Maddie, and his hands itched to grab her. She wore an oversized soft pink tee and gray sweats. Relaxed clothing, incredibly sexy, and he'd seen her in a lot less.

"Gio..." Her gorgeous eyes widened. She swallowed, and he wanted to kiss her throat.

"Hey."

Maddie arched an eyebrow. "I'd ask what you want, but the more urgent question is how did you find me?"

He smirked. "I'm a good little stalker."

As for what he wanted...she wouldn't like his answer.

His statement tugged the corner of her mouth up, but her brow was still quirked. "Well, why?"

"Why what?"

"Why'd you hunt me down?" She let go of the door and crossed her arms over her breasts.

He struggled to tear his eyes from that temptation, and met her hazel ones. "I…wanted to talk to you."

That honey-colored eyebrow shot high again. "You could've done that all day. You barely said a damn word." Maddie tilted her head, studying him. "Or, I dunno. You could've called. Texted. Emailed. What's so urgent?"

*You.*

Not like he could fucking say that. He couldn't explain that *she* was the answer to dull the voices in his head, either. She always had been, even eight years ago. She hadn't known him long then, but she'd helped him get through his mom's passing. Sorta. The alcohol helped, too.

Gio's mouth went dry. Anything he said would make him sound like a liar. Something he'd already done to her today, even if she didn't know.

He took a step forward, then another, forcing her back inside the apartment, and he followed, using his much larger frame to make her give enough space to close the door. He did so with a well-placed kick.

Her feet were bare, which made him tower over her even more.

"Gio, wh—"

He snatched her to his chest, and covered her mouth with his.

Maddie was right with him. There was no delay in her opening and kissing him back, so score one for him.

Their tongues danced and dueled, only this time she wove her arms around his neck and pressed closer, her soft curves melding into his chest. She didn't have a bra on from her tiny peaked nipples brushing against his torso. That made him groan.

Gio slanted his lips over hers again and again, tasting her until she sagged in his arms, and his head spun. His zipper bit into his hard cock, and damn, he wanted her.

The burn for her was familiar, but his desire *ached*; it'd been so long since he'd held *this* woman in his arms.

The sense of rightness holding onto her that used to tease him back then, even though he'd been too young to want it, cascaded over him like it had before. But this was different, too. Stronger. More urgent.

Now, he didn't want to let her go.

"Gio," Maddie breathed into his mouth.

"Do me a favor, don't lie to me." His statement came out low, guttural.

She pulled back and stared up at him, those eyes amber with arousal, just like he remembered.

He bit back another groan.

"Lie to you?" She panted, pushing her impossibly soft breasts into his chest even more.

"Don't tell me you don't want me."

The crimson stain on her high cheekbones spread, deepening and going up to her ears. She was so beautiful. So much *more* than he remembered.

He expected her to look away, but she didn't.

Maddie didn't pull from his arms, either. "I—"

"You what?" Gio demanded softly.

"Is that what you came over here for? Sex?" Her demands didn't hold enough accusation for any real bite. She still remained his in embrace, her breasts to his chest, her hips glued to his.

There was no way she couldn't feel his erection.

"I don't know."

Maddie cocked her head to one side and her hazel stare bored into him. "Really?"

"You're the only one who can quiet the noise in my head." The bit of honesty made him wince, but her face softened, and his heart skipped.

"It's your dad, isn't it? Did you come from the hospital?"

"No. The casino." He couldn't lie to her again, not about his stupid father.

*Sorta.*

"How's your dad?"

"No change."

It wasn't untrue, even if he didn't know the details. Elise would've told him if something about their father's medical condition had worsened; or improved. Big Tony was still in the hospital, and Gio still couldn't go.

"Oh, Gio."

Guilt made him feel like a liar after all. Again.

She'd told him all those years ago that half-truths were just as bad as lies. The same for lies of omission.

Maddie squeezed her arms around him and pushed to her toes to kiss him.

Gio quickly took control, and the lip-lock went on until his balls pulsed painfully.

Her hands opened and closed on his biceps, but she made no move to pull away. "We shouldn't do this. It's a horrible idea," she whispered as they both struggled for normal airflow.

"You're probably right."

That gave her pause, and those green-flecked golden eyes were so fathomless as she scanned his face. There were so many questions there, but Maddie didn't ask him anything.

Should he mourn or rejoice?

"Do you want me to leave?" Gio whispered.

Why the fuck was he giving her an out?

The hovering guilt gave him an answer he wanted to ignore. He was playing off her sympathies regarding his father to get in her pants. That was *worse* than lying.

Was he using her?

"When you kiss me, it feels like it did eight years ago. More than that, it feels like no time has passed."

He had a feeling the confession wasn't planned, because her gorgeous face lit up all over again, a more appealing shade of pink than he'd ever seen.

Gio cleared his throat. "Same for me. I tried to say that yesterday." This, at least, was a truth he could confess.

Maddie's eyes went misty.

His tongue glued to the roof of his mouth. He should've teased her instead of gone for the truth. It was too heavy, old emotions making something more out of this than the lust he was trying to ride out. The lust he needed to concentrate on.

Maddie had been right about one thing yesterday.

Eight years *was* a long time. However, when he held her, kissed her, Gio felt he same about her as he had at twenty-three.

That couldn't spell anything but disaster. Worsened of course, because of her case.

He wanted to say something—anything—but words wouldn't form.

"I'm sorry for threatening to go to Olinsky. I don't want you kicked off the taskforce." Her voice was soft, and she averted her gaze. "I'm not afraid to work with you. You're a detective now, and all your coworkers say you're a hell of a cop. You *can* help my case."

"You want to talk about this now?" He sure as hell didn't, despite the compliment that was no doubt Hector-originated. Gio needed her body to be the distraction he'd been seeking. He needed to bury himself inside her and forget. At least for a little while.

Maybe he had come to her place for sex, after all.

He couldn't let himself feel the guilt. He cared about her—whether he wanted to or not—so he *wasn't* using Maddie.

Those hazel eyes flared when he rolled his pelvis, pushing his erection into her belly.

Maddie rocked her hips right back and he groaned. Her attention landed on his mouth. "Not really."

He smiled, slow, intentionally sexy, and a bit triumphant.

Madison Granger never could tell him no.

"Wanna show me where you might have a bed in this place?"

M addie cradled her face in her hands. She was in her bathroom, planted on the closed toilet. She'd…run from Gio so she could…think.

*What the* hell *are you doing?*

Something she had no business even considering—ever.

Besides, it was too soon. She'd just gotten back in to town.

*Yesterday.*

Somehow, none of that mattered.

His kisses were just as potent as eight years ago. *He* was just as hot as then, too. No, maybe more so, since he'd grown into a real man, more seasoned, more muscled than the rookie cop, twenty-three-year-old Gio.

The kiss in the office supply room was like a preview.

For him showing up on her doorstep? Or for an X-rated movie?

She'd spent the day pretending not to notice him, trying not to spare him any glances as he'd posted himself, fairly brooding, in the corner of the conference room her taskforce had taken over at the PD.

He hadn't said much, so she'd failed to see him in real action. No proof of what Olinsky and his coworkers had raved; Gio was the best detective on the squad. Hector Garcia had especially had nice things to say, but she suspected a little hero-worship. Not that he wasn't worthy of that.

If anyone asked him anything, Gio stated he was considering the evidence and would let them know when he had a plan. Who knew, maybe that was his normal way of investigating. Perhaps, since no one contradicted him.

Maddie had let it all go; she was trying to avoid him, after all.

Speaking of brooding, she'd mulled over what he'd said about his father since he'd declared Big Tony couldn't possibly be laundering money.

Her initial investigation hadn't been able to prove what the Chicago accountant, Cesare Fratelli, had claimed. *The Giovanni* had been started by mob funds traced back to the Falcone crime family. It was heavily suspected, but rumors were rumors—hearsay that didn't help her at all.

Regardless, Gio's father had kept his nose clean.

For over forty years.

The latest activity they'd detected had been new. Less than a year ago in origin.

She'd asked herself a dozen times what'd changed. So far, her delving into the financials only revealed that something was off. The details were fuzzy, which is why she'd gotten the go-head to come to Sin City and fully check things out.

So maybe Gio had a point.

Maybe *that* had been part of the reason she'd promised to let him prove his father's innocence, as he'd claimed he would.

Maddie wouldn't report his tie to the casino to Olinsky. Even after only meeting and working with the guy a day and a half, she could tell the fair-haired man was on the up-and-up, and would yank Gio off the taskforce in a heartbeat.

Not making the case harder on him would have to extend to his father's health. No matter what the full investigation uncovered, there'd be hurt for Gio and his family. She'd always liked his siblings, especially his sister, Elise.

Maddie could only hope getting reacquainted with them didn't involve too many jail cells. Research had revealed Elise worked in accounting at *The Giovanni*, and as much as she hated it, the beautiful girl she'd called a friend eight years ago was implicated, too. She wouldn't speculate. Only cold, hard evidence from a real investigation mattered.

She also wasn't naïve to the meaning of Gio's declaration, *"I'll prove it,"* either. He wasn't going to involve her—or the taskforce—in his mission. His behavior today shouted that.

One of the things Nico Giovanni did best was embody *I am an island*. She'd have to push her former lover to open up about anything he discovered. They'd argue tons. That was so Gio, too.

*Former lover.*

Maddie sucked back a gasp and called herself all kinds of nutso.

Nico Giovanni was in her bedroom.

Probably naked in her bed by now.

One kiss at her front door and she'd fallen hook, line, and sinker for every word out of his mouth. She *hated* that she'd melted at his declaration *she* was the only one who could quiet the noise in his head.

Where the fuck was her resolve?

She'd rejected him in that supply room — but that'd come with a pack of lies, too. She'd told him she was over him. Had been for years.

*Liar liar.*

Maddie snorted and scanned the small bathroom attached to her new bedroom. A set of plastic drawers she'd used in Chicago to organize her girly things sat on the floor with a cardboard box on top of it. She'd already stocked the medicine cabinet and put a few towels in the built-in cupboard in the corner, but only because she'd needed to shower.

This was her third night in the new place and the only room she'd entirely unpacked was the kitchen.

Funny, she'd been too tired to do any further unboxing when she'd gotten home from the PD. Now? Unpacking was a damn good idea.

A better idea than…

*Gio.*

She'd told him she needed a minute.

Maddie really needed days…months…years?

She gulped.

The familiar guilt regarding Jake swirled in her gut.

*Yeah, but I don't have to fuck him to make up for it.*

She snorted. Not like sex would "make up for it" anyways.

He still wouldn't know about their son, and she would've added another mistake to her belt concerning the half-Italian, half-Greek demigod in her bed. All work-case-stuff aside, of course.

*Would've? Who am I kidding?*

She was *totally* going into that room to have sex with the man who'd fathered her son.

Even if she lied to herself that she didn't want to.

The knock on the door made her jump.

"Maddie? You okay in there?"

She'd wanted him from the first time she'd seen him, then she'd been addicted, even though he was younger, drank too much and was too reckless as a cop.

Then he'd lost his mom, and since hers had died when she was barely grown, she'd had even more of an excuse to see him; they could commiserate. She'd made Gio's comfort her mission. Hadn't been able to stay away; or out of his bed.

"Maddie? You're starting to freak me out."

His second query jarred her, and she almost fell off the toilet. She braced herself on the nearby sink in the tiny room. The slapping noise made her wince.

"What was that? Did you fall? Maddie."

Her name was all warning, much darker than his two questions.

*Answer him, dumbass.*

Her words scattered from her brain to her mouth, so she had to clear her throat and try again. Had she locked the door? Damn, she couldn't remember.

"Umm…I'm fine. I'm…good. Be out in a minute."

There was a pause before he spoke again. "All right."

Very Gio, not to ask if she wanted him to leave. He'd already dutifully inquired at the front door.

She actually hadn't answered, but there also hadn't been a delay in her bringing him to her bedroom when he'd asked *that*.

Of course, she hadn't been smart enough to order him to go.

She shot to her feet and shucked her after-shower sweatpants, berating herself the whole time. Stomped her feet to free herself, then stepped away from the soft gray cotton on the floor by the tub.

Maddie needed to command a shutdown on her mind, really. Maybe her conscience. Her body still roared for him, so she needed to go with that.

*Right?*

She'd never gotten to say goodbye.

*Okay, loser, you can scratch that, because you ran from him, remember?*

Ran because she'd been afraid—deep down—that he *had* heard when she'd told him she was pregnant. Heard her and didn't give a shit.

For years, she'd wrestled with the idea Gio had avoided her *because* of it, before settling on the fact he *had* actually been too drunk. He hadn't comprehended her very important news, flung at him in a moment of hurt at his rejection. He'd told he didn't deserve her. Told her he couldn't handle a relationship. Told her he'd been too much of a mess.

Maddie had been the bigger one.

*I should've reached out to him.*

She'd only told herself *that* eleventy billion and five times.

Yes, she needed to tell her conscience to take a hike.

Her hormones were totally on board with that.

She yanked her shirt over her head and forced her feet forward, ignoring the shake in her hand when she reached for the doorknob.

Maddie hadn't put a bra back on after her shower, so she kept her panties on, and luckily she'd chosen simple lace. They were black, lightly sexy, and at least not her normal granny-panties, as Jamie would accuse.

Maybe subconsciously she'd known she was getting laid today?

Or fate was fucking with her.

With her luck, probably the latter.

She hadn't bothered with nice undies since she'd brushed sex off the table. It'd been a while. The few liaisons she'd had had been casual. No relationships there and no one that'd mattered. An FBI agent she'd been drawn to for his Gio-like qualities—if she was honest; a college acquaintance, an old boyfriend once. All of the above had left her with a reality check; single mothers shouldn't be accomplished at casual sex.

Her tummy somersaulted. Shouldn't matter how long ago it'd been since she'd lain with a man. She'd been with Gio before.

So why *did* it matter?

After all, she'd had a baby since then, and even though she was in shape, her body was different.

She needed him to want her like he had eight years ago.

Maddie sucked in air to fortify her courage to tug the door open.

Their eyes locked. Desire glittered in those darkening sapphires.

Gio's nostrils flared, like he was breathing her in, and his expression intensified. His Adam's apple bobbed.

She shivered, but not because she was cold. The way he was looking at her made her feel like a goddess.

Hunger, raw and honest was in that gaze, like he hadn't had a meal in months.

*Check. He still wants me.*

Maddie tried to control her tremors and rubbed her arm.

He didn't speak, and the longer the silence lasted, the further her nerves descended into hell.

Gio had taken his shirt off, and his jeans were slung low, belt open, zipper down. Gray boxers peeked out, as well as an obvious tent.

He wasn't just hot, he was incendiary.

He'd always had a nice body, but what was before her proved he'd continued a gym regimen—unless he really was a demigod.

His pecs flexed as if they liked her watching, and she stopped counting the abs when she got to six on each side.

Gio always had a nice ass, too, but the way the jeans hugged there, and the thickness of his thighs told Maddie he kept up with his running.

"Mads, God, I—"

*Mads?*

The Gio-only nickname dissolved her on the spot. There was no hope of escape.

A wave of emotion that had more to do with love than lust, and *completely* forbidden, smacked into her. She had to swallow. Twice. "I missed you, too."

*Dammit, why'd you say that?*

Maddie made her eyes dart all over the mostly unpacked room. She needed to say something.

Nothing came.

She studied the open boxes stacked in the corner, then her desk, with a few more still taped up and resting on top of it.

He didn't speak to her confession, and that didn't help her discomfort.

"Gio—" she forced his nickname out, but still couldn't look at him.

He darted forward, claimed her waist and the small of her back with huge warm hands. His lips settled over hers, absorbing her surprised gasp.

Anything else she might've said was ripped away. Coherent thought fled, along with all the rest of the stuff—guilt, reservations, everything.

Maddie let Gio kiss her, let her body respond.

No other lover had ever made her feel like this. Only *him*.

She wanted to experience him again.

And she *would.*

The kiss she'd told herself she hadn't wanted in the supply room didn't count. Maybe the one at the front door didn't, either.

This one was different. *More.*

He dominated her mouth, and his hands were on her ass, kneading, squeezing, making her squirm against him.

His chest was so hot against her breasts, and desire shot low with a pulsing demand already between her legs. The lace was in the way.

"You're so fucking gorgeous." Gio pushed the words into her mouth amongst nips and licks.

"Fucking…that's a good word," she panted.

He pulled back, and those blue orbs seared her from the inside out. "It was never just fucking with you, Mads. It won't be now, even though it's been too damn long."

Maddie's heart inverted. She wanted to shout a quick denial—a speech like that wasn't good for her, and he'd never spoken of feelings before, why would he hint like that after eight years?

*He's right, though.*

She shivered.

Gio kissed her again, dissipating her need to answer yet again. His fingertips on her back made her tremble. Then his big palms covered her breasts and she whimpered.

He pinched her nipples, not painful, but stimulating.

It made Maddie beg for more.

"Always so damn responsive," he murmured. "So glad that hasn't changed."

"Only for you," she blurted. "You turn me inside out."

He leaned away and smirked when their gazes brushed. "*Inside* is a good word, too." As he spoke, Gio slid his hand into her panties, moving up and down her already-slick sex, then shoving his finger inside her.

She gasped and grabbed his wrist.

He stilled. "Did I hurt you?"

"No." Maddie shook her head.

"You never had the patience for me teasing you." He flashed a sexy grin with enough genuine warmth to liquefy her even more, and tugged her underwear down in a quick move.

"Your teases were never fair." She stepped free of her bikinis.

"You always came harder."

Heat flushed to her toes and her core throbbed against the heel of his palm cupping her. "Maybe."

Gio chuckled, and the sound was as good as his touch, like the thumb currently circling her clit. "Nah, it's a sure thing."

"Gonna…stand here and…talk all night?" Maddie struggled through words as he revved her up even more, adding and taking away pressure on her ultra-sensitive nub.

He laughed again, but shook his head and kissed her, hard and fast.

It was over much too soon, and she quivered when

he pulled his hand away.

He swung her up into his arms. "I intend to make you scream my name all night."

"Prove it."

Gio growled, then showed he was a man of action, like he always had been. He dropped her to the middle of her bed and shoved his jeans down.

She couldn't tear her eyes away from every inch of flesh he bared, especially when he nixed his boxers.

*Damn,* he was even hotter fully naked. Hotter than before.

He stalked to her bed and mounted it like she needed him to mount *her.*

"Gio," she moaned his name. She heard the plea, and when he licked his lips, she couldn't control the shaking in her whole body.

Anticipation. Desire. Need.

She'd likely come in the first two seconds, she wanted him so badly.

He wasted no time wrenching her legs apart at her knees, and she thrust her hips up when he came down to her, hovering his chest over her breasts. Gio's blunt nipples brushed hers; his chest hair tickled, and a whimper breeched her lips.

Maddie was going to combust if he didn't touch her. Kiss her.

Get inside her.

"I want to taste every inch of your body to see if you're the same, but I need to take you first." His voice was deeper than moments before, almost guttural.

Good to know he wanted her just as badly.

"Inside me," Maddie begged.

Gio perched on his haunches and grabbed his erection, letting out a groan.

Somehow, he was even more intoxicating in that moment, touching himself and unable to hide a tiny sound of pleasure.

"Condom?" he asked.

"I have an IUD." She couldn't bear being separated from his body, even by a thin layer of latex, but she couldn't tell him that, either.

She reached for him when he dipped toward her.

Their bodies came together from head to foot, and he filled her with a quick jolt forward.

They both gasped.

*Rightness*—the same as eight years ago—hit Maddie, and she bit her bottom lip to keep from crying like a big baby. Tears during sex weren't something she'd done before, certainly not before they'd really gotten started.

She needed to concentrate on the pleasure he was already giving her. There would only be more, like it'd always been with Gio.

He stilled above her, his gaze intense. "You okay?"

"Yes. I need you to move." She closed her eyes and tilted her head back as he answered with a grunt and obeyed.

He drove forward hard, keeping the ecstasy sharp and her thoughts scattered as she could only hold on to keep up with him.

She avoided the tenderness in his sapphire eyes, despite how his hips pistoned.

Gio gave as he took, and her heart couldn't handle it.

Maddie tugged him down and crashed her mouth into his. He didn't hesitate to kiss her back, winding her higher and higher as his tongue matched his thrusts.

She wrapped her arms and legs around him, lifting her pelvis to take him deeper, to move with him, under him, against him.

Until it was all too much and she exploded.

She jerked her mouth off of his and screamed his name. Orgasm made her vision go black and her whole body clench.

Gio was right with her, shoving forward once more like a bulldozer. Her new bedframe creaked a protest as he stilled and threw his head back. He gritted through his release, his powerful form tight as he held himself above her.

Then he collapsed on top of her. "God, Mads." His hot breath caressed her cheek and Maddie only wanted to get closer.

His softening cock slipped from her sex, and a sense of loss cascaded, despite the no-space between their bodies.

She whimpered.

He stilled. Pulled back and tugged her chin up.

She called herself a coward for smashing her eyes shut, but she gave a small smile when he kissed her eyelids so gently it only intensified the unwanted emotion hitting hard.

"Mads?" he whispered.

Maddie tried to take a *subtle* fortifying inhale so

she could look at him, but her breasts lifted into his chest.

"Mads?" Gio repeated. "You okay?"

*Nod. Just nod.*

"More than okay." The words came out a croak, but his answering smile was brilliant and made her heart stutter.

"Me, too. More than you know."

Damn, he looked *happy*.

She couldn't avert her eyes like she wanted to. Couldn't risk the third degree, and really didn't want to wipe that expression away. It resembled one Jake wore when her son was excited about something.

*Shit. Jake.*

Her heart flip-flopped for reasons other than forbidden emotions for the hot cop holding her.

Gio still didn't know about their son, and she'd just had sex with him.

She'd conveniently used the case and getting her taskforce settled as excuses the last two days, then jacked up the avoidance after the kiss in the supply room.

Maddie couldn't dodge telling him for much longer, and how could *this* make her look?

He relaxed in her bed as if he didn't have a care in the world, one arm tucked behind his head on her pillow. With the other, he urged her to him, and started rubbing her back in large soothing circles.

Gio closed his eyes, contentment dominating his handsome face, but her stomach had never been knotted tighter.

*Dear God, what have I done?*

G ian cursed long and hard. What the hell was he going to do?

How the ever-living-fuck had Elise's cop brother found out he wasn't the unassuming Marco Fratelli?

After the news of Cesare Fratelli's "disappearance" and likely arrest by the feds, this could only spell trouble. The cop not liking him was one thing; finding him out was something he couldn't abide.

Something that might have to slap murder on the table after all. His favorite knife, one of the tactical police variety, was in his pocket and he knew how to use it.

He'd always preferred knives to guns. Guns required little skill to kill. Knives, on the other hand made killing an art. Gian just usually didn't do that kind of thing himself. After all, his family had people for that.

Did Fratelli's disappearance have anything to do with his fiancée's brother outing him?

Nah, the oldest Giovanni was local heat, not a fed.

Gian didn't want to contemplate the *why* of the

discovery; maybe the asshole was looking out for his sister and had done a background check. Even his fake docs couldn't substantiate a lifetime paper trail...he hadn't paid enough for that.

He couldn't afford to take time to kick himself about it, nor would it be helpful. His situation was what it was.

He was going to have to call Uncle Dino, but it was a risk; for more than one reason. He tried to keep their contact at a minimum, and they weren't due for another phone meeting or another transfer of money for a week.

The man hadn't called him back after he'd ended their call, and Gian didn't want to admit his uncle might be right about them slowing down, or taking a break. He was in a hurry to get back in his father's good graces. A break, even for a week, hurt his target. It was an impressive amount, to show his dad he *was* worth it.

He could handle anything.

No, he didn't want to call his uncle. He had to solve this problem on his own.

"Dammit," he muttered.

Well, was his cover really blown?

*Yes.*

Even if he couldn't pinpoint the current level of danger, he was no longer secure in his little Vegas bubble.

"Fuck." Gian ran his hand through his hair and glanced at his Rolex. His father had gifted it to him for his sixteenth birthday, and the damn thing made him think fondly of the asshole, if only a little.

It was barely ten p.m. and there were two more

hours of this torture, the annual gala.

Just because Nico Giovanni had released him from the wall and dropped his declaration, didn't mean the cop would let things go.

Quite the opposite, most likely.

His fiancée had nothing but good things to say about her big brother, and raved about how proud she was of him being a police detective. The glory boy had made detective at age twenty-seven or something. She never discussed him around their father, of course. Big Tony always grimaced at any mention of the son who everyone seemed to call *Gio*.

Maybe old habits did always die hard.

Antonio Giovanni had been best friends with Gian's father Luciano, along with Cesare Fratelli, where they'd grown up in Chicago. Gian's grandfather had then run the family business—the Falcone Syndicate, as his own Daddy Dearest like to refer to it.

Big Tony, Luciano and Cesare had gotten it in their heads to establish a casino in Vegas, following Bugsy Seigel's footsteps of course, and had "borrowed" some money—a *lot* of money for the times—from Grandpa Falcone, or so the story went.

His father *never* discussed what'd happened afterward, but somehow Luciano and Cesare had ended up out in the cold, and *The Giovanni* had been born.

Cesare Fratelli went on to open his CPA firm and handled the Falcone finances on the "it looks legal" side of things. His job was to keep federal noses and alphabet soup agencies where they belonged. Out of

Falcone books and assorted "businesses."

Uncle Dino had always refused to explain what'd happened surrounding the casino. His father's younger brother either didn't know or was too embarrassed to say. *Or* had been sworn to secrecy, maybe paid off, knowing his family.

Who the hell knew?

That ledger was supposed to tell Gian, and he still couldn't fucking find it. He needed to take another shot at the office, but hadn't safely had the chance.

His grandfather had been rather ruthless, so why Big Tony had been allowed to live baffled Gian. If his father had taken the full blame for missing money, that purpose hadn't been solved, either. It wasn't unheard of for a mob-boss to whack his own son, but Gramps hadn't laid a finger on Luciano's head. Maybe his father hadn't had the balls to off someone he'd grown up with, but that didn't seem much like Luciano, either. His dad was a lot like ol' Grandpa.

The man hadn't hesitated to kick Gian to the curb over a little disagreement. Okay, a lot of disagreements, but still. His mother had begged his father not to disown him, but the plea had fallen on deaf ears.

He hadn't called her since the night of the big fallout that'd caused him to leave Chi-town. Uncle Dino was the only Falcone he'd had any contact with. He didn't regret his father—at all—but even as a grown man, he had to admit he missed his mother. A little. She'd always been good to him, duchess of Italian guilt or not.

Conversations and the clinking of glasses and

silverware on plates were background noise to the calculations going on in his brain. Soothing music played from a live band on the stage, so the dancing must've started.

What the fuck was he going to do?

Gian scanned the huge ballroom. The gala was in full swing.

Could he slip away?

If he did, what the hell was he going to do anyway? Brood in the penthouse he shared with Elise?

He'd like to take another run at Big Tony's office, but even if all known Giovannis were present in this room, it wasn't a good idea to try again so soon. There was no logical explanation for why he'd be in that room. He couldn't risk getting caught.

His identity was already blown by big brother, and Gian hated to admit he didn't know what the fucker was going to *do* with that information.

He didn't want to run to his uncle for a few reasons. Didn't want Dino to try to rescue him, or tell him, *I-told-you-so*, especially since the older man had wanted to delay the money laundering. After all, his uncle had been down with his plan all these months. He also didn't want the only Falcone who didn't hate him to have a reason to see him as weak.

He'd have to handle Elise's brother, and he couldn't kill the bastard.

Yet, anyway.

It was smarter not to have a body trail, especially starting with a dead cop, future family, or not. He'd for sure have to figure out everything the fucker knew beforehand. No one except Uncle Dino knew Gian's whereabouts, so if he did need to dispose of Nico, he'd have to do it himself, and he'd never been fond of the mess of killing. Didn't trust anyone to outsource it, either.

He growled and reached for his phone. Started a text for Uncle Dino to call him, but then deleted it and pocketed the device in his Armani tux. He didn't have the burner and he didn't want to risk anything on his "real" cellphone.

"Hey, where are you right now?"

Gian jumped and sucked back a curse at the low inquiry. He met Elise's dark brown eyes, trying to smile away her obvious concern. "No worries, *tesoro*. I'm here." He grabbed her hand and brought it to his mouth, pressing a kiss to her soft knuckles.

Only one corner of her mouth shot up, missing his mark. "You look really worried." As she spoke, her brow knitted.

He leaned down and pressed a quick kiss to her lips.

Gian intended to marry her after all, and even if he *was* trying to steal her family's business out from under them, there was nothing that said he couldn't *like* her, right?

His fiancée's expression softened a little. "The gala is going great, so you're not worried about that. So, what is it? You and I make a great team."

Elise was always trying to 'diagnose' him like that.

"You're right. We do make a fantastic team, and I think *you* worry too much."

She cocked her head to one side. "Probably. There's a lot to freak out about these days."

"Don't think about your dad, babe. Even *he* said for you to enjoy tonight. He'll be out of the hospital before you know it, and we will be able to talk him into chemo. It'll work out."

They'd had to endure a phone call with the old bastard earlier that evening, and of course, since Big Tony didn't think Elise should handle the affairs of the huge casino; he'd had to be present, too. Like the old man required proof of life that his legacy wouldn't collapse from him being in the hospital for the last few days.

Her smile was sad, like she doubted him, and she averted her gaze. She took a big inhale that made her fantastic tits rise, and strain against the hot Versace platinum number she'd poured herself into.

Gian wanted to make her smile for some reason. He cupped her face. "Did I tell you how scrumptious you look?"

She granted his wish, her luscious mouth curved up, in 1000-watt territory.

"Thanks. I think so, but I don't mind hearing it twice." Elise eyed him up and down, and tugged on his jacket's lapel. "You don't look so bad yourself."

His libido awoke with a jolt down his spine. He growled and leaned down to nip her mouth. "Don't make me spirit you away from here."

She grinned, and it made his balls ache. "Sorry, honey, we need to stay until this shindig is over. Dad said Giovannis need to be visible, and he's right about that. We can't have big money nervous. There are too many casinos around. It's all about amenities, remember?"

"Your brothers are here."

Elise sobered. "Sam and Dom aren't enough, unfortunately. *I* have to be here. You, too, are integral." She paused, biting her bottom lip. "Brothers… You're not worried about what happened with Gio earlier, are you?"

He feigned appropriate surprise. "Hell no."

She cocked her fair head to one side and he wanted to sweep those glorious pale locks off her neck and kiss her there. That always made her melt into him.

Damn, he needed to get a hold of his…lust for her.

"You sure? Don't worry; I'm going to kick his ass for the stunt he pulled."

Gian forced a laugh. "He just cares about you, *tesoro*. I don't blame him for trying to protect you. He didn't know about me, after all."

The asshole had been clever citing big brother duty; he had to give him that.

However, what had kept him rattled the rest of the night was what the fuck he would've said if Elise *hadn't* come down the hallway. He *needed* an answer that made sense to keep Nico off his back.

It was only a matter of time before her brother would force the issue again.

Only knowing what the cop had uncovered about him would make him feel better. Would help determine his next move.

A guilty flush of pink kissed her cheeks. "I'm

sorry. I just didn't know how to tell him. Gio is…well, like you said, always protective. Dad approving of you is only another reason to make him contrary. You know how they get along."

Gian tapped her pert little nose. "Don't blame him. I feel the same way. Protective is a smart way to be, concerning you."

She beamed again. "I love you."

He told himself to relax. It was a *good* thing she loved him. He was fully *in* with her, and they really did have Big Tony's blessing.

"Me, too." He stopped short of saying the words. Love was weakness, and not something he'd ever felt for a woman, other than his mother. He didn't love her. Would never love her, as much as he admired her smarts. Gian never returned her three-word-declaration with anything other than, *'me too'* or *'ditto'*. She'd never called him on it.

Elise was a good business woman, but *he* was better. She was too trusting, which was a damn good thing, or he wouldn't have accomplished all he already had.

When she wrapped her arms around him, he pulled her in and held onto her for a moment.

"Hey, wanna dance with me?" he whispered above her ear.

She pulled back and smiled again.

Elise Giovanni certainly was a beautiful woman, especially with those killer dark eyes and naturally blonde hair that made them even more striking. High cheekbones and a heart-shaped face added to her appeal. He couldn't complain about her appearance, or her skill in bed.

"Sure. We only have to last until twelve, then I'll dance *for* you."

"Oh yeah?"

She nodded, a twinkle in those midnight orbs. "Naked."

Gian's cock liked that idea. He smiled; this time it was genuine. "Deal."

His fiancée giggled, and he guided her out to the dance floor.

His troubles we far from over, but maybe they should both follow Big Tony's advice and enjoy the evening.

K<br>♥

Gio's head was blissfully quiet. Maddie and pleasure were the only things consuming his thoughts, absorbing his concentration. He wanted to draw it out. Make it last.

Maybe forever.

That should scare the shit of out him, but it didn't. His life hadn't been right since she'd walked out on him eight long years ago.

He might've only seen her again thirty-six hours ago, but that didn't seem to hit his radar either.

Gio cupped her shoulder and dragged his palm down the soft skin of her biceps, elbow and her wrist. She lay in her bed with her back facing him, deliciously naked, and her ass tucked into his thighs as he lay behind her.

When he neared her hip, he caressed her there, then moved on, skimming his fingers over her perfect bottom. It was made up of just the right amount of muscle and roundness to hold it high and tight, and make him want to bite her there; nibble and tease her flesh, but his tongue also tingled to taste her elsewhere.

He tugged her onto her back, and drew his fingertips over her lower belly, then lower between her legs.

She moaned, but didn't open her eyes. Maddie lifted her arm and tucked her hand behind her head on the pillows, elbow bent. A soft smile curved her mouth, as tempting as she was.

Her delectable breasts shifted with her movement and caught his eye; Gio watched her nipples. He leaned down and sucked one into his mouth. At the same time, he started to rub her clit.

She gasped and buried her free hand in his hair.

He smiled against her plump breast, and ran his tongue around her areola. "Hmmm, Mads, I want you again." He ran two fingers up and down her slick folds, and slipped them inside her.

She was already wet for him.

Maddie gasped and pulled his hair.

Their eyes met.

"I won't be able to walk tomorrow."

Gio chuckled. "Guess I'm just that good."

She smirked. "That, and the fact it's been forever for me. And you're a fan of rough sex."

He stilled, then frowned. "Did I hurt you?"

Maddie's golden locks scattered with the hard

shake. "No, Gio. You always give it to me the way I need it. The way I need you."

His heart thumped and words evaporated. He wiggled his fingers inside her and she tilted her chin up, making a sound in her throat.

"You're so damn tight. How many lovers have you had after me?" He cursed the question when it fell out. Didn't really want the answer. Kinda wanted to shoot any man who'd touched her.

Her pretty hazel eyes widened when their gazes met. "You're really asking me that when you're inside me?"

Gio groaned. Her choice of words gave him ideas that only his hands on her—fingers *in* her—wouldn't satisfy. He twisted his wrist and she gasped, reaching for him. He grabbed her hand with his free one, and entwined their fingers. "Never mind."

Maddie bit her bottom lip and averted her eyes. "Not as many as you, I'm sure. And no, I don't want to know." Her voice shook, as if she was hurt at the thought of him with another woman.

He had to swallow *again*, and squeezed her fingers.

Jealous, he could handle. The idea pleased more than he wanted to admit.

Hurt, he couldn't deal with; especially if *he* was the culprit.

Sure, he'd had sex after Maddie. He was no saint, but he hadn't been a whore, either. The only lovers he'd had were when shit had gotten to him and he'd needed a release. Always quick interludes that didn't mean much. Not like *her*. He was a guy, after all. It might be a cliché to state a man had needs, but it didn't make it less true.

No matter the female, they never quieted, contented, his brain like she could.

Maddie had always been on his mind, even then.

"I don't want to hurt you, so what if I just taste you instead of taking you?"

Her expression was grateful, as if she appreciated the subject change. Or maybe it was just his proposal. "If you want."

"Want? Driven to, is more like it."

Finally, she smiled a little.

Gio released her fingers after pressing a kiss to her knuckles and shoved her thighs wider. He settled his shoulders between her legs and inhaled the honeyed scent of her arousal. Closed his eyes and smiled, then dipped down to lick her.

Maddie gasped and grappled for a hold, but he planted her hands at her sides.

"I know you don't like giving up control, but let me make you feel good, Mads. I want to. I love this."

She nodded. Something darted across her eyes, but it was gone before he could question what.

He kissed right above her pubic hair, and continued downward, tasting, licking, nipping her tender swollen flesh.

Gio kept his fingers inside her, but rocked them, instead of thrusting hard like he wanted, since she was worried about being sore. His cock had been inside her for two rounds, and he'd take her as many times as Maddie let him, but he'd never want to hurt her.

She whimpered his name.

He swirled his tongue around her clit and sucked her into his mouth, reaching for her G-spot inside.

She bucked off the bed and lifted her hips, but he didn't slow or stop his ministrations. She buried a hand in his dark locks and tugged again, but he didn't give a shit if she yanked it out. Not when she was shaking in his grip like she couldn't get enough.

Hell, *he* couldn't get enough.

Maddie's free hand flailed, and her nails scraped the back of his shoulder and left biceps, but it didn't matter if the touch had a bite.

The only thing that mattered was how she tasted, and how her impending orgasm flooded his mouth with more of her essence. How her sex clutched his fingers, and how her clit pulsed under his tongue.

Gio crooked his fingers, rubbing her most sensitive spot on the inside, and intentionally nicked her swollen nub with a tooth.

She tossed her head back, making her hair fly, and screamed his nickname. Her thighs quivered and her sex constricted and relaxed in waves as the climax rolled over her.

Maddie came in his mouth. His tongue coated with the sweetest thing he'd ever tasted. He lapped up every drop.

She collapsed to the bed panting, and he couldn't tear his eyes away.

*She* was the most gorgeous thing he'd ever seen.

Her skin glistened with sweat, sporting a rosy glow from head to foot, from arousal and coming hard.

Maddie's hair was mussed from thrashing on the pillows, and an extra slash of crimson was across those high cheekbones up to her ears.

Gio couldn't breathe.

That look, *this* woman was what'd been missing from his life for eight long years.

He had to pant to get air down.

Gio shot up her body because he needed her in his arms. Burned to have her entire length against his. His cock was so hard it ached, but he didn't give a shit.

"Gio..." Maddie whispered, burying her face against his neck as soon her breasts touched his pecs.

He couldn't bear to have her face hidden. He cupped her cheeks and tilted up.

Gio stared into her eyes, still heavy lidded and dark amber with desire. Dipping down, he took her mouth and kissed her until his air was restricted again.

Until his chest was even tighter.

Couldn't put his finger on why; whether it was physical or mental. All he knew was if he didn't get Maddie closer, if he didn't hold her, kiss her, he'd not survive the night.

T he dreaded morning after.

Maddie's guilt was a live wire, snaking around her spine and threatening electrocution.

She didn't want to look at him, so it was a damn good thing when he'd kissed her after one cup of coffee and told her he needed to go home before they both headed to the PD.

It was Friday, and she told herself she only had to endure one workday being around him. They wouldn't work over the weekend, unless something really broke with the case.

She wouldn't allow herself to think of the next two days alone in her apartment.

Gio was *definitely* not invited. They couldn't have a repeat of last night.

She needed to tell him about their son.

Inspectors Griggs and Bailey should be in today at some point. They were trying to get a search warrant signed by a federal judge, since Maddie had put together all the probable cause affidavits from the info they had via FBI reports, IRS tax info, and the legwork she'd done. Whether the judge would agree they had enough evidence was a tossup. If not, they'd do more work and try again, but she'd been thorough on her PC paperwork.

Maddie stared at the door closed in Gio's wake. It was still early. She had enough time to shower and actually do her hair.

Everything was strange. This was her place, but it didn't feel like it. He'd been back in her bed, like no time had passed. She was back in Sin City, the City of Lights, a place she'd never wanted to be.

The night in his arms had her thinking…wanting.

That was more dangerous than a shootout.

Back in Chicago, she'd dreaded seeing him again, and now what had she done?

Met him one day, fucked him the next—almost as bad as when she'd first gotten together eight years ago.

*Ugh. Resistance is futile, and all that.*

He'd kissed her awake at 5:30 but they hadn't had sex. He'd touched her, tasted her again, then held her.

*So tender.*

She'd wanted to reciprocate—this man was the only one who'd ever brought out the urge to give a blowjob, but he'd stopped her. Told her she didn't have to, and he wanted to shower before she did that. A sweet sentiment, but it hadn't mattered.

Maddie had capitulated and just let him hold her, but after rocking her world with his mouth, that just put her heart in more peril. She'd drifted back to sleep, but Gio had woken her gently and told her he had to go.

After the coffee, he had.

She'd assumed he'd shower at her place, but he'd said he wanted fresh clothes.

Why was she mourning his departure as much as she felt guilty for *still* not telling him about Jake?

It should've been the first thing to leave her lips that morning.

Hell, it should've been the first thing she'd said in the storage room on day one. Or the first time she'd seen him in the hallway.

"Ugh," Maddie whispered and gripped the steaming coffee mug with both hands. She needed to get her ass moving instead of wading in sorrow and guilt at her kitchen table.

Her son's smile kept flashing in her mind, making her feel worse. It was Gio's lopsided grin in miniature.

She hadn't *exactly* forgotten what the man looked like over the past eight years, but not seeing him in person had dimmed the reality of how much her little guy resembled his dad.

"Damn." That just made the wallowing even worse, like she was in the swamps up to her torso, fighting not to drown.

She closed her eyes, sucked in much-needed air, and shoved the chair back.

Maddie should really capitalize on the rare quiet-time because when Jake and Jamie moved in, there would be no such thing.

Quiet made her…think.

Remember.

Compare sex with Gio back then to what'd happened last night.

*God, there is no comparison.*

He was better. Wine clichés were usually reserved for describing women, but Gio had aged like a fine wine.

She smiled in spite of the negative feelings warring with the good. Didn't regret being with him. "But it can't happen again."

Maybe saying it out loud would make her believe it.

Maddie scoffed at herself as she went back to her bedroom. She could still smell him there, in the air. She didn't dare sniff the sheets, because he'd be there, too.

Healthy male, aftershave, the musk of sex, and something that was just Gio; something she'd never forgotten.

Who was she kidding; when she finally managed to tell him about Jake, he'd probably be so pissed she'd *have* to savor last night. Because he'd never touch her again.

He was a good man, so he'd likely want to be involved in their son's life, and that was okay, but she wouldn't blame him if he needed time before dealing with *her*. *Away* from her. He'd probably rage at her, and she wouldn't blame him for that, either.

Her shower was quick, and she had to squeeze her thighs against the ache in her sex. It was a cross between pleasant and accusatory.

She'd have nothing to say if Gio demanded, "how could you?" when she finally told him about their son, *and* when he wanted to know why she'd slept with him before revealing the truth.

*Because I'm an asshole,* was all she had.

Damn, she was stupid.

So so so stupid.

*Fuck my life,* was pretty much her new mantra.

If only she could shut her brain off—or leave it at home.

"Damn, get over yourself." Maddie shook her head, making her pony tail tickle the back of her neck. She'd nixed the idea of doing her hair; it would only bother her later when she was poring over financials.

She and Foster had made it further than planned the day before. They would continue on, and she could conveniently ignore Gio like before. She wouldn't *have* to look at him if she was busy, right?

*Ugh, you're getting more pathetic by the minute.*

"Just take your pathetic ass to work. Woman up." She slammed her apartment door, earning a raised eyebrow from a neighbor retrieving a newspaper down the hall, and her ears burned.

*Sure, make them all think the new chick is weird.*

The five minute drive was uneventful, but the Ducati was already in the parking lot when she pulled up.

Maddie's heart battled her stomach for supremacy.

How was she supposed to function all day long?

Her vertebrae were bound to pop out of her back and abandon her. Sweat dotted her brow, but her palms were clammy.

She swallowed—twice. Then a third time, and was suddenly grateful she'd not consumed more than coffee.

"Good morning, Inspector!"

She jumped and cursed when the stocky Hispanic detective came up beside her.

Maddie must've been transparent, because Garcia's expression was immediately contrite. He reached for her forearm to steady her. "I'm sorry; didn't mean to startle you."

"I was just lost in thought." She laughed, but it sounded like a nervous titter to her ears.

His smile was easy and genuine, and somehow it made her like him even more than she had when she'd met him. He was so damn personable.

"It happens. Rough morning?"

"It's okay, I could use more coffee, and maybe some breakfast."

"Oh? Late night?"

Maddie startled, as if this guy could read her mind, and her cheeks heated. One thought of sex and Gio had mini earthquakes going off in all her unmentionable places. She squeezed her thighs before she fell into step with the man. "Yeah, just moved into my place and I was unpacking."

"Ah, if you need any help—"

"Oh, that's nice of you, but I'm good." Her ears crackled with fire.

She'd never be able to look at Gio without combusting, and being paranoid everyone would know they'd had a lot of sex the night before.

*Stop. It's not like you're wearing a sign.*

"Well, I mean it. If you need help, gimme a holler." Garcia scooted around her and put his keycard against the sensor, then grabbed the long handle and held the frosted glass panel open. He gave a half-bow and smiled again.

"Thanks." Maddie told herself not to read into his behavior. He wasn't like the leering captain; he was just being a nice guy. He was on her team, after all.

They chatted on the way to the conference room, about inane things, but at least that helped her gain her bearings. She hoped her face wasn't as red as an overripe tomato.

She felt eyes on her even before the detective repeated his earlier behavior and urged her to enter their investigation headquarters in front of him.

Gio's blue gaze seared her from across the room, instead of focusing on his computer screen. His focus moved to his colleague, and back at her. He flexed his jaw, like he was bothered she'd walked in with Garcia.

Maddie arched an eyebrow, but Garcia snagged her attention again.

"There're bagels and donuts over there, Inspector. Breakfast awaits." He winked, and gestured like Vanna.

She couldn't help her smile. He was charming. "Call me Maddie," she said as she made her way to the food.

"Oh, sure…Maddie." Garcia returned her smile. She could see how most women would think him handsome, despite his lack of height.

He was stocky, but the bulk was muscle, and he had a trimmed goatee. His skin was a natural bronze, a testament to his heritage. His fitted black button-down was a bit tight around his biceps and pecs, hinting at a chiseled physique under the fabric. The same could be said of his khaki's, hugging what had to be toned thick thighs and a nice high ass. Hector Garcia was…cute.

The detective grabbed a jelly donut and offered another grin as he took a bite and retreated, going to conference with Detective Foster, who was already studying some of the reports the FBI had filed and shared with the Marshal Service.

Before Maddie could spread the cream cheese on the cinnamon raisin bagel, she felt a blast of warmth at her back. She didn't have to turn around to know Gio stood too close for comfort, but why the hell was he hovering over her…at work?

She should yell at him.

"Maddie, huh?"

There was a sneer in his inquiry but his handsome face was placid when she met his eyes over her shoulder.

She offered him the same arched eyebrow as before. "Yes, that's my name. And we'll be working closely."

He smirked. "How closely?"

That same heat slowly crept up the back of her neck again, and Maddie instantly regretted the intentional tease. She was pretty transparent when it came to Gio—hated to admit that—and she really didn't want the rest of their team to see it.

"Inspector Granger!"

The shout saved her from having to endure her former-turned current-lover's response. Whatever it might've been.

*Thank. God.*

All eyes landed on the two people in the doorway.

Senior Investigators Griggs and Bailey had finally arrived.

The male marshal from her former office held up a piece of paper. "We got a search warrant."

K<br>♥

Gian's phone rang, and when he took it out of his breast-pocket of his favorite dove-gray Armani suit, he frowned at the screen. The number wasn't in his contacts, but the area code was familiar.

Chicago.

With a swipe of his thumb, he put the cell to his ear. "Yeah."

"Listen to me." Uncle Dino's voice was commanding, urgent.

"Why are you calling me at this number?" Irritation inched up his spine, and he crossed his office in *The Giovanni* executive suites in two strides, closing the glass door.

No one was around, since it was still about thirty minutes before the admin support staff were scheduled to come in, but he didn't want to take any chances. He'd left Elise asleep in their huge bed earlier than normal, because he'd hoped for another go at Big Tony's office. He'd been about to head there.

"You know better than to call me on this phone."

"Tried the other number. You didn't answer."

Yeah, he didn't keep the burner phone on him, in

case Elise might see and become suspicious of him having more than one cell. It was in his personal safe in their penthouse, and she even didn't know he had the secret lockbox. It also held his stash of passports, a few identities, getaway cash and two weapons.

He'd hoped to never need them.

"Get the fuck out of the casino. Now."

"What? Why?" Paranoia skimmed over his limbs. Gian darted his eyes around.

The offices all had glass walls and doors, and most of the lights were dimmed or off. He was alone, but his legs tingled and he fought the urge to run.

"Got some intel this morning. The feds have search warrants."

"What! Who knows I'm here?"

His uncle cursed in Italian. "Just me. If you want to keep it that way, get the fuck gone."

"I can't just disappear."

"Leave for now. Feds know who you are. No one can see you. Your cover is compromised."

Gian hadn't told his father's youngest brother about the would-be confrontation with his fiancée's cop brother. Now probably wasn't a good idea either.

His heart skipped into overdrive and slipped downward. Did the conversation before the gala have anything to do with a federal search warrant?

No, it couldn't. Elise's brother was a local cop, not a fed.

Doubts swirled, and he stomped them away. He couldn't lose his shit.

Gian was in control. This was his operation. His

mission. He *would* succeed. He'd done a hell of a job for the past nine months, on all fronts.

"Dammit, Uncle Dino."

"*Nipote*, listen to me. Now. Get gone."

"I can't fuck this operation." Desperation and shock, mixed with rage churned his stomach. Dread and a sense of loss at the wasted time and money made him want to stab something. He grabbed his knife inside his pocket and squeezed it until his fingers ached.

He was supposed to end up owning this place, not be forced to flee.

"You covered your ass with the numbers, right?"

"Yes, always." Gian was a smart launderer. The paper trail was slight and well disguised; he prided himself on that.

"Then you have nothing to worry about. They won't find jack shit. Disappear for the day. When the cops leave, you can go back. Assess the need for damage control. If it's a lost cause, get your ass back to Chicago."

"Fuck, *zio*, I don't want to lose the work I've done here, not to mention the money." That would fuck him even more in his father's eyes, not endear him.

"I know, *nipote*. But bars wouldn't look good for you, either. Just get out. Lay low."

It was Gian's turn to exercise his cussing muscle, and he used multiple languages.

Uncle Dino let a bitter laugh loose in his ear. "It might be okay if no one sees you. Just get the fuck out while you still can."

"Might? Fuck that. I've worked my ass off here. Fucking feds. Does this mean Fratelli talked?"

"We don't know yet, we're working on it."

"Work faster; everyone has a price."

His uncle laughed again. "Including you and me, *nipote*. It's a challenge to get info and keep your and my ass out of it. My sources are limited."

"You've done it before, do it again." This was a hard order.

Dino growled, a rare show of temper from the normally easy-going older man. His uncle had always been a better soldier than commander. It was probably why they worked so well together, and also why his youngest uncle would never be the king. Not that *he'd* ever point that out.

The man had spent his coming-up years as an enforcer for his brother, and his father before that. He knew some creative ways to dispose of someone and wasn't afraid to do it.

"Let me handle Chicago, and you cover your ass in Vegas," his uncle said finally, but he was mostly even, normal.

"All is not lost," Gian said.

*It can't be.*

He refused to believe he'd wasted the last nine months of his life in the desert, let alone his father's money.

"You'd better hope they don't find anything, then."

"They won't. I know what I'm doing." He ended the call, refusing to let even one tiny niggle of doubt inch into his brain.

He left his cellphone on his desk and locked his office on the way out. Hopefully, he could get his shit from the safe without running into his fiancée.

# Chapter

## TWELVE

*We got a search warrant.*

The unfamiliar male's statement reverberated in Gio's head, as excitement swept his teammates. The room was cheery and triumphant, but he wanted to puke. Wanted to demand what, who, where, when, why and how, as if he was writing a report on an event he hadn't witnessed.

The more positive the vibes in the conference space, the less the air flowed. His chest constricted and his head spun.

The light-skinned black man who'd made the announcement at the door strode into the room, a petite redhead on his heels. The guy had a moustache and a bright white-toothed smile to go along with his declaration.

Maddie snatched the paper in his hand and Gio watched her eyes scan each typed line, then again, as she went from top to bottom.

She smiled. A wide and genuine one; proud.

Bile rose up to meet the lump dominating his throat.

She made quick introductions of the new

newcomers to the team, but his head was fading in and out, and he barely remembered anything about meeting Senior Inspectors Roger Griggs and April Bailey, except the man had striking green eyes that stood out from his burnt caramel skin.

They shook hands, but his was clammy against the firm shake and no amount of ignoring it was alleviating the need to spew the coffee he'd had at Maddie's place.

This couldn't be happening.

There hadn't been enough time.

Sure, they had docs from the IRS and FBI that showed mismatching numbers, but how was there enough probable cause for a federal judge to sign off on a search warrant?

He hadn't been able to prove his father and sister weren't involved.

Gio couldn't panic, but that was the exact emotion slithering around his spine like a snake. A venomous viper that would sink its fangs into his brainstem as soon as it was fully seated.

The pretty female marshal wore an odd expression when they finished shaking hands.

His crazy must be showing, because he felt like he was losing his mind.

Always observant, Maddie's gaze landed on him, and her brightness faded.

Her coworkers from the Marshal's Service made their way to the food table and she assured everyone they would talk warrant-executing logistics in a few moments.

"You okay?" she asked, her eyes scanning his face.

Gio forced a nod, sliding his arms across his chest to steady himself. He wanted to wipe his palms on his jeans, but resisted the need.

"Can I have a word with you in private?" she asked.

An awkward hush sucked the anticipation from the room.

All eyes were on them, but he didn't give a flying fuck. In the back of his head, something whispered for him to get a hold of himself, and it echoed, becoming louder, reminding him his privacy, his secret, was going to be exposed.

Maybe his nickname had scattered people's brains enough not to ask if the casino was tied to him in some way, but he worked with a bunch of smart people, and even if they didn't always ask nosy questions to his face, maybe they all knew.

Maybe they'd all whispered behind his back.

If so, why had Olinsky let him remain on the taskforce?

Was his name the reason Inspector Bailey had peered at him so strangely? Was she whispering the query about Detective Giovanni and *The Giovanni* casino that seemed so obvious?

Was it in neon lights on his forehead?

Maddie's hand landed on his wrist, and she practically dragged him into the hallway, but she looked around and shook her head. It clearly wasn't secure enough for her tastes, so she guided him down the corridor to an interview room. She shut the door behind them.

His head was on some chaotic loop, ideas of what he could and couldn't do flying back and forth. Walking the line between legal, moral and ethical, mixed with worries his connection would be discovered, down to him being implicated in the investigation.

It wouldn't quiet.

He didn't know what to do. Or say.

Gio didn't miss her making sure the camera in the corner of the room was off.

Maddie whirled on him, her hands in front of her, as if she wanted to reach for him but had thought better of it.

Neither of them made any move to take a seat at the small table.

"Maybe you should sit this one out." Her voice was low, a tad hesitant, as if she was afraid to give an order, even though it was her right as leader of the taskforce.

His anger was whiplash fast, helping to clear some of the anarchy in his brain. He glared. "Hell no."

"Gio—"

"Fuck that, Maddie." He gritted his teeth and tried not to use his body's size to intimidate her, despite them being alone. Gio made tight fists at his sides, opening and clenching his hands until his fingers hurt, because he didn't know what else to do with them. His whole form was made up of twitches, as if tweaking on meth.

Rage boiled beneath the surface and he started pacing.

Couldn't help it. Couldn't meet her eyes.

"This is my fucking *family*, Mads." He fizzled out.

"I know. That's kinda my point." She used that same even-keel soothing tone.

Maddie really didn't need to *try* to calm him, because her presence always did it; it was a normal thing for him.

To be calmed by Maddie, like he'd told her the night before.

This…it was different, wasn't it?

"You said you'd let me prove his innocence. My sister looks guilty as fuck, too, and she sure as hell never cleaned a dime of mob money in her entire life."

"Gio—"

He jerked back when she reached for him again, but his lover was undeterred, and stepped into his chest, wrapping her arms around him.

Gio froze; half-surprised she'd hug him at work. Even when he was swept into a giant headfuck.

It was only about two seconds later when his arms pulled her closer of their own accord. He closed his eyes, laying his cheek against her soft hair and took in her scent.

After last night, he'd always have fresh-cut wildflowers wrapped around his olfactory system. Not exactly a bad thing.

She slipped away too soon, as if she'd remembered where they were. "The fact remains, money was laundered at your father's casino," Maddie said softly. "I need assurances, Gio."

He swallowed for the thousandth time. "He didn't

do it. She didn't do it. My dad's still in the hospital, for Chrissakes." He ignored her last statement, because he knew what she wanted, and she should know him better that. Better than needing a verbal confirmation.

Gio was a cop first, and a damn good one.

He wanted to yell at her.

Her pretty eyes finally landed on his face. "Assurances," she repeated.

He stared in silence.

"If you come; if you're there to assist executing this warrant, I need assurances you'll turn in *any* evidence you find. No matter *who* it might implicate."

He refused to give her what she wanted. Not because he wasn't going to do it; he wasn't stupid, he loved his job and wouldn't break the law, but he couldn't tell Maddie what she needed to hear because there wasn't going be anything *to* turn in.

Gio couldn't find the words to declare that, either.

His family wasn't guilty.

He probably should reveal Elise's fiancé wasn't who he claimed, but he didn't share it. He should want to, right?

If it could help exonerate his dad and sister?

Gio couldn't say who the guy really was, but he could do the math. There was no funky financial record exceeding nine months in age.

The cockstain had no personal records before the same period of time, and had been the dingleberry hanging from his father's ass the same amount of time.

But who *was* the fucker, if he wasn't Marco Fratelli?

If he was the one cleaning mob cash at *The*

*Giovanni,* how was he going to prove it?

"I need you *fully* on board. We have some facts, but not enough to make a concrete case," Maddie admitted.

"Then let's go serve the fucking warrant."

K ♥

For once Gio didn't arrive at *The Giovanni* on his Ducati, or park in the employee parking garage. He rode with his team and the newly-arrived marshals, and he wouldn't be entering a back door with a fob.

Gio was…embarrassed.

The only thing that would fix this was if he caught Not-Really-Marco the fuckwad doing something arrestable.

He was relieved his father wasn't on the premises, but that was odd, wasn't it? Hadn't he always dreamed about showing Big Tony whatfor?

Well, not like *this.*

The search warrant would be presented to his sister before the team went to town on the executive and accounting department offices. That was going to be bad enough. He hoped he could be scarce for that part.

Gio might not survive her shock and hurt, since *he* was there to help locate evidence that would prove their father — prove Elise — was guilty of federal crimes.

Crimes that resulted in years of prison time. Crimes he knew in his heart, down to his bones, his family members were not guilty of.

Perhaps at one time he would've considered Big Tony capable, but not really. His father might've been born and raised in Mobtown, but he'd never committed a crime, to Gio's knowledge. Why would he start laundering money *after* running a successful casino on the Vegas strip for the last forty years?

Big Tony Giovanni wasn't hurting for cash—far from it. Even Maddie had to admit the suspected dirty money through his father's casino had been a recent thing.

Nine months recent.

*Not-Marco-the cockstain.*

He slammed the van door shut, then adjusted his bullet-proof vest to a more comfortable position. He made sure the straps were secure, and his badge swayed on the chain around his neck. Securing it would be better, but he didn't really give a shit at this point.

"You okay?" Maddie asked.

Gio grunted.

She'd insisted on the protection, and although it was standard protocol, it was ridiculous in this instance. It was a search warrant, not a dangerous arrest or retrieval mission, and besides, his sister was the executive they were going to be meeting.

Did Maddie think Elise would meet them at the office door with a bazooka?

The idea almost made him smile. His sister *was* a badass.

"Great, we're relegated to Neanderthal communication skills?" she grumbled.

"Gio's never been a big talker." Hector Garcia chuckled, and patted the back of Gio's shoulder.

He wanted to sneer at his buddy. Instead he

maintained his silence and arched an eyebrow at them both.

Their two vans were on the far side of the vast building and civilians roamed everywhere, even though they weren't facing the strip.

*Stupid tourists.*

They'd opted to execute the warrant immediately, since *The Giovanni* was a twenty-four/seven operation, and they wanted to enter the offices during regular business hours.

Gio had to commend Maddie for not addressing him specifically for answers about operations when they'd returned to the conference room. He also had to admire her ability to pull herself together and brief the whole team like nothing had happened between them in that interview room.

Like nothing had happened between them last night.

She had her game face on.

Back when they'd first met, and she'd been a part of a joint fugitive squad, he'd only been support personnel when they'd located the bastard, since he'd been a uniform patrol cop. Gio hadn't gotten to see her in real action. He'd never doubted her ability to do her job, but it was nice to see her at work.

Or, it would be if she wasn't trying to bust *his* family.

Still, Maddie Granger was a tough broad, and that was sexy as hell.

It was hard to stay mad at her.

Was he mad at her?

This investigation, as wrong as it might be, wasn't Maddie's fault. Maybe he knew that deep down, unless his dick was still doing all the thinking?

Gio didn't want to know the answer, and he wasn't about to involve any other organ; especially the one in the vicinity of his chest, so he'd just have to ride with this.

Do his job.

Prove his father and his sister weren't laundering money for the mob. They weren't capable of something so egregious — or stupid.

He might not jive with 'ol Pops, but his father and sister were brilliant in business. If it was otherwise, *The Giovanni* never would've lasted all these years, through recessions and back stock exchanges crises.

"Listen up," Maddie said, her commanding voice thick with confidence.

His embarrassment really was going to eat him alive. It roiled his gut, and he was probably going to end up with symptoms of the worst case of indigestion in history.

Yet, being there, seeing things for himself, was better than the alternative.

"Remember where your assignments are, when we get in there. Bring anything of notice to me, or Inspectors Griggs or Bailey. We do this safely, and as thoroughly as we can," Maddie continued.

"No one gets hurt," Griggs cosigned.

Gio wanted to roll his eyes. *No. Shit.* His sister was innocent. Not to mention unarmed.

Of course, there was armed security on the

premises, but it wasn't like it was security POS to draw down on the cops.

He did want to get his hands—deadly force had appeal—on Elise's fucking fiancé, but he couldn't share with the class until he knew more.

Maybe if nothing else, today would result in a positive ID of Not-Marco the cockwad.

M addie's instincts told her to stay close to Gio, but she questioned her own motives. He was more than brooding. If he was a comic strip character, he'd have a thundercloud over his head. With lightning. A lot of lightning.

Despite telling him she needed assurance, she *did* trust him. He was a good cop by all accounts of his coworkers, and she knew him to be a man with integrity. A man she cared about. The man who'd fathered her son.

She stopped mid-step. Maddie didn't have time, nor was this the headspace for Jake, Gio and her guilt. This was one time where it legitimately needed to be for later.

*Well, this is the rest. You got this, girl.*

She needed to maintain that, pin it to her brain and *handle* this. As she'd told the team, she didn't anticipate danger, but they all needed to prepare for any possibility. Like any time they did an op. Serving warrants went sideways all the time.

"Inspector Granger? You okay?" Garcia asked,

close to her ear.

"You bet." She forced a smile.

Gio shouldered past the shorter detective to come up beside her, as if he didn't want his friend so near her. He still didn't speak, and Garcia quirked a knowing smirk.

Maddie ignored both men and led the group of marshals and LVMPD's finest into the massive casino. She headed straight for the first uniformed security officer in sight, and demanded access to the executive offices.

She wouldn't state their purpose until she had to, out of respect for Gio. If the team thought it odd, no one said. For that, she was grateful.

No doubt Gio had access of his own, but she didn't want to blow what he'd referred to as his privacy.

Besides, it gave her plausible deniability of their connection. If no one managed to uncover her past cases, and discovered her little trip to Sin City eight years ago.

*Conflict of interest* floated around in her head and she ignored it. It wasn't like rules hadn't already been shattered. The man had spent the night in her bed, after all.

Awareness zinged down her spine, partly due to her too-vivid-for-its-own-good memory, and partly because Gio was at her side.

Evidently, he agreed with her idea of the two of them sticking together. He'd insisted *he* would be the one to search his father's office, so when they got there, Maddie would go with him.

The young security officer's eyes went bigger than a jackpot winner, and he raked his gaze over their whole unit before finally settling and locking in on Gio.

Obviously, the man knew who he was, and she commended him for not publicly shaming him, or even addressing him by name.

Gio's family would see his involvement with the warrant as a traitorous act, since the investigation would seem as if it'd come out of the blue to them.

She closed her eyes for a split-second and took what she hoped was an unnoticeable fortifying breath. She'd always adored his siblings. Especially Elise.

As soon as the younger woman recognized her, any shred of friendship they'd ever had would be ripped away. Torn to pieces and whipped into non-existence.

The security officer got on the radio, and two more uniforms joined his podium. They also leered at Gio with recognition in their eyes. Silent recognition, like their counterparts, so perhaps the gods were with them this day. For his sake, anyways.

Maddie tried not to spare him a glance, but her periphery couldn't escape, and his Adam's apple bobbed a few times, as if he couldn't stop swallowing. She inhaled through her nose and prayed he wouldn't hate her forever. There was no way he didn't blame this situation all on her, even if she was just doing her job.

She suddenly wanted to be anywhere but at *The Giovanni*, especially in *this* capacity.

Two of the officers escorted them to the executive offices. The farther away from the casino floor they got, the more the blinking wildly colored lights and beeps, bings, dings and sirens faded, and it was disconcerting, making the walk an awkwardly mute affair.

The noises of heavy boot-steps, keys rattling and leather gear creaking enveloped the corridor, and for some reason it made her want to flee.

Elise Giovanni met them in front of the huge curved dark wood receptionist desk with her hands on both shapely hips.

The vivacious college student Maddie had met and made fast friends with eight years ago had become an ethereal beauty, with shoulder length blonde hair and a killer body she didn't seem too shy to show off.

The fire-engine red business suit fit her like a second skin, and the pencil skirt stopped right above her knees. Her three-quarter length sleeve blazer was buttoned, the white shirt beneath still hinted at cleavage. She even had a jeweled brooch of the casino's logo on her lapel.

Her shoes were no doubt Louboutins, matching her outfit, as did her cherry-red lipstick. If her narrowed eyes and pursed lips were any indication, she wasn't happy they were there, even if she couldn't know why.

*Yet.*

Maddie's stomach inverted and she inhaled. Expensive-smelling and appealing perfume teased her senses.

They had an audience of more than the rest of her taskforce. People stared through the offices' glass walls, down to the brunette receptionist behind Elise, who looked on with her mouth parted and her eyes wide.

Gio's sister appeared to scan their unit before meeting Maddie's eyes.

Unlike the security officers, she didn't pay special notice to her brother standing to Maddie's right.

"Excuse me, what is this about?" Polite, but a demand nonetheless.

"Ms. Elise Giovanni, I'm Senior Investigator Madison Granger," as if the younger woman could've forgotten who she was. She plowed on, "with the US Marshals Service. We have a warrant to search your executive offices and your accounting department records, as well as to seize all equipment that may have been used in the commission of federal crimes."

"What?" Elise glanced at Gio now, her fair brows tight even as she took the warrant from Maddie. She scanned it, and her pretty face paled. Her throat worked, and one hand shot up to her mouth. "Federal crimes? You've got to be kidding." She pinned her brother with wide dark eyes. "Gio? What *is* this?"

None of the team said a word in the tense quiet, but Maddie wanted to groan.

There was some uncomfortable shifting behind her.

That couldn't be good.

There wasn't a doubt that those questions would be dancing through their heads, but she hoped to Heaven they waited to say anything.

Gio didn't answer his sister, but his expression betrayed pain before he schooled it whiplash-fast. He straightened his already impossibly broad shoulders and his chest heaved.

Maddie clear her throat, hoping he wouldn't want to answer. She needed to speak fast, just in case. "The sooner we get started, the sooner we'll be done."

*Remain professional*, became a chant in her head. Not that it'd be a cure-all, or a cure-at-all, for her genuine grief and discomfort.

Elise's eyes were so dark they made her beauty even more stunning, but when they misted over, Maddie felt like shit for the first time since she'd agreed to lead this investigation.

Her first command was becoming a shitstorm.

*Do* not *look at him.*

Gio had always been super protective of his siblings. There was no way he'd abide his sister's tears.

She needed the team to scatter. Stat.

She whirled to face her guys and gals, because even she needed a reprieve from the honest-to-God shock on Elise's face. "Everyone has their assignments."

Elise snapped her fingers. "Hold on. I will require my security team to remain present, especially if you're intending to go into restricted areas." Her voice was hard; no trace of tears, and Maddie admired her backbone.

She offered a nod. "As long as they don't interfere with our search, that's fine."

The younger woman nodded.

The receptionist handed her a radio. No shocker that the brunette was hanging on every word of their exchange.

"Call Paul Allemand's office. Tell him to get his ass down here. No partners or associates. Paul himself," Gio's sister barked to the receptionist before she held the button down on the small radio.

The brunette immediately obeyed, dipping her head and speaking lowly when someone answered on the other end of the call.

Of course the big casino was represented by one of Sin City's most famous bulldozer law firms. Even Maddie had heard of the man. She'd never heard if he or his large firm was suspected to be involved with anything illegal or had mob ties, so it was smart for *The Giovanni* to be aligned with prestige on the up and up.

There was no awkward downtime, waiting for Elise's security guys. In less than a minute, six men in dark gray suits, not uniforms, poured into the executive offices' lobby like a marine unit on a combat mission.

Maddie studied their hardened implacable faces. Their demeanor screamed that one or more of these men were ex-military. They were the elite security of *The Giovanni*, Gio's family's version of the Secret Service, and for some reason she wanted to smile.

One of the men stepped forward, while the others stood as a unit, shoulder-to-shoulder, not exactly glaring at their invasion, but almost.

"This is Chase Warren, Director of Security for the casino, and he'll assist you." Elise's delivery was even stronger than the previous time, but it was colder, too. She was mega-pissed.

Chase Warren was likely in is mid-thirties, and his suit jacket was well-fitted without fully disguising his massive biceps and pecs. He was handsome, and his sandy hair sported a jarhead cut, as if he'd been discharged the week before.

He accepted the warrant when his boss handed it to him, and his eyes went narrower as he read, ending up tiny slits by the time was done. His nostrils flared and his jaw was set in a hard line.

*Perfect, he'll love to assist us. Hope they're not armed.*

"Chase, please show these *gentlemen* to the areas they require." Elise's words held a deadly edge, and she'd said 'gentlemen' like a racial slur.

Yeah, Maddie had never seen the leggy blonde so irate.

Chase Warren offered a curt nod and handed the warrant back. "Ma'am."

When Maddie's team—save Gio—split off, each accompanied by a security officer, she tried to take in air, but for some reason her chest was tighter.

"Mr. Allemand is on his way, Ms. Giovanni, but he's coming directly from court, and may be delayed," the receptionist said. "He'll be here as soon as he can."

No one acknowledged the brunette.

"Gio," his sister hissed through clenched teeth. "What the *hell* is going on here?" She grabbed his wrist and tugged.

Maddie looked from sibling to sibling, trying not to chew on her lip.

He pinned her with a stare and broke physical contact with his younger sister. "Inspector, we need to search the president's office." He whirled in his shitkickers, completely ignoring Elise.

Undeterred, she followed, her five inch heels *click-clacking* on the tile floor and her irritation shooting up as she repeated his nickname.

*Oh shit.*

K<br>♥

Elise was going to fucking slaughter him for doing this to her. Maybe she'd slide the dagger-shaped mail opener from their father's desk into his back.

Right. Now.

It would put him out of his misery, so maybe it'd be all right.

"Nico Antonio Demetri Giovanni!" His full name from her would've been amusing at any other time, considering the last person to break it out had been their mother, he-couldn't-remember-when.

He just hoped to God no other cop had heard her. Logically, after she'd addressed him by nickname in front of the group to ask what the search warrant was all about, his coworkers would draw some conclusions. If not, well they were too dumb to be cops, and he just wasn't that fucking lucky.

Maybe the captain had known all along, despite Gio guarding his privacy in a vault. Maybe it was some sort of don't-ask-don't-tell sitch.

Olinsky had been his immediate supervisor for a few years and it'd never come up. The same inquiry as before danced back into his brain…if the guy really did know, why *was* he allowed to stay on the taskforce?

Well, he wasn't going to make inquiries, for damn sure.

Maddie was behind Elise, but the only one was speaking—shouting—was his sister.

"Gio, seriously. Tell me what the fuck is going on here, *now*."

He stopped right inside their father's inner sanctum and whirled on her. That brought to mind the last time he'd stood there.

The other night, when he'd first met Armani-the-cockstain.

Elise crossed her arms and stopped a few feet from him. A serious scowl marred her pretty face. She was wearing a red skirt a few inches too short.

Unlike usually, he didn't give a shit that she was *trying* to look like a hot little number, or that her rage was as bright as the red hue of the fabric.

He could deal with the anger. When she'd faced him out by the main receptionist desk, and her dark eyes had misted over with helplessness, he'd wanted to shoot himself.

Gio might've tried to blame Maddie, but at that moment, his guilt was the size of a grizzly bear that'd already ripped chunks from his body, only to leave him for dead until it could come back for more.

The beast was already on its way to finish him off.

He headed to the nearest filing cabinet and tried to open it. When a lock stopped him, he went back to his dad's desk and opened the top drawer, grabbing a set of tiny keys from the corner of the sorter-tray. The long slender drawer was the only one without a lock.

His father had always been a "keep it locked" kind of guy, so it was odd the keys were right there. But he'd question that later.

"Where's Marco?" he said without preamble, still ignoring Elise's demands.

The small key worked on the first try, and he slid the first metal drawer open before his sister answered.

Maddie scanned the room, too. She probably wanted to get this shit the hell over with, too.

Before the attorneys showed up.

Big Tony had had Paul Allemand on retainer since before Gio could remember. The man had started his firm about the same time his father had started the casino, and they'd grown their businesses side-by-side. Had been equally successful. Paul had known them all since childhood. He was a hell of a lawyer, too.

He'd fight to exonerate his father, and destroy Maddie's case.

*Isn't that a good thing?*

He had a reputation for obliterating cops on the stand. Half the force was shit-their-pants afraid to be subpoenaed if he was the attorney of record.

Gio wouldn't want her humiliated, even if she was wrong about his dad.

His sister's voice pulled him out of his head.

"He's not answering the damn phone," Elise admitted at the same Maddie asked, "Who's Marco?"

When he spared both women a glance, his sister's gaze was on her phone, and her thumbs were furiously flying over the screen.

There was nothing worse than angry-woman texts, but he didn't feel for the twatwaffle. He was disappointed the fucker hadn't been with Elise when she'd met their team in the office lobby.

"I've tried to call him ten times. It goes straight to voicemail, and I haven't seen him since he left our place this morning." She didn't stop texting, even though she was speaking normally, without the same fury.

Gio scowled. They were living together?

He didn't like that.

One. Bit.

He slammed the filing cabinet shut and went to the next drawer. The top consisted of a series of mostly empty hanging file folders. Nothing of interest. As if the four-drawer cabinet was for show.

"Who's Marco?" Maddie repeated, this time with a little more force.

"My fiancé, Marco Fratelli. He works here at the casino. He's one of the VPs." His sister sounded distracted, most of her attention on her phone.

He froze with his hand on the second silver handle and closed his eyes.

*Mother. Fucker.*

Why had she had to say the cockstain's fake last name?

"Fratelli?" Maddie's question was so loaded Gio feared one word could pierce his skin with such force his Kevlar wouldn't have a chance in hell to stop it.

He didn't want to turn around. He couldn't crush his younger sibling even more, by publicly outing Armani, especially since he didn't know who the asshole really was.

As for his lover, he'd be lucky if she didn't actually flay him open when he confessed the truth. Or shoot him. His woman always carried.

Both females would want him dead in a matter of seconds.

Maybe they'd take turns hanging his balls from their mantels, or the hoods of their cars.

"Yes. Marco Fratelli," Elise supplied again.

Gio sucked in air, hoping it wasn't his last.

Maddie was silent, and the furious *click-click* from the letters on Elise's phone screen was the only sound, other than his freight-train nervous breathing.

He hoped he was the only one aware of *that*.

Gio tried to open the second drawer, but it only came toward him about halfway. He tugged, to no avail. "It's stuck," he said, more to himself than either pissed off woman.

He yanked the drawer with all his might. It opened so fast, he stumbled back and barely avoided tripping over his own feet and falling on his ass. Gio threw his arms out for balance.

*Thanks, Karma?*

Something small and dark went flying in an arc and landed on the carpet with a soft *thud*.

"What the hell?" he asked as he bent to retrieve the small book.

It was dark brown, leather-bound and looked old; the cover was scarred with fold-marks as well as scratches on the surface. The spine revealed that someone had often tucked the cover behind the back, as did the curve of the pages.

His sister and Maddie crowded him as he straightened and opened it.

"What's that?" Elise asked.

Gio met her eyes. "You've never seen it before?"

She shook her head, making her loose pale locks dance over her shoulders. "No, have you?"

"Nope."

"Lemme have that. It's evidence," Maddie said.

Gio and his sister both glared at her.

He tightened his grip on the little book.

She pulled, and they played a mini game of tug-o-war, until he relented, so it wouldn't come apart.

It creaked in protest.

The only thing he'd been able to make out before he'd relinquished the book was his father's name written in cursive on the inside cover, as well as a date forty-odd years back.

Maddie pulled an evidence bag from her back pocket, but she thumbed through what he'd found instead of sliding it inside and sealing it. "No mob ties, huh?"

"What?" Elise squawked.

"No," Gio said, but it was more a whisper of disbelief than the harsh bark he'd intended.

Maddie held the petite tome open. Someone had drawn lines and columns with a black pen, as if the book had been intended for a journal more than a record-keeper or ledger. They were neat and straight, as was the writing in each column. Initials and dollar amounts filled each one, as well as the date for each transaction. Much like an old-fashioned bookie's records.

*Fuck. Me.*

His heart resumed its dive to his gut. "Just because—"

The radio on Maddie's hip squelched to life.

"*Granger, we're done here. Hard drives from the accounting department are secure.*" Griggs' voice sounded and Gio could've kissed the man for his timely interruption.

Maddie reached for the radio to answer, and Elise grabbed his hand.

"What's she talking about? Mob ties?"

His heart galloped and he wanted to look anywhere but at his sister's astonished face. "Lise, I'll explain later…"

"No. Right. Fucking. Now." She put her hands on her hips and glared at them both. She didn't often utter his favorite word, and she'd dropped it a few times since they'd headed to their father's office. A testament to how upset she was.

*Well, duh.*

"We've gotten what we needed, so let's to meet the team in the lobby," Maddie said, hooking the radio back to her belt.

His sister's expression could've peeled paint. She shot a new scowl at Maddie. "I'd say it's nice to see you again, but it's *not*." Her full mouth was a hard line. "I have a right to know what the hell is going on here."

"You lawyer will explain," Maddie said at the same time Gio said, "You will. Soon."

He tried to reach for her but she wrenched away.

Her face went even harder. "You'll be hearing from our attorneys." Her dark eyes flashed with renewed fury at Maddie.

"When you hear from your fiancé, we need to talk to him." Her cheeks were tinged pink, but she his met his sister head-on, so he had to admire her for that. She handed her a business card. Or tried to.

Elise took the little paper rectangle and ripped it in half. "I know how to reach my brother, thanks," she snarled, but she wasn't looking at Maddie.

Gio had never considered himself a coward, and he'd never wished for a sinkhole to swallow him alive, but one conveniently located under his feet would've been super fucking helpful.

Maddie didn't know whether to feel triumphant or sick to her stomach. Executing the warrant had gone smoothly, all things considered, but she couldn't look at Gio, for reasons other than the sex they shouldn't have had or the fact he still didn't know they shared a child.

She just wanted this day to be over so she could escape to her new apartment and lock the deadbolt until Monday morning. Until she had to face him again.

Or maybe she could foist her command off on Griggs and run all the way back to Chicago. Tell her old boss she'd changed her mind about the transfer and grab up her son in a hug and never let him go.

Maybe she could ask for a transfer to Alaska.

She also wasn't looking forward to the inevitable contact from Paul Allemand and his law firm. It was a wonder they hadn't stormed the police department already.

Maddie had done nothing wrong, and she had confidence in her PC affidavit, but it would no doubt be the first thing he requested to see, as was his right.

"Great job today, Granger." Griggs grinned.

She jumped five feet. She'd sunk into her own head, and had tuned out the excitement floating through the conference room back at LMVPD.

The man's smile faded and his moustache twitched. "Everything all right?"

*Hell no.*

"Yeah, of course. Great job to you, too. Thanks for getting the warrant."

"No worries."

Gio brooded in the corner, staring at the little brown book he'd found in his father's filing cabinet.

They hadn't gone over every page yet, and it was a mystery what a forty-year-old ledger could have to do with a recent nine-month-old money laundering scheme, but time would tell.

Would it reveal motive? Show the history Gio so staunchly denied?

Maddie had plans to go over it with a fine-toothed-comb if she could wrestle it away from him.

Scratch that, he was probably relegated to *former* lover again, after today.

That was a good thing, right?

It was what she'd wanted this morning, wasn't it?

Somehow the idea of never touching him again, kissing him again, made her ache; not in a good way.

"Granger, did you hear me?"

She met Roger Griggs' stunning green eyes. "Sorry, what was that?"

"I said, with Captain Olinsky's blessing, I've already sent the hard drives we gathered off to our federal tech squad, and I'm not sure how much time it'll take."

"Ah, well if they find definitive proof, they can take as long as they want."

He smirked. "Not all of us want to be stuck in Vegas forever."

Maddie managed a smile, and her eyes wandered back over in Gio's direction. "Come on now, Vegas isn't that bad."

"What's the deal with you and him?"

She whipped back to her colleague. "What? What d'you mean?"

"First, the private conference before we left, and then the weird interaction with him and the chick at the casino." He dragged his hand over his bald head.

His skin-tone, as well as the hue of those pretty eyes suggested he was bi-racial, but she'd never asked.

Griggs wasn't bald because he didn't have any hair, he shaved it all off. In Chicago, their fellow marshals teased him about it, claiming he must have to oil his head to make it shine like it did.

She'd always liked him, and he had an all-business way about him; no bullshit, no nonsense. It usually meant he wasn't all up in anyone's business, either.

*Looks like the buck stopped.*

*Perfect.*

Maddie told herself to meet his curious gaze head-on. "You don't have anything to worry about."

He narrowed his eyes. "His name's a little coincidental."

Her heart slid to her toes.

"Just tell me if we have a conflict of interest."

Griggs lowered his voice.

She scanned the room. Everyone on the team was busy with a task. Navarro and Foster chatted at the whiteboard, markers in hand, and Garcia and Inspector Bailey were at the computer together.

Olinsky had gone back to his office after being debriefed, and he'd told them he would update Deputy Chief Patton himself.

Gio hadn't moved, or stopped his perusal of the little book, the plastic evidence bag in one hand.

The old ledger had never made it all the way inside to be sealed away, and she agreed with that for the moment. She wanted to determine what they'd found, too.

Maddie told herself not to even glimpse his direction. "We don't have a conflict."

Her Chicago teammate studied her for a long moment, then offered a curt nod. "I won't ask anything else. For now. But I'm not the only one who's noticed."

"I know." She winced at the audible defeat in her answer.

"Does Captain Olinsky think it's a problem?"

"Would he let him remain on the taskforce if he did?" She ignored the heat that kissed the back of her neck and put on her best poker-face. Her question-answer was a lie—sort of. As far as she knew, Olinsky didn't know about Gio's tie.

"Would you tell me if you thought there was a problem?" Griggs arched a dark eyebrow and narrowed his vivid eyes again.

*Act natural. Don't take a breath.*

"Of course." Maddie hoped to God her response hadn't cracked, as she'd suspected. She didn't need to tell him about her promise to let Gio prove his father and sister innocent. Couldn't tell him; not now, not ever.

It would confirm there *was* a conflict of interest with her lover.

"Griggs, c'mere!" April Bailey called to their fellow marshal.

She sent up a silent prayer for the distraction.

The pretty redhead gestured to their colleague, urging him to join her and Hector Garcia at the computer.

"Granger, we'll pick this up later."

*Oh, please, I hope not.*

When she looked at Gio again, frustration tickled beneath the surface.

How could she want to hold him close and shove him away at the same time? Comfort him while she condemned his family?

There was something wrong with that—with her—wasn't there?

His long frame was reclined at a table, and his shitkickers were perched on the edge, as if he hadn't a care in the world. He still poured over the pages of the book, but his shoulders were as tight as his brow.

He was really bothered by what he was reading, despite his casual posture.

Maddie sighed and approached.

Gio didn't spare her a glance.

"You have something to tell me, don't you?" she

asked.

He still didn't look up. "Do I?"

She narrowed her eyes. "Marco *Fratelli*? Elise's fiancé?"

Gio closed his eyes and exhaled. "Oh. Him."

Maddie shoved his feet off the table, but she didn't feel any satisfaction as his body jarred to an awkward position, and he shot his hand to the table's edge for balance. She crossed her arms over her chest.

"Jesus, Mads, you're gonna knock me on my ass." He scowled as he straightened and centered said-fine-ass on the chair.

"Don't call me that here," she hissed. "You falling on your ass is no less than you deserve. You *knew* and didn't tell me."

He winced, but it didn't make her feel any better. "I know you don't like secrets. Sorry."

*Secrets? Shit.*

Guilt smashed into her and almost knocked her out of her skin. Her arms fell to her sides, as her eyes spun and her heart cantered.

Jake's smiling face danced into her head.

*Secrets.*

The biggest secret of her life.

Maddie screamed at herself to focus. This wasn't about Jake. This was about relevant information regarding her *case*. Something Gio had kept from her.

*Work. Work. Work.*

"Secrets?" she squeaked, but didn't give shit, and made herself keep going. "That's not the half of it. You kept information regarding this case from me. That could be considered obstruction." She worked to maintain low tones. Didn't want to drag him from the room for this conversation and risk more whispers about them. Or about how they'd disappeared this morning before the warrant.

"You promised I could prove my family has nothing to do with this. You had to know I'm gonna do it my way," he retorted, meeting her gaze. His eyes were defiant, not remorseful, and that made her blood boil.

He didn't move, still maintaining the semi-casual posture, and somehow *that* made her pulse kick up even more. Like she was just supposed to *accept* whatever was coming out of his mouth.

"I shouldn't have to tell you full disclosure has to be a part of that," Maddie barked.

A hush fell over the conference room, and she didn't need to scan around to confirm all eyes were on them.

*Fuck.*

Gio shot to his feet and towered over her. He tucked the book under his arm and narrowed his eyes. "I'm done with this issue, Senior Inspector Granger."

He strode from the room, leaving wide stares, hanging jaws and a shit-ton of silence from their team in his wake.

Maddie was going to kill him.

# Chapter

## FIFTEEN

Gian shut the penthouse door quietly with his return. The gorgeous view of the Sin City's radiance, even though it was only early evening, caught his attention, with its thousands of tourists scattering the strip like tiny ants on the sidewalks. The place was glowing, never sleeping, and he'd always loved standing here surveying his kingdom.

If they were in Big Tony's penthouse, the only other residence on this floor, he'd be able to see the giant fountain in front of the casino. He'd always liked to watch the water dance. It was calming for some reason. Shame it wasn't visible from this angle of the building.

"Where the fuck have you been?" Elise's demand held a deadly edge he'd never heard before.

He turned away from the lights and gave his fiancée a once over. Tried to appear surprised at her choice of words, but he'd always liked her spunk.

Her hair, normally neat no matter how it was coiffed, was down over her shoulders and looked more than a little windblown, like she'd been running her hands through it over and over. She wore an oversized black silk robe falling off one bare shoulder. She was all ready for bed, much earlier than normal.

A thick belt encircled her tiny waist, but her top peeked through. It was a pale pink, spaghetti strapped nighty she was fond of. It had matching shorts that stopped *right* below her perfect ass-cheeks.

If he didn't know why she was upset, his fiancée could pass for rumpled after some fantastic sex. His cock liked the idea, but her expression shouted he wouldn't be getting laid for a long, long time. Unless of course, he played his cards right with cleaning up this…situation.

"I had something I had to take care of. I'm sorry it took so long."

"You didn't answer your phone all day!"

Gian suppressed his odd urge to comfort her, and wipe away the tears forming in her big brown eyes. He donned his best chagrin. "I hate to admit this, but I lost it."

Her fair brows furrowed. "You lost your cellphone?"

"I did. I'm sorry. I'll replace it in the morning."

Elise averted her gaze, but when she met his eyes again, she appeared to be unable to speak. Her bottom lip wobbled. After a few moments, her chest heaved, lifting her awesome tits. "S-something…horrible happened today."

His heart stuttered and he told himself it had to do with the fucking search warrant she didn't know he knew about, and *not* the expression on her beautiful face.

*Shattered.*

He didn't like it.

Gian scrambled for words and made himself rush to her side. "Is it your dad? What happened? I'm so sorry I was out-of-pocket when you needed me, *tesoro*." He kissed her cheek, and she threw herself into his arms, sobbing in earnest.

He had no choice but to hold her, and he stroked her back, whispering calming Italian endearments. She'd always liked when he spoke dirty in his second language, but of course, that wouldn't get him inside her right now.

"Wh-where were you?" Elise demanded between sobs, not looking up from his chest. "With you gone all day...considering what happened, it...made me think...you knew what was—"

He rested his hands on her shoulders and squeezed, tilting her away so he could meet her eyes. He needed to pull his acting skills together, *stat*. Needed to be a concerned, *innocent* fiancé.

Enough to take an Academy Award.

"What're you talking about? Tell me what happened." Gian wanted to demand she stop crying and shake her. However, the urge to comfort her equaled that unwanted urge. He'd deal with that later.

Much later.

Or not at all.

She was a mark and didn't mean anything to him.

"I—"

When she wiped the tears and running makeup from her face, he let her take a few steps back, but those mocha eyes still implored too much for his comfort.

Like only *he* could restore order to her world.

"Let's sit, *tesoro*. Tell me all about it." He kept his voice even, and disregarded the skip of his heart. It had to have something to do with all the info she was about to reveal. Now, he'd know for certain just how fucked he was.

His fiancé nodded and allowed Gian to lead her to their L-shaped black leather sofa. It was overstuffed and extra wide. Two people could sleep side-by-side on it.

More times than he could count, he'd bent Elise over the back of the cushion and taken her from behind with the lights of Sin City as the background. His little half-Italian firecracker could be a dirty girl.

Instead of sinking into the plush cushions and relaxing, she perched on the edge and let her knee go to town, hammering up and down until her nerves skittered down *his* spine.

He took a seat next to her. Grabbed her hands and squeezed. All for her benefit, of course. "What happened, Elise?" Again, he employed that calm tone, sounding more shrink than fiancé. He'd pat himself on the back if he could.

"Cops."

"What?"

"Not just cops. Feds." She hiccupped.

"Start from the beginning." Gian plastered the appropriate shock on his face, and caressed the back of her hand.

"US Marshals showed up with a warrant. They

wouldn't say what it was for, only what they were there to seize."

"US Marshals?"

*Not FBI?*

Interesting. Uncle Dino had said the FBI had arrested Fratelli.

Elise nodded. "My brother was with them."

He made his eyes widen and opened his mouth in a half-gape. "What? That's terrible. What did he say?"

Her pretty face darkened with instant rage. "*Nothing.* The jerk didn't even give me a heads-up. He was just *with* them, like a freaking stranger."

*Also interesting.*

Why had her brother not mentioned he knew Gian *wasn't* Marco Fratelli? Strange to keep the truth to himself in investigation like this. Had he figured out who Gian really was?

Had he told the feds?

He cleared his throat, ignoring the quiver in his stomach. "Have you talked to him since?"

"He can go to hell." She stuck her bottom lip out in a tempting pout, but he knew better than to lean over and suck it into his mouth, no matter how he might want to.

Gian gave into a smirk that was too hard to fight. There was her fire again. He admired it. "I take that as a no?"

"He's not taking my calls, but Paul said no contact is better for now. He's the one who told me what the warrant was for."

"Paul Allemand?"

She nodded. "He made it here after they left."

"What did he say?"

Elise's eyes clouded with tears again. "He said he reviewed the paperwork from the cops."

Gian had to admire her ability to keep from losing it all over again. "And?" he prompted when the seconds ticked by and she failed to speak.

"It's bad, Marco, it's so bad… I don't know what—"

"Elise." He gripped both her hands and held them in what he hoped came off as a comforting, confident grip. "Just breathe and tell me."

"Money laundering."

He reared back and forced a gasp of appropriate horror. "What?"

She nodded. "When I couldn't get a hold of you all day, I freaked out. My mind went a whole bunch of scary places. I thought… I mean, I know you. I love you, you could never—"

"No," Gian said with enough hurt and volume to get her eyes back to his face. He frowned and flattened his lips. "You know me better than that; I could never be involved in something like that. I'm not a *criminal*."

Elise startled at his emphasis on the last word, then studied him, as if looking for something to confirm his words. Her mouth trembled. "Then…where were you?"

It was his turn to inhale, as if he wasn't over being offended that she'd thought the worst of him. "I went to LA."

"LA? Why?"

"There's an oncologist there that specializes in late-stage cases. I didn't tell you, because I didn't want to give you false hope. I know your dad doesn't want to be treated, but I hoped if this doctor knew about his case, and I could get him out here to talk to Big Tony, maybe…" He shrugged and made his voice catch, as if he was about to lose it over her poor-cancer-ridden daddy.

"Oh, Marco." She threw herself into his arms again, and he caught her up, rubbing her back again. "I can't believe I thought… Oh, God, I'm so sorry." When she pulled back, she trembled all over. "I'm a shit. I mean…can you forgive me?"

*Damn, I'm good.*

Gian donned another appropriate expression, instead of giving into his internal pride and beaming. He should join the Actors' Guild. He *did* deserve an Oscar. "Say no more. I understand. I disappeared, and you couldn't get a hold of me. It's only natural for you to suspect the worst, especially given what happened. I would've thought the same."

Elise clung to him again, and he patted her shoulders until she stopped shaking. She was crying again, and he didn't want her to spiral.

He had to regain control. Needed more information about what the feds had seized. "Then I lost my phone somewhere between here and there," he said with a light edge to distract her, and offered another shrug.

She straightened and wiped her fresh tears away. "We'll get you a new phone. I love you."

He nodded. "Ditto. My lost cell is the least of our worries, *tesoro*. We have to handle what happened today. What else did Mr. Allemand say? What did they take from us?"

Her expression softened, like it always did when he called her his 'treasure' in Italian, and when he acknowledged her love for him, but there was more than silly feminine approval in her dark eyes.

Gian could read relief.

*Feel* her relief.

This was good. It could work in his favor.

"I knew you'd help me fix this."

"Of course, *tesoro*. We've worked too hard to modernize this place. To make it ours."

"Maybe it wasn't worth it. Maybe something like this wouldn't have happened if we hadn't overhauled the accounting programs and software."

"Hey now, stop that. We'll figure this out." He tilted her chin up and brushed his mouth over hers so she would smile.

She did, but it still had a forlorn edge he didn't like.

"Did you call your dad?" he asked.

Elise shook her head. "No. I don't have the heart to bother him with it. I'll tell him when I don't have a choice. Not…yet."

He nodded. Knowing the old man, he'd leave the hospital AMA and storm the police department. It was better for Gian if Big Tony was in the dark. For more than one reason.

He needed her to focus and tell him the rest. "Does Allemand feel like this has something to do with our software?"

Of course it didn't. Gian wasn't an idiot. He didn't plant his numbers where they could be discovered easily amongst the legit financials from the casino. They were hidden, well-placed, as if they belonged where he'd put them. He excelled at making numbers lie.

"I don't know. It's all I can think of. It has to be some mix-up. Maybe we got hacked?" His fiancée sounded so damn optimistic, he wanted to agree.

Should he give her false hope?

Nah, Elise Giovanni was many things, but an idiot wasn't one of them. Unfortunately.

"I don't think the feds would've been able to get a warrant over a hack job."

"We haven't laundered any money!" She punctuated her shout with a stomp of her foot.

"I know, *tesoro*. Take a breath and tell me the rest. I promise we'll figure this out. What did they seize? What did the lawyers say is the next step?"

Gian tried not to pitch himself on the edge of the couch like she was, or seem too eager as she ticked off the items the feds had taken that morning.

Every item could amend his plans. Or quite possibly be the fuel that fed Uncle Dino's drive for him to cut his losses and hightail it back to the Windy City.

In disgrace.

*No, thank you.*

His time here wasn't done. He was going to own this place. Gain—no, own—his dad's respect.

"This is good."

"Good?" Elise demanded, with another flash of

anger in those big brown eyes.

"Yes."

She wrenched away from his hold. "How?"

"They didn't get anything we still don't have access to. We have backups. Remember all those redundancies we put in place? *Two* off-site server locations."

Elise pushed off the couch and started to pace. "Off-site servers?"

Gian forced a smile, because she was displaying her sharpness, and despite the turn of this conversation being *his* fault, he didn't need his fiancée launching a mission. She was too smart for her own good. "Exactly," he managed.

"I can fix this," she breathed. She smiled. A little. "I can prove we *didn't* do this." Relief engulfed her whole lithe form; lifting her shoulders and making him see the normally confident woman that drew him no matter his resistance.

"Hold on a moment, before you go off half-cocked."

She frowned. "I need your help right now."

"And you have it. Always. But what did Allemand say to do?"

"He said investigators from his office will meet with me in the morning. I need to order the back-ups. To start analyzing the data."

"I think we need to do what the firm says," Gian said, pushing the caution forward. He needed her to calm her damn jets.

"What? But you were right. I can see almost

everything the feds can. I can—"

"Hey. Breathe." He shot to his feet and grabbed her shoulders again. "I'll help you wherever I can, but I really feel we should follow Allemand's lead. You don't want to hurt the case, do you? Or make it look like you're tampering with evidence."

Elise's expression fell; all the hope fleeing as if it hadn't been there.

He couldn't care how she felt. Not that he did. He had to cover his ass. Her uncovering his real identity hadn't computed in his calculations, and he *needed* it to stay that way.

"You're probably right," she whispered.

"I don't want to be right."

She nodded. "Will you come to the meeting tomorrow?"

"Of course."

"Then we can reassess?"

He nodded. "We'll see how it goes. You might want to order the back-ups to give to Allemand's investigators."

"Yeah, I will first thing."

"Good. It'll be okay, *tesoro*. One day at a time…"

"One day at a time," Elise echoed.

"Do you want me to go beat up your brother?" he offered half-heartedly.

She laughed. It was genuine, and made him return a soft smile.

"No offense, my love, but I fear he'd wipe the floor with you." The playful twinkle returned to her eyes.

Somehow, Gian liked that.

"Hey! I feel insulted!" He grabbed his chest and she giggled.

Her expression sobered so fast, he frowned.

"Speaking of my brother…"

"He can go to hell, remember?" He didn't need her reaching out to the asshole tonight. His identity was still in danger. Her brother knew too much.

The feds had a case.

There was a lot of work to do. He could clean things up with his fiancée to put her off his trail, but *she* wasn't the real danger.

He had no intention of telling his Uncle Dino. Gian needed to know what Fratelli had told the feds, too.

"Yes, but it's not that." Elise's luscious mouth rippled as if she was fighting another smile. The frown won, and her lips turned down. He could feel her perplexity. "He did find something else."

"What?"

"A little brown book. It looked old."

His heart skittered to a stop, then tripped into overdrive. He prayed she couldn't make out his genuine *'oh, shit'* face. "What? What was in it?"

"I don't know. They took it before I got a chance to see inside."

D amn, he needed a drink.

Maybe he needed to have his head examined.

Gio stood at her apartment door, and the golden numbers mocked him. He stared, not having the balls to form a fist to knock. When he shifted on his feet, the number four of 472 glinted more than the other digits in the fading light peeking in from the hallway windows.

*Take your ass home.*

He didn't move.

There was no way she'd want to see him, not after his very juvenile outburst in the conference room, or how he'd fled like a thirteen-year-old caught whacking it by his mom.

Gio had gone right out of the PD, threw the little book into his bike's saddle bags and had hit the road. He hadn't gone back to work for the rest of the day, and someone must've covered his ass because he hadn't gotten any calls or texts from Olinsky to ask where the hell he was.

*Maddie.*

Why she would've done it was a mystery, but he didn't doubt it was all her.

He'd traveled the city streets of Vegas, then moved away from the strip, finally ending up on the highway, studying the mountains in the distance and the desert that surrounded where he'd grown up.

Gio had ended up at his childhood house, in the suburb of Boulder City, which his father had sold not long after his mother's death. The old man had moved into one of the two penthouses at the casino. Elise lived in the other one, with the sleazeball, he suspected.

He'd stopped short of pulling in the driveway of the huge Mediterranean home, built in the style his mother had loved so much.

Minutes or hours passed as he'd observed the place. Happy memories flitted through his mind, even ones where his father had laughed and played with him and his siblings. That had to have been a hundred years ago, because it'd been more common for them to see the man inside the empire he'd built. Big Tony had worked *a lot* when they were kids.

Gio remembered his mother pretending not to cry, and holding it together for her children. Damn, Sam had to have still been in diapers. Their mother, Helen, had hated *The Giovanni*.

He restarted his bike, finally moving away from the old house when he'd gotten some weird looks from neighbors — no one really *had* to take the trash out twice, while subtly holding their cellphone, as if 9-1-1 poised — and forced his Ducati to take him back to the city. Last thing he needed was for someone to call the local police for the weird guy in a leather jacket on a motorcycle that really didn't appear to be suburb material.

He hadn't been able to go home, or back to work. He'd wasted a ton of gas.

Beyond a few calls he'd let go to voicemail, his sister hadn't texted or phoned. Not that he blamed her, but Dominic had.

Angry messages that promised violence had filled his voicemail from his brother. Messages that made him worry they would never be able to smooth over their conflict.

*This* was a crapton worse than Dom getting a DWI.

He hadn't heard from Sam or his dad, and if Big Tony was finally going to reach out, why not when his oldest kid had brought a group of cops to raid his legacy?

Gio crushed his eyes shut.

How could he be more fucked up than before Maddie had come back to town?

He must be some sort of masochist to want to seek comfort from the source of the problem.

Then again, it wasn't *really* her fault. He must know that on some level, or really be FUBAR to show up on her doorstep like he had last night.

It wasn't like she was going to throw the door open naked, and demand he take her.

His dick, the little fucker it was twitched at the image.

Nah, it was more likely she'd meet him at the door with her Glock.

Not-Marco-fucking-Fratelli was the culprit of this whole thing, *not* Maddie. Sure, she was the investigator in charge and all that, but that little cocktwat was the one who'd made his father and sister look guilty of money laundering.

It had to be him.

How to prove it?

*Tell Maddie the whole truth about what I found, and work with the team to prove it,* his conscience chided.

She *did* need to know Marco wasn't who he said he was, and she could help him find the truth; she was damn good at her job.

Maybe she'd forgive him for keeping it from her.

Gio snorted.

"Is everything all right?"

A tremulous inquiry snagged his attention and he whipped his head to the left.

It was a little old lady, eighty if she was a day, wearing a floral-printed moo-moo and peeking around the door of the apartment a few doors down and across the hall from Maddie's. She had stereotypical white hair with a blue sheen.

Great, she'd seen him languishing on the welcome mat, if her worried expression was any indication.

*I'm not a stalker, for real,* wanted to pop out of his mouth. He cleared his throat to make sure he could talk. "Uh, yeah. My girlfriend just moved in here."

Her wrinkled face lit up with a smile. "Ah, she's a pretty girl. I saw her this morning."

"That she is." Gio made a show of lifting his fist, preparing to knock. "You have a nice evening, ma'am."

Just as the door flew open, the old woman mustered an answer, but she didn't retreat into her apartment.

Nice, Maddie's new place came equipped with a nosy old lady who wasn't shy about it.

"Gio." His name was a curse, and she regarded him with narrowed eyes.

"Uh, hi, Mads."

"What're you *doing* here?" It was an incredulous demand. "And where the hell is my *evidence*?"

If the elderly woman wasn't hanging on every word, he might've mentioned he had colossal balls.

"Uh, I was talking to your neighbor…"

Maddie sobered immediately and peered around him at Nosy Nellie. She cast her eyes to the ceiling, as if in prayer, then flashed a very fake smile, but didn't address their witness. She clamped her hand on his leather-clad arm, and dragged him inside.

The door snapped shut just short of a slam.

Maybe he should thank the old chick for getting him in, because had she not been watching, there wasn't a doubt Maddie would've sent him packing. Immediately.

Or shot his ass.

He should scan the place for the nearest firearm.

She whirled on him and her scent enveloped him, scattering any thoughts but carnal ones.

Visions of her naked in his arms, her taste, her lips, her scream when she came, dominated his brain and whatever he'd planned on saying eviscerated.

"Well?" she demanded, her hands on her hips.

She was dressed in pink again, but this time it was a tank top with alternating white stripes, as well as a pair of darker pink shorts that stopped right above her knees. They were cut-offs, as if she couldn't stand them in pants-form and had grabbed the scissors.

Unlike the oversized tee from the night before, the tank top clung to everything he shouldn't look at. She didn't have a bra on, either.

His mind was still in the gutter. Or in her bed.

"Well what?" fell from his mouth like an idiot.

"Where's the little book?" Maddie's fair brow was drawn tight, and her full mouth a hard line he wanted to make time to soften with his lips. His tongue.

"I have it," Gio croaked.

"It's evidence."

Couldn't argue with that. "It is."

"Hand it over." She put her palm out, high and flat.

How on earth did she know he had it *on* him?

Like a guilty kid, he dug into the inside pocket of his leather jacket and pulled out the little tome. He refused to feel bad for snatching it.

He had a right to study it, didn't he?

*He* was the one who'd found it, so it wasn't like his keeping it *really* effected the chain of custody.

"It's my dad's writing," he admitted, studying his shitkickers for a moment. He might've been estranged from his father for years, but he'd recognize the serial-killer-scrawl anywhere. He sounded like he was sulking, even to his own ears, and he couldn't meet Maddie's eyes for seconds that felt like hours.

Maybe he shouldn't look at her at all, since he

couldn't focus on anything but the heat between them.

Heat that felt one-sided at the moment.

He'd already gone over all the reasons he shouldn't be there when he'd been on the wrong side of the door, so he wasn't shocked. He *was* still a fool. There would be no jumping into his arms.

"What do you make of it?" she whispered.

Gio met her eyes. That was the last thing he'd expected her to say.

There was no triumph in her expression. If anything, she was regarding him cautiously.

Thank God there was no pity in her pretty hazel orbs.

He had to take in air before he could find his voice. "It seems like an old school bookie's log. Although, there's no indication as to what the money was for."

"No record of bets? Can't tell if it was horses? Cards? Fights?"

He shook his head. "Just initials and dollar amounts."

"Weird." Maddie thumbed through the pages that were thick and sturdy, despite the age of the leather-bound book.

Gio didn't speak as he observed her. She was so damn gorgeous, especially with the expression of concentration she wore as she studied what he'd already gone over multiple times. "Do we have to stand right inside your door all night?"

Her head shot up. "Who said anything about all night?"

He bit his lip so he wouldn't smirk. "Why're you

so defensive? Don't know how to host a guest?"

Maddie guffawed. "I'd say I hosted you quite well last night."

He chuckled. "I wouldn't disagree, but don't multiple orgasms at least earn me a seat?"

She giggled.

Damn, this woman. No one had ever had the same effect on him.

He was tied in fucking knots.

Their eyes locked, and time froze, until she finally looked away, her cheeks flushed a delicious shade of pink.

His dick was half-hard and it took all he was made of not to touch her.

"Do you want a drink? I have bottled iced tea, or beer." Maddie said, but she wouldn't meet his gaze again.

"Mads…"

She glanced back at him expectantly over her shoulder on her way to the fridge, but words failed him.

What the hell had he wanted to say, anyway?

"What, Gio?"

"I'll take tea, thanks."

She nodded, but it seemed like it was more to herself than him. "Make yourself comfortable in the living room, and I'll meet you there. Have you eaten? I ordered a pizza. Should be here soon."

"I could eat." He stood there, instead of heading the few feet to her living room. The open floor plan, featured the wide kitchen to the left of the front door, and the simple pecan-wood dining table with four chairs behind it. The spacious living room was to the right, where a brown couch, single recliner and long coffee table faced a generic flat-screen television sitting on a stand, obviously not plugged in.

"Yeah, you could always eat," she said, but he was distracted, watching her long legs move in those cut-offs. For a shorter woman, Mads knew how to accentuate her killer stems.

He had to stop thinking about sex. He shuffled his feet forward, moving to the couch and ordering himself to sit.

Maddie offered him a frosty bottle of sweet tea. She held a beer for herself dangling at her side.

He was glad she hadn't asked why he was abstaining. Gio reached, and their fingertips collided. "Yeah. Eat."

The crimson flush up to her ears told him she knew he wasn't talking about food anymore.

"Gio, it's just not a good idea."

He nodded. Couldn't disagree; even though his dick did, with a vehement throb of protest as he readjusted on the couch.

"Let's just eat pizza and relax." She sat, leaving a cushion between them. "I'm tired, and it's not like staring at that little book will decipher it." Maddie gestured toward the kitchen table, where she'd left his dad's old ledger.

Did her suggestion mean she wasn't putting him out on his ear?

"TV's not hooked up." He broke a somewhat companionable silence.

"Aren't you observant?" She took a sip of beer, smirking, but he couldn't help but wish her lips were around his cock, instead of the brown glass bottle's rim.

"Comes with my job, I guess." He winked. "Sucks we can't add a movie to that 'relax.'" Gio shot his fingers up to make air quotes. He'd almost said, *Netflix and chill*, which read; hot sweaty sex, but didn't want to push his luck.

"Cut me a break, I've been working nonstop since I arrived. It's bad enough I haven't unpacked everything." She gestured to several stacks of boxes around the room. "And Jamie will be here—" Maddie tensed and snapped her mouth shut.

"Jamie? Your sister?"

She nodded, but it was terse, obviously uncomfortable.

A knock on the door interrupted them, and she popped to her feet as if she'd been shot.

"Pizza." Maddie all but ran to the door.

Gio grabbed paper plates from the kitchen counter, and met her back at the couch, but the woman's movements were still stiff and unnatural.

What had he said this time?

"Your sister's moving in with you?" he asked. Anything to break the tense silence.

She dropped a slice of pepperoni and cheese on his plate. She nodded, but didn't speak.

"Is something wrong?" he ventured after his first bite. He wanted to close his eyes as the flavors burst on his tongue, but he didn't look away from Maddie.

He loved *Papa's Pies*. It was a small chain with a

few stores in the Vegas area, and there was one right down the street.

She shook her head, and reached for her beer.

A few more quiet seconds passed, and she frowned. "Yeah, actually."

"What?"

"Something *is* wrong."

"What?" Gio repeated, glancing at her face after two more bites. He needed another slice.

"Who the hell is Marco Fratelli?"

He groaned and dragged his hand down his face. "Mads—"

"I ran his name and only came up with a little boy who died a long time ago. From a heart condition. He's the son of the accountant for the Falcone crime family. Cesare Fratelli, the guy the FBI snagged, and sent me down here."

"Shit." He should've known she'd be able to discover the same information he had in about two seconds.

"Gio?"

"I believe he's the person responsible for the money laundering at *The Giovanni*."

Various emotions dashed across her pretty face at his confession.

She opened her mouth to speak, but had to try more than once. "Why the fuck would you *not* tell me about the person you suspected committed the crime, to make your sister and father look guilty?" Her face was red again—part anger, part two beers—and all he wanted to do was claim her mouth.

Gio made his smile lazy. "I thought you were tired, and didn't want to talk about work? No case talk? Pizza and relax?"

"Gio." His nickname was all warning, and Maddie glared harder.

"I needed to find out who he was first."

*Which I still don't know.*

"What the fuck *for*?" She punctuated her demand by bristling, and pushed to her bare toes. Her fists her at sides, but the movement made her breasts bounce. So distracting.

His tongue was flooded with the memory of her clean skin and his cock went from half-interest to zipper bitten in a few seconds.

Why was she so hot when she was mad?

"You said I could prove my dad was innocent, so I was doing it my way. You *knew* I'd do that. I told you that this afternoon. Don't act all shocked."

She narrowed her eyes so hard, if she'd been Superwoman he would've been incinerated on the spot. She had lasers, they just didn't have murderous power.

*Thank God.*

For some reason, he wanted to cover his balls with both hands.

"Why do you always make me want to kick the shit out of you?"

"Why do you always make me want to kiss you?" Gio retorted.

Maddie froze, and her gaze burned his again, but the desire that flared gave him hope she wouldn't rip his junk off after all. "Gio." His name was breathy on her lips, but her expression said she hadn't wanted it to come out that way.

He stood and took her hand, never breaking their eye contact. "Please, Mads. You said it. We can't figure out the book tonight, and we can't delve into who my sister's fiancé really is until we go back to work. Do you want to do that tonight?""

"No," she admitted. Her tongue darted out to moisten her bottom lip.

He'd been so driven to discover the truth, hadn't he?

Why was he pushing her *away* from the case?

Was Gio letting his dick do all the thinking?

He sure as hell wanted it to do the acting, at least right now.

He dipped down and took her mouth until she moaned and ground her hips against his.

Then Maddie twined her fingers with his and dragged him to her bedroom.

# Chapter
## SEVENTEEN

"Oh. Fuck."

Maddie's fingers wandered down the goosebumps on his abs, and Gio trembled under her touch. "Do you want me to stop?" she whispered. A sharp intake of air next make her smirk.

"Hell no."

"Damn good thing tomorrow's Sunday."

"Why?"

"Because you've kept me up all night the last two days." She gripped his cock, marveling at how he hardened against her palm. "So much for relaxing my first weekend here."

"You don't find…this, relaxing?" He didn't open his eyes as he asked, but the fact he was already panting from her touch made desire curl low in her belly.

"Not exactly." She grinned and started to pump him.

They'd spent two blissful days in her bed, only leaving to seek fast-food, breakfast, lunch *and* dinner.

Then there'd been the takeout, since Maddie hadn't made but one quick trip to the grocery store the day after she'd moved in. She only had the bare minimum in the cupboards and fridge. Coffee, sugar, creamer and some junk food. She'd need to do full food shopping before Jake and Jamie came into town, but she could do that…tomorrow.

Jamie. Jake.

She'd almost blurted it when he'd teased her about the TV being unplugged.

*Jesus.*

That would've been a nightmare.

She buried her face in her pillow as the now-familiar guilt scorched her ass, because she *still* hadn't told him about their seven-year-old. Time was ticking, and she was ignoring all manners of clocks.

Gio and sex wasn't how she'd seen herself spending her first weekend back in Sin City, *ever*, but Maddie couldn't regret it.

They hadn't talked about the case much, either. They'd gone over the little book a bit more, but Marco Fratelli hadn't been mentioned. They were in a little pheromone-filled cocoon until Monday. Somehow it was a relief she needed. Keeping reality at bay for as long as fate would allow.

It was an odd sensation, going from case-obsessed to having it on some backburner she'd not known she'd possessed. How could she "not care" about it so suddenly?

The man in her bed was going to ruin her.

Gio's laugh was cut off by a gasp. "Who's…keeping who…*up*?"

Maddie giggled. "*Up* is another one of those good

words."

He didn't speak, but then again, she didn't blame him, since she slowed her pace, varying her grip.

Tingles raced all over her body as his thick tip disappeared and reappeared in her hand.

How she could be aroused when she was giving *him* pleasure was a wonder, because she'd never wanted to do what she was doing to any man other than Gio. Especially the next part.

She scooted down the bed, lying across his long legs, resting her breasts on his thighs.

He pinned her with those sapphire orbs. "Mads, you don't—"

Maddie sucked him into her mouth.

"Shit, Maddie," Gio panted. His powerful chest heaved as he struggled to breathe normally.

She didn't want him reined in.

Maddie flexed her hand on his impressive erection and dragged her tongue around the underside of his tip.

"Fuck. Me," he gasped.

She smiled against his shaft and glanced up. "I'm trying to make you feel as good as you made me feel with your mouth. More than once." She squeezed him and tugged once for good measure.

"You…are."

"Good." She licked his entire length before taking him back inside her mouth.

"Mads…" He cupped the back of her head, burying one of his huge hands in her hair and pulling. The tension on her scalp wasn't painful, but just enough force to invigorate her attentions. He tangled his fingers in her locks, and his sac tightened. She loved it; all evidence he was losing control.

She wanted him unbridled.

Scream her name like he'd made her.

Maddie moved up and down, taking all of him, rubbing her tongue on his most sensitive part—the underside of his thick head.

He shifted his ass and tilted his hips as if he couldn't help it, and she smiled again.

"More, Gio," she whispered against his dick, nipping at his skin. "I want all of you."

Her lover threw his head back in answer, and lifted his pelvis off the bed.

She gripped his thighs and took all of him in her mouth, sucking hard as she moved up and down. Cupped his heavy sac and squeezed gently.

Gio gasped and grunted. He grabbed one of her hands. "I'm close, Mads. You can stop."

Maddie shook her head and gripped the base of his erection. Squeezed and pumped harder. Ran her tongue around his tip again, and tasted the salty preview of his release.

He grabbed at her shoulders, but she didn't stop.

His body went stiff, his muscles taut. He gripped her wrist almost painfully, but yelled her name as the warm rush of his orgasm filled her mouth.

She swallowed every drop, stroking his thighs with one hand, and entwining their fingers with the other when he reached for her again.

He'd barely popped free of her lips, when he

yanked up to his chest, jarring her.

Gio crashed his mouth into hers, pinning her to him and kissing her breath away.

Maddie's head spun, but she clung to him, slipping her arms around his neck and kissing him back with all her might.

When he ended it, he pressed his forehead to hers. "Damn, you blow me away."

She smiled and cupped his cheeks, thumbing his stubble, remembering the scratchiness against her inner thighs. It'd been heaven, heightening things. A tremor shot down her spine. "Good. I wanted to."

Gio kissed her again, and held her closely, wreaking havoc on her emotions.

The oral sex had happened a few times this weekend. This was the first time she'd gone down on him, but he'd done it to her after they'd had phenomenal sex so many times she'd lost count. She really was going to be sore as hell, but she didn't give a shit.

It was after three a.m., and words regarding Jake still didn't seem as if they would surface.

Maddie told herself for the hundredth time to do it.

She'd convinced herself after she rocked his world, she'd tell him.

Now, as she looked at Nico Giovanni with his eyes closed and satiated contentment all over his gorgeous face, she couldn't muster the whole truth.

Guilt swirled low, jumping up to take a bite out of her heart.

The feelings she'd had for this man from eight long years ago came slamming down so fast she couldn't return them to the vault where they'd resided since he'd broken her heart.

When he'd said the word '*love*' in regards to going down on her, that first night he'd shown up at her place, she'd wanted to order him gone.

It didn't matter he'd been referencing oral sex, or a physical act in general. It'd hurt, because of how he'd said it.

What it *didn't* mean.

*Now I'm thinking crazy. I owe him the truth.*

Contradictory thoughts were bound to make her brain hurt.

"Mads?"

"Yeah?" When the word came out a croak, she cursed.

Gio cracked one eye open. "You okay?"

"Better than okay."

The truth was the truth, even if she hated it.

*Still not the truth I need to tell him.*

She couldn't.

That just made her feel guiltier.

"You're not kicking me out, are you?" Now both of those incredible eyes were open and pinning her with sincerity she wanted to ignore.

"No. It's late, why bother now? Besides, you stayed last night, why would tonight be different? We don't have to work until Monday."

"No case talk, remember?"

They'd agreed the weekend would be about *them*.

His cell vibrated from her nightstand. Gio grabbed it, and silenced it without so much as a peek at the screen.

He'd done that tons of times.

"Are you sure you don't have to get that?"

"Nope." He lifted the device again. "It's off now."

"But it's late, so it might be important."

"Don't care." His smile was serene, as if he'd *really* put everything on the back burner.

Again, it swirled in her mind. How could she have not only *agreed* to put the case aside for a few days?

Gio had agreed, too, even though his sister looked so guilty, and they hadn't been able to figure out what the little book meant.

It was still her case, her work. She'd always been driven to see things to the end. Without distraction.

"Maybe I can talk you into letting me inside you once more?" He waggled his eyebrows.

It wouldn't take more than a simple kiss, but Maddie couldn't admit that. "Don't get cocky."

Gio winked. "No other way to be."

Her heart raced all over again, as if she was running a race.

*I'm so screwed.*

K ♥

The buzzing sound repeated and Gio rolled over. He blinked to orient, but the unfamiliar sound didn't click in his brain.

He caught a whiff of something sweet on the pillow next to him. Something that'd been gone from his life for nearly a decade.

*Maddie.*

His Mads.

He was in *her* bed.

The woman who'd fled from him. The woman he should've chased.

Flashes of the weekend danced across his memory and his dick jumped. He wanted her again, would *always* want her.

Memories of her whirlwind arrival back into Vegas, and his life all seemed to coalesce, starting with that kiss in the storage room, to him showing up on her doorstep that first night, to serving the warrant and finding the book, crushing his sister.

He wasn't supposed to be thinking of the case. The pair of them needed the weekend off. Especially him, to quiet his headfuck. He'd needed *her*.

She'd agreed without much protest, but then again, he'd always been great at distracting her. They'd looked at the little leather book to distraction and frustration, but had set it aside for carnal pursuits.

They'd pick all the emails, phone calls, and demands back up on Monday. It would all hit—when it had to.

He'd had two days in her bed, inside her body, but it was far from enough.

This time…Gio wasn't going to let her go.

Had he made a decision to keep her in his life? How could he even go about it?

Maddie had said her sister Jamie was going to move in with her, but other than that one mention over pizza Friday night, she hadn't mentioned her again, and there'd been something weird about it. She'd stiffened as if she'd said the wrong thing. Or it was a secret.

Why?

Did Jamie at her place mean Maddie was *staying* in Vegas?

He really should ask. They hadn't had much time for *talking*.

Damn…she'd been exquisite.

Every. Single. Time.

Better than he remembered. Made his balls ache with the mere recall; especially with her mouth on him, but he'd always had a great memory where Madison Granger was concerned.

Maddie had shown him how a woman wanted to be touched, tasted and kissed. It'd always come naturally with them.

Then again, the fire, the drive, the desire to possess each other had always been there.

Gio had never had a lover like Maddie since then, and like that old Garth Brooks song, it wasn't often he hadn't thought of her, even when he was having sex with someone else. Could be mid-act, as shitty as that made him.

The infernal buzzing repeated, this time it was intermittently short and long, like someone was laying on a—

"Fucking doorbell," he spat and swung his feet over the side of Maddie's bed. "Mads?" he called. He paused, but didn't get an answer.

She wasn't in bed.

Gio could hear water running from her bathroom. Why had she showered without him? They could've had fun in there.

Over the last two days, they'd showered together several times. This was the first one she'd taken solo. Then again, they'd had sex under the steamy spray every time. Maybe Maddie just wanted to get clean. She'd always been a girly girl who'd loved a long session with hot water.

Her cell on her nightstand vibrated madly, and at the same time, the doorbell buzzed again.

The phone quieted only to start the routine over again.

He did the math and cursed. Whoever was calling was likely at the door, but he didn't get nosy and peer at her screen.

Gio scanned the room to locate clothing. He whipped his jeans off the tan carpet and shoved his legs into them, not bothering with his boxers, but he made sure to tuck his boys in to avoid the zipper. Haste could make for *ouch* on the frank and beans.

He didn't bother with a shirt or shoes. "Guess *I'll* get the door," he muttered and stomped his way there, running his hand through his hair.

Two turns of a deadbolt and doorknob's lock, and he whipped thing open, prepared to bark at whoever dared bother her on a Sunday. The inconsiderate ass.

Eyes that matched Maddie's went so wide the whites showed. The girl's arm drifted away from her face, going limp with a cellphone in her grip. This had to be Jamie, the younger sister.

She was blonder than Mads, but he didn't think it was from a bottle. Pretty, with a youthfulness to her cheeks that put her under twenty-five. Despite the multiple mentions even back then, they'd never met. She was the younger version of Maddie.

"Uhhh…" she said.

Gio's urge to yell dissipated. Movement behind her caught his attention.

A little boy regarded him, head tilted to one side, staring with eyes just as wide.

*Jamie's* presence made sense, since Maddie had mentioned her sister was moving in, but who was the child?

Unlike the young woman, the kid's eyes were blue. Very blue. His dark hair dangled just over his eyebrows, and a large toy airplane hung from one hand. His facial features were somehow…familiar. High cheekbones and a jawline that would only become more sculpted as he grew into a man.

He could spot that, despite the childish roundness of his cheeks.

"Who are you?" the boy asked. Not a demand, just a curious question.

Something nudged from the back of Gio's mind.

This kid reminded him of something—some*one*.

*Wait.*

It was like looking at pictures of *him* and his brothers when they were little. Their resemblance to each other was unmistakable.

His heart dropped to his gut.

*He looks like* me.

"Gio, what're you—"

Maddie's inquiry was cut off by a gasp, and he glanced over his shoulder.

She was standing next to the kitchen table, about ten feet away, wearing a baby pink robe and sporting bare feet. Her glorious locks were loose and darker since they were wet, but the towel in her hand slipped to the floor.

His lover blanched, paling so much he was concerned she'd faint.

Her gaze locked on the two people in the doorway.

"Mommy!" the kid yelled and darted into the apartment. He threw his little arms around Maddie's waist and buried his face in her stomach, but she was imitating a statue.

Her eyes stayed on Gio. Unblinking, with *'oh shit'* written all over her gorgeous face.

*Mommy?*

"Oh, shit is right," Gio muttered.

His Mads had a kid?

A kid that looked suspiciously like *him?*

The math added itself up in his head, like some sick, cackling robot calculator. It scared the shit out of him.

Jamie slid past him and followed inside, stopping between the pair of adults. "Maddie?" Her eyes were still saucers, like when he'd opened the door. "Surprise?" She shrugged, but a glare from her older sister nixed the slight curve of her mouth and froze her shoulders half-shrug.

"Jamie…" Maddie stuttered. Her arms went around the kid, and the boy dropped the large plastic airplane to the floor with a clatter.

"I got us a cheap fare, and thought we'd surprise you since I'm off the next few days, and I snagged an interview…"

Maddie knelt in front of the kid and gave him a proper hug. Whispered to him, and even though they weren't all that far apart, what she'd said didn't carry.

"I missed you, Mommy!"

Gio could only stare. His brain was ignoring what he'd already computed.

Maybe denial was keeping him from comprehension.

How could Maddie have *fucked* him—all weekend—and kept a *kid* a secret?

*My kid?*

He blinked. Reached for anger, but only shock was there.

He was numb. His limbs were heavy, shaky.

With all the shit about the case, his dad, his sister, the cockstain, the casino; wasn't it worse to heap something *else* on him, right?

Had that been her justification?

Where were his words, so he could *ask*?

His voice had moved out.

*Holy. Shit.*

Gio wandered away from the door he didn't remember closing, ending up next to Maddie and the boy in front of the couch.

She straightened, and he waited for fury to fill up

inside him, but when his eyes landed on the kid, he didn't get angry.

He *couldn't.*

The child's face resembled his so much…he was so beautiful, Gio could barely breathe.

The kid slid his hand into Maddie's, and even though she hadn't said more, she didn't shove him away.

Those eyes, so much like his own, landed on him and the little boy quirked his dark head to one side, like he'd done when the door had first opened. Even the inquisitive expression resembled Gio's own reflection.

"Are you my dad?"

# Chapter
EIGHTEEN

Maddie flushed to her toes and suppressed another gasp.

How the *hell* could Jake have deduced the truth?

*Everyone* was looking at her. Even Jamie's eyes burned.

Jake and Gio wore identical stares. Wasn't that some shit?

Of course she'd noticed her son resembled the man who'd fathered him. Knowing it and *seeing* it would've rendered her speechless under normal circumstances. *This* was nothing even close.

Seeing them *next* to each other was striking.

Like lightning hitting her brain.

"Mommy?" Jake asked.

"Mads?" Gio echoed. His voice was calm, not filled with rage.

*Why?* How was *that* even possible?

History had displayed his temper many times, including the night she'd told him she was pregnant. He'd been so intoxicated.

Nico Giovanni was a mean-as-hell drunk. Any girl

with half a brain would've fled, instead of trying to hug him or converse with him.

Maddie had been a smart girl that night.

Hadn't she?

She sucked in air, but it didn't lessen the spinning in her head. She opened her mouth but nothing came out, so she cleared her throat and tried again.

*Might as well rip the Band-Aid off.*

Maddie closed her eyes and told the threatening tears to go to hell. Explaining was going to be unavoidable but she could start with the simplest answer. The truth.

She opened her eyes and met Gio's. Then looked at her — *their* — son. "Yes."

Gio sat, hard, like her words had cut the tendons in his knees.

The couch creaked as it caught his weight, but considering she'd expected shouting and cursing, she'd take it.

"Mads..."

Her nickname was loaded with all sorts of emotions that made her insides wobble.

Again, she didn't hear or see the fury she deserved, and that freaked her out even more. She should thank him for not yelling, for the sake of their son, but *why*?

No sign of his infamous temper? Maybe the shock hadn't worn off.

Jake tugged free of her grip and went to the man he looked so much like. He thrust his hand out. "I'm Jake. I'm seven."

Damn, only *her* kid would...

Maddie trembled from head to foot. Tears spilled; she had no control.

Gio's baby blues went at his child. His hand rose to shake Jake's, but it was probably just automatic pilot. "Uh, hi. I'm—" He laughed with a nervous edge like nothing she'd ever heard before. "I guess *'Dad'* is good. Jesus—" He exhaled audibly, and that powerful bare chest heaved a few times. He glanced at her again, and shoved his free hand through his short hair.

Her little boy grinned and she was grateful he didn't seem to sense the tension in the room. He was usually pretty astute, so it had to be because of *who* held his attention.

"But I want your name! Mommy's name is Madison, but Aunt Jamie calls her 'Maddie'. I'm not allowed. She gets mad if I call her that. Aunt Jamie's name is Jamison, which is a boy's name, but *she* gets mad when I say that. There's a boy in my class named Jamison."

Maddie tried to regulate her respiration, as she listened to her son babble, as if this was the most natural thing in the world, and the walls weren't crumbling around her.

Jamie still hadn't said a word.

That was just another super weird thing. Her sister was normally a chatterbox.

Gio told Jake his name, and his nickname.

"I'm sorry, Maddie. I had no idea—"

Her eyes shot to her sister's at the pain-filled whisper. She shook her head. "It's fine."

Jamie was wringing her hands like she did when

she was little and Maddie had caught her doing something forbidden.

Jake had picked up the same habit.

Her stomach took another dive to her toes.

*This* was so fucking *far* from fine, but she didn't need her sister to be as much of a wreck as she was.

Jamie sidled up to her. "You had him over and didn't tell him? Wait, you didn't..." Her sister's gaze roved her face and robe. Then she reddened to the tips of her ears and her hazel eyes widened. "OMG, you *did*. Madison Susan Granger!"

Maddie groaned. "First of all, keep your voice down. Secondly, mind your own damn business, Jamison Kimberly Granger, since we're popping out full names. Thirdly, don't *speak* in text. Use your words."

The twenty-four-year old grinned; the obvious discomfort that'd been evident when Gio had opened the door was nowhere in sight.

*Of course,* her little sister had no problem composing *herself.*

She studied the two males.

Jake's instant comfort with Gio should've bothered her, but it just spun her heart into more chaos. Maddie didn't know whether to laugh or cry.

She'd been obsessing about her case and Gio and his family drama. The sight before her blew that out of the water. Her case wasn't even on her radar.

The more her son spoke to his father, the more relaxed Gio appeared, too. His smile—even his laugh—sounded more natural.

Jake was the only one *not* freaked out.

Later, when she got him alone, she was going to quiz her son about his guess.

"Jamie, did you tell him his dad was in Vegas?" She whispered, forcing the inquiry to remain free of the demand she really wanted to make.

Her sister reared back, as if she'd slapped her.

At least the shock *seemed* real.

"No, Maddie. I wouldn't do something like that. Promise." Her fair brows drew tight and she frowned. "I'd *never*—"

"Okay, I believe you. How the hell did he know?"

Jamie snorted. "Dude looks *just* like him. Maybe he saw it."

"Right. He's seven."

"And far from stupid."

Maddie shook her head. She'd still ask him later.

"May I say—"

"No, you may *not*." She made a cutting gesture with her hand.

Her sister grinned, completely unrepentant. "You don't even know what I was gonna say."

"Yes, I do, and I don't wanna hear it. Nor do I want you ogling him."

Jamie scoffed, but her grin didn't fade. "Jealous?"

Maddie rolled her eyes and didn't answer.

"Can I hug you?" her son asked Gio.

Her breath caught and they all froze at Jake's innocent wish.

Gio's eyes found hers.

Her chest ratcheted up even more.

"Uh, sure, champ. C'mere." The man opened his arms and the little boy rushed into the embrace.

Tears spilled instantly at the sight of her child in the arms of the man who'd fathered him. There was no stopping the hot trails down her cheeks, despite how hard she tried.

She'd always wanted this, right?

Jake *with* Gio.

Even if she'd never admitted it—woman power, *I am woman, hear me roar,* and all that—raising him without his father had left a canyon in her heart.

Not *just* where Jake was concerned.

Maddie had *missed* Gio.

Why were her emotions all over the place?

Because she'd loved this man once. She ignored the voice that accused she *still* loved Nico Giovanni.

She didn't. She wasn't that stupid, right?

Maddie had been the biggest fool, *ever* to think she could sleep with him again, kiss him, touch him, have him *inside* her and have her heart emerge unscathed.

Hadn't worked worth a shit the first time, only then he'd left her with a piece of him.

Was this time going to be easier?

She didn't kid herself. Having him as a lover was temporary. No matter that her new post was permanent and local.

Was Gio going to break Jake's heart, too?

She'd *kill* him.

Jamie squeezed her arm, and she forced a watery smile.

When her little sister slid an arm around her

shoulders, she let her comfort her, leaning in to her slender side.

Her sister couldn't know everything that was racing through her head.

"It'll be okay, Maddie. This'll be good, for *both* of you."

She didn't answer. Didn't know what the hell to say anyway.

Maddie could only watch her son interact with the man she'd fled.

K<br>♥

"So, I guess you're Jamie?" Gio stood and thrust his hand out, smiling at Maddie's younger sibling.

The young woman blushed scarlet and offered a shy nod, eyeing his hand, but not giving him a shake.

He didn't miss Maddie rolling her eyes beside them.

His son clung to his other hand and he didn't have the heart to dislodge him. *Jesus Christ, I have a kid.*

"Aunt Jamie, why're you bein' weird?" the kid asked, as if on cue. His expressive blue eyes transferred back and forth between all three adults.

Jamie gasped and glared at her nephew. Then she shook her head, but didn't answer.

Maddie snorted and hid a smile. "Wow. She's never speechless. Ever."

Gio found himself grinning. Like he hadn't in ages. His brain must've packed bags and moved out.

Finding out he had a son with the one that'd gotten away should've rocked him to his core. Instead, he was…okay with it?

Standing here chatting like it was the most natural thing in the world, and teasing her younger sister?

Maybe his family's sitch had finally fucked with his head so much he *had* lost it.

"Bite me," Jamie muttered.

"Language, little ears." Maddie gestured to the boy.

"Those weren't bad words, Mommy." Jake had one dark eyebrow arched, and Gio snorted.

"It's still not nice, and I better not hear you repeating it, sir." She ruffled his hair and for some reason, Gio's gut clenched.

This was *his Mads*.

With *his son*.

Maddie glanced at him and sobered. Her eyes asked if he was all right, and he forced a nod. "I have an idea."

"What?" Jake asked, his little face open, curious. His small hand was still tucked into Gio's as if they did it all the time.

*He* wanted to fidget, too. Not from discomfort, which made him feel even more out of sorts. Holding the child's hand wasn't making him feel anything negative.

Only the opposite. As if he'd accomplished something.

*Take that, Big Tony.*

Gio cursed his father popping into his head. He might've only met his son today, but he'd never treat him the way Big Tony Giovanni had treated *him*.

He wanted his siblings to meet his son. Let the little guy know he had two uncles and an aunt other than Maddie's sister. They'd love the boy, no doubt about it.

Elise was going to shit. Dom would be a bad influence. Kids always loved Sam, they gravitated toward him.

What would his old man say about Jake?

Did Gio care?

Well, he might have to wait on the 'ol family introductions, considering his sister probably wouldn't talk to him, even if he did return her calls. Dom wanted to kick his ass — literally. He hadn't heard from Sam, but he hadn't checked his phone since he'd exercised the *off* switch.

Would the news of, *it's a boy*, change how his family felt about him regarding the case?

*Probably not.*

"How about if Aunt Jamie takes you for breakfast?" Maddie looked at her sister. "There's a café around the corner that has great pancakes."

The mom and pop they'd ordered-in from yesterday. Gio had licked syrup off Maddie's nipples after their brunch. He straightened his spine through a shiver and concentrated on his son.

Instead of agreeing, or smiling, Jake wore a frown. "But Mommy, I wanna stay here. See my room. My dad's here." He pointed those blue eyes up at Gio.

His heart skipped.

*My dad.*

*Shit. That's* me.

Jamie grabbed the little boy's free hand. "Breakfast

is a great idea. I'm starved. Mini pretzels on the plane didn't cut it."

Jake clung to Gio, not letting him release him. "Dad."

This time, his stomach jumped and he fought a physical jerk. Had to clear his throat because he didn't trust his voice. "Yeah, champ?"

"Will you be here when we get back?"

His peripheral vision caught discomfort on Maddie's beautiful face.

She was gnawing on her bottom lip. Her eyes were misty, which shot a tremor down his legs. Maddie was dreading being alone with him, no doubt.

"Absolutely."

The smile he got as a reward made his pulse pound.

"Okay. Let's go, Aunt Jamie, so we can get back." He released Gio's much larger hand and stood next to Maddie's sister, then pulled on her arm.

His mother kissed his cheek and he wiped it off then stuck his tongue out.

Gio chuckled. "That's not nice, champ."

"Well, wait 'til she does it to you," he said with all the drama a seven-year-old could muster.

"Actually, I like when your mother kisses me."

Jake appeared doubtful, and Jamie grinned.

Maddie was too quiet. Avoided his gaze.

Her sister broke the silence before it could get more awkward. "Want me to bring anything for you guys?"

Gio politely refused and stayed glued in the living room as she walked them out. He blew out a huge exhale when the door closed.

*I have a kid.*

Jake seemed to be the only person *not* freaked out by the revelation.

Maddie stopped by the kitchen counter, about a dozen feet away. Clearly maintaining distance, as if she was afraid to return to him all the way. Her eyes scanned his face. "It just hit you, didn't it?" She cringed.

"Maybe." More words piled against his lips and pushed, but he held them back. Maybe part of him wanted to yell and scream now, but it wouldn't change a damn thing.

Besides, it was too much like something Big Tony would do, so that made Gio want to rage even less.

"Thanks for being so great about this. So calm," she whispered, inching close, but not as close as he wanted...*needed.*

As much as that didn't make sense, considering the bomb she'd dropped on him. Then again, she hadn't really, had she?

Jamie and Jake had surprised her, too.

Was she going to tell him?

*When?*

They'd been alone together for two days. She'd had ample opportunity. They'd worked together a few days before that, to boot. Hell, he'd cornered her in the closet that first day. She could've told him then.

He really should be pissed as shit.

Gio was known for his hot, short-fused temper. His whole life. Where was that now?

He shrugged and buried his hands in his jeans. "I

have a few questions, but I'm not sure now's the time."

She shook her head, making her gorgeous locks flow over her shoulders. "I can't tell you how sorry I am, and…I'll tell you anything you want to know." Her expressive eyes—something he'd always loved about her—went misty, and his gut clenched.

"Don't cry, Mads." He darted over and put his hand at the back of her neck, bringing her closer, and urging her into an embrace.

Maddie pushed against his chest. "Just…stop it."

"Stop what?" He didn't release her, but he loosened his hold, gripping her upper arms lightly.

"Stop being so great. I did you wrong. For *years*. I didn't tell you about *your kid*. Then I let you in Thursday and fucked you. I didn't tell you then, and you came back Friday. I fucked you for two more whole days, *still* without telling you. Be mad at me, yell at me. Cuss at me. Push me away. Something. You're being too nice."

Gio smirked and thumbed her tears away. "What did I tell you about that?"

"What?"

"It's never been fucking. This weekend sure as *hell* wasn't. Every. Time."

Maddie blinked. "You don't regret this weekend?"

"Hell no."

Although, everything she'd said were valid points. *I must be batshit crazy.*

She stared up at him, her lips slightly parted.

"Besides, with all the other shit fucking up my life, my dad's cancer. My sister looking guilty right beside him. The casino. The case. What the fuck? One more thing to heap on. I can take it."

She snorted.

He cupped her face and tilted her chin up, then took her mouth. Kissed her until she went limp in his arms and clung to his chest.

Until his dick was hard, and his zipper took a bite. Gio pulled away only because he needed air. Hoped to alleviate the ache in his balls, because he wasn't getting laid again right now. He wanted to, but they needed to talk. "Were you going to tell me about Jake, Mads?"

"Yes," she panted.

"Then, that's all that matters. For now."

"Stop it," Maddie begged. "You have a bad temper. Is this a trick? Will you be psycho later?"

Gio chuckled. "No."

Her pretty eyes raked his face. "Why?"

"I've changed a lot in the last eight years. We can't go back to change the past. I'm sad I missed a lot of his life. But I can't focus on the hurt, at least not now. We can only go forward."

"That's too grown up to be what you really think." She sagged against him.

He sighed.

She was right.

He was shocked, too, but everything he'd said was truly how he felt.

Maybe it *would* hit him later.

Concerning his dad, he was already rocking the *fuck my life* thing, so why scream and holler about the little boy who resembled him much he couldn't deny him if he wanted?

"I can tell you one thing I regret."

"What?" she whispered.

"Losing you." His heart was getting a workout this morning, because it stuttered as that new bit of truth fell out. Gio should've told her so last night when he was in her bed, or the night before. Or hell, even Thursday, the first time he'd done doorstep duty. He'd felt it from the first kiss at the PD, really.

Now, it seemed to matter more, since they had a son.

Maddie stared. So long and hard he wanted to squirm from the way she was looking at him.

Hell, *he* didn't have a clue why he hadn't exploded.

A kid?

He'd knocked Maddie up eight years ago?

Gio had to pant to fill his lungs. His head spun. Maybe wobbled on his feet a little.

She grabbed his arm. "Oh shit. *Now* it really just hit you," she whispered.

"Yes," he confessed.

"Hate me yet?" She scrunched up her face like she was going to cry again.

He shook his head because speaking wasn't going to happen. Still wasn't sure why, but the expected rage wasn't born.

*I'm better than my father.*

"He's really great, and he…well, you noticed."

"He what?" Gio croaked.

"Looks just like you." Maddie averted her eyes.

"Yeah, I did notice. But he has your nose."

Her eyes welled with tears and spilled, and he cupped her face and wiped them away.

His chest was still tight.

Flight, fight, or freeze was supposed to be instinct. *Fight* was Gio's usual go-to.

However, as the woman who'd fled from him stared up at him silently all over again, his heart shot to his throat.

"What do you want from me, Mads?"

"I…don't know." More tears misted over, but the low statement was like a gut shot in a dirty fight.

"You don't know?"

She shook her head, and he wanted to run his hands through her hair.

Gio's emotions didn't make sense. His mind circled it all again, as if the cycle of confusion couldn't help but start over.

Repetition didn't clarify it, either.

He *should* be angry. He *should* be hurt.

Why wasn't he?

Hurt, check. But…not for the reasons he should be.

Sad, yes. He'd missed every day of his son's life until *today*.

He was more crushed at the idea that Maddie might not want *him*.

"What did this weekend mean to you? Nothing? Because it sure as hell meant something to me." Gio winced as the confession tacked itself onto what should've been a demand. It'd all come out pained whisper. Not something he wanted to show her.

"It wasn't nothing."

"Good."

Silence fell and they stared at each other.

"I know something I want." Maddie spoke finally, but the whisper was tremulous, as if she was being more brave than honest.

"What?"

"I want you to be involved in Jake's life, but I need you to *want* to be there."

"Done."

She tried to stifle a sob, but it exploded from her mouth at the same time new tears cascaded. She covered her mouth with one hand.

Gio's whole body stuttered and he drew her to him, rubbing her back over her silky robe. Minutes that felt like hours passed and he comforted her, trying to breathe normally as he put the whole morning under a microscope in his head.

Maddie pulled back gently and swiped at her cheeks. "Just like that?"

A flash of irritation darted up from his gut and he swallowed so he wouldn't yell, as the negative emotion finally made itself known. "Newsflash, I would've been there from the start, if I'd known about him, so do me a favor and don't sound so damn surprised."

Maddie winced and regret replaced the frustration.

He hadn't meant to hurt her.

"I'm so sorry," she blurted. She clung to his chest, her arms tight around his middle. "I know you would've. No matter what happened between us, I know you would've been there for Jake. I'm so sorry."

Gio sighed and closed his eyes. "I don't want to make you feel like shit, Mads."

"I already do. There's pretty much nothing I can say or do to make up for it."

"That's where you're wrong."

She blinked. "What d'you mean?"

"*I* want something, too."

"What?" Maddie squeaked.

"You want me to be in Jake's life, and I want that, absolutely. But I want to be in *your* life, too."

G ian's burner phone rang, wrenching his mind from its obsession about the stupid ledger that was firmly in the hands of law enforcement. He jumped, dug the device from his breast pocket, and cursed as he brought the small device to his ear. "Yeah."

"I got you a gift." His uncle's gravelly voice sounded pleased.

"What's that?"

"You'll need a pen."

"Gimme a second." He opened the top drawer of his desk and tugged out sticky notes with the casino's logo on them, along with his favorite Montblanc.

"Go to this email, but only if you're on a secure connection." Uncle Dino rattled off an address and the password.

"What will I find?"

The old codger chuckled in his ear. "You'll see. And you're welcome, *nipote*."

With that, his uncle hung up.

They always tried to keep their calls short and to

the point, but ghosting with no info was a bit ridiculous. Gian had never been a fan of riddles, either. He was too impatient.

He cursed as he unlocked the bottom drawer of his desk and tugged out an iPad he kept there, because it wasn't safe to keep in the penthouse. Elise didn't know about it, and it was encrypted, complete with its very own internet connection; one separate from the casino's.

It only took a few touches of the screen to pull up the email Uncle Dino had directed him to.

There were two unread messages, and the 'from address' was listed as *unknown sender.* Both emails had no subject.

Curiosity got the best of him, and he opened the first one. The text was short and sweet and didn't have a signature, any more than the specific sender.

*US Marshal running the taskforce.*

Gian opened the attachments, which were a series of photographs of a fair-haired woman. One had to be a driver's license or work ID picture, with the standard blue background and not much of a smile.

Other shots were of her in what appeared to be a conference room, and another of her crossing a populated street with a takeout coffee cup in hand.

Several depicted a badge around her neck on a chain, and a gun holstered at her hip, but she was dressed mostly in khakis and dark long-sleeved button-downs.

The woman was really pretty, probably in her early thirties, with wavy, honey-colored hair kissing her shoulders. Most of the shots had her locks bound in a ponytail, and in only a few she wore it free.

The close-up shot revealed hazel eyes, a heart-shaped face, and a full mouth that could do some damage to the right man.

The last two pictures showed her holding the hand of a small dark-haired boy. A third person stood beside them, a younger woman with blonde hair a few shades lighter than the marshal.

Was the kid hers? Who was the girl?

The shot was from a distance, so it was hard to judge age on either additional party, but if she had people she cared about, and he could identify them, it could help in the long run.

None of the images had been taken in Vegas. He recognized downtown Chicago. He'd know the city he'd grown up in from any distance. Knew those streets like the back of his hand.

So the cat chasing his mouse was from Chi-town?

Pity he'd never run into her before. Blonde was his type, after all.

Gian opened the second email. The little paperclip indicated another attachment.

When he touched the icon, a PDF opened instead of a picture. "Madison Granger, huh?" he whispered, and kept reading. "Senior Investigator, Organized Crime Drug Enforcement Department."

The document was a complete dossier, including her residential address and ID for the two others in the photos.

The kid was her son, Jake, and the girl, her sister, Jamie.

Her address was *local*.

Google told him it was an apartment building off the strip, but only a ten minute drive.

"Thank you, Uncle Dino." He grabbed his miraculously re-located cellphone and snapped a photo of the dossier and two of the photos before stowing the iPad and locking the drawer.

He probably shouldn't do it on his regular phone, but it wasn't like the device wasn't password protected, and the burner phone had a shitty camera. On his iPhone, he could zoom if he wanted to reread the marshal's stats.

His uncle had done his homework, but that info packet on Marshal Granger was definitely not from a PI, or the like. Uncle Dino had mentioned everyone had a price, and it looked like that held as truth.

Be it FBI or the Marshal's Service, someone from the *inside* had provided the information, and perhaps the pictures of the woman trying to catch him laundering money.

Well, she wasn't going to succeed, because he was too smart to get caught, and now…well, he could turn the tables on her.

Oh, the things he could do with these details.

Gian leaned back in his chair, grinning.

"Knock, knock," Elise called from his open door. "It's nice to see you smiling. Get good news or somethin'? I could use some about now."

"Just thinking about you, *tesoro*."

His fiancée cocked her head to one side, as if trying to decide whether or not to believe him, but her answering smile was sweet. "That's better than worrying, I suppose." She sauntered into his office and plopped in the single chair on the other side of his desk.

Sitting hiked her already-short black skirt mid-thigh, and his mind went to the forbidden. They hadn't had sex in forever. Her mind had been on the investigation, and he hadn't been able to convince her to relax enough to let him inside her.

For the first time since he'd been with her, Gian was tempted to get laid elsewhere.

*He* was stressed, too. Needed a release his hand couldn't satisfy. Maybe he'd give her one more chance before he did something 'drastic.'

It wouldn't take much effort. He could order an escort; there were even some girls that worked *The Giovanni*, but something was holding him back.

Funny, his relationship with Elise Giovanni wasn't real, despite his intention to go through with the marriage, but with past girlfriends, genuine ones, he'd never been faithful.

Sex with one woman had been a foreign concept. He'd *only* been with Elise since he'd been in Vegas. Nine months. One pussy.

It was a wonder he'd not grown tired of her, but she was sensual and responsive, and it kept his blood at a constant simmer. A constant want. He could barely keep his hands to himself.

"What's up?" he asked, to distract himself from

stupid ideas, along with a half-hard cock.

"Did you finish compiling the finance reports Paul's team wanted?" She smiled again, as if to let him know her question wasn't really a demand, but it was.

"Sure did. I was about to get them from the printer and bring them to the conference room. Are they still in there?"

"They should just be getting back from lunch. Did you eat?" Elise's brows drew tight, her instant concern on him.

"I'm fine, baby. I was hoping you and I could grab dinner together later. Let me take you out on a date."

She frowned. "Oh, I dunno, there's so much to do—"

Gian leaned across his desk and grabbed her hand. "You need to get your mind off things. Let me help."

*Let me in your bed again. In your body.*

He seriously needed to get laid.

Her expression softened. "You've already helped so much over the past few days. If I didn't have you by my side, I wouldn't be able to handle this stuff. Seriously."

He forced a smile. "Happy to help. But I want to help you on a more personal level." Gian waggled his eyebrows and was pleased when she managed a small laugh. "Let me pamper you, *tesoro.*"

"The past three days have been hell," she mused. Elise let out a little sigh, but her smile widened. "I suppose I could do with some pampering."

He'd won. Gian told himself this was all about getting laid, but he loved that look on her face. In his direction.

Adoration.

"Well, I don't call you my treasure for nothin'," he teased. "You have standards to maintain. You need shined and buffed once in a while."

His fiancée rolled her eyes, but her delectable mouth was still curved up. "Thanks, Marco, I don't know what I'd do without you."

"Don't think on it. It's not a possibility." He kissed the back of her hand. "You're holding up wonderfully. Running this place, and dealing with this investigation. No one can tell how stressed you are. You're a queen, really."

Her obvious relief sagged her shoulders and lifted her gorgeous tits with a large audible inhale. "Oh, good. I'm falling apart. I still haven't been able to tell my dad what's going on. I just can't. The doctors have him stable and say no stress. This wouldn't help at all, and he can't do anything anyways. Dom and Sam are as pissed at Gio, as am I."

"Have you talked to him yet?" Gian was dying to have her ask her cop brother about the ledger, but he couldn't justify why he'd want to know something that was none of his concern. How the hell had they found it so easily when he'd searched several times and managed a whole lotta nothin'?

She'd said it had been in Big Tony's office.

Damn, he wished he could've seen it just once.

Elise frowned again, and it was full of sadness. "No. Paul still thinks no contact is better for now. I don't really know what I'd say to him anyway. Dad always worried Gio's career choice would come between the family, and…" She shrugged. "I guess he was right. For something we're not even guilty of. Dad would be heartbroken. Will be, when I finally break down and tell him."

Why did Big Tony worry about having a son in law enforcement? Maybe he hadn't forgotten his roots after all? Had he really been running a *completely* clean business all these years?

Gian couldn't remark on it, of course, but it certainly gave him things to ponder. From what he'd understood, Big Tony's falling out with his eldest son had been years ago, not long after his wife's passing. Had it been because he was a cop?

His fiancée had never been decisive in her explanations. It was another thing he couldn't ask for clarification on.

Elise sighed and rested her head on the back of the chair, staring up at the ceiling for a few seconds.

Again, he was struck with that odd urge to comfort her.

He wheeled his chair closer, around the side of his desk so he could grab both her hands. "Hey."

She met his eyes and seemed so damn sad it almost slayed him.

Gian cursed and plastered on what he hoped was a soft smile. "It'll be okay. Why don't you grab those reports, and I'll meet you in the conference room in a few? I have a call I need to make."

"Everything okay?" she asked, her fair brows drawn all over again.

He nodded. "Nothing concerning here. Are you guys getting anywhere on the financials?"

Frustration settled in her expression. "They're supposed to be freaking forensic accountants and they say nothing stands out. But they're determined to figure out what the feds saw. Paul says there has to be an explanation."

Of course there was.

The files he'd provided them were all legit. He'd also removed several hard drives—the ones with his real records on them—from the boxes when they'd been delivered from the off-site server warehouse, and snatched the manifest.

He'd reported that he'd checked all the items off, and every record was accounted for. No one questioned him, and why would they? No matter how good Paul Allemand's team was, there was nothing to find on what he'd given them. Gian had white-washed the accounts, and controlled what he'd released.

It was a damn good thing his fiancée had put him in charge of that facet of the exoneration investigation.

He was a good little helper.

"Don't stress about it." He squeezed her hands. "These guys are the best, and these things take time. Poring over financials, line by line is tedious, too."

She blew out air and puffed her bottom lip out. "I know you're right, but the feds got a head start. It's a matter of time before arrest warrants are issued."

Gian shook her head and kissed her knuckles. "That's a worry for another day."

Elise frowned. "Is it? I'm implicated in this. *I* run

accounting. My dad has *cancer*. We both could see the inside of a cell if there are indictments. I'm scared shitless, to be honest. We're *innocent*."

He stood and tugged her into his arms. "I promise that will never happen, *tesoro*. The feds have bigger fish to fry than a sick old man."

"What about me?" she whispered in a very small voice. Her arms, which had been around him, fell to her sides. She deflated.

He met her eyes. "That's why we pay Paul Allemand the big bucks."

She nodded, but gnawed on her bottom lip.

"Let me make my call, and I'll be there to help the team, okay?" he said.

Again, his fiancée nodded, and when they parted, he bumped the edge of his desk. His phone tumbled to the hardwood with a *thunk*.

They went for it at the same time, and Elise enclosed her hand around it first.

The screen lit up, displaying the last thing he'd accessed.

"Why do you have a picture of Maddie?" She cocked her head to one side, one fair eyebrow arched.

*Damn phone.*

Why hadn't it locked, like normal? It should've needed his face to access it.

"Maddie?" he asked.

"She's the marshal that served the warrant." Elise's expression darkened.

"Exactly," Gian said.

"What?"

"I asked Security to get me her picture, so I could recognize her if she comes back. She's the leader of the taskforce, is she not?"

He read the acceptance in her dark eyes, and he thanked God — or maybe the devil — he was a good liar.

"Senior Inspector Madison Granger," he mused with a purpose — a fishing expedition. "You called her 'Maddie'. Do you know her?"

"That bitch."

He had to hide a smile. She was so damn fiery and he…loved that about her.

Gian pasted on an expression of appropriate offense. "Such harsh words, *tesoro*." It was really difficult not to grin in appreciation.

"She's earned it. I knew her years ago, when I was still in college. We were close, but I guess none of that mattered. She doesn't know the meaning of the word, 'loyalty'. She also used to date my brother, and left him without a backward glance. He was devastated. She can go to hell. This crap is *all* her fault. Even if we were still friends, we're not any more. I will never forgive her for *this*. As Dad would say, she's dead to me." Elise gestured around his office, but he knew she'd meant the whole casino.

"Which brother?"

"Gio."

*Interesting.*

He sucked back another smile, and leaned down to press a kiss to her cheek. "I won't be too long. The reports are on the big copier."

She nodded and departed.

Gian pulled up Marshal Granger's dossier on his phone, zooming in to read it again. She had a few commendations in her file, and she'd been with the Marshal's Service for almost eleven years. He had to give it to whoever his uncle had paid; the info was thorough and helpful.

Gian swiped over to the first photo he'd saved, and his fiancée had inadvertently seen. Although he'd had to do some quick thinking, he was grateful she'd seen it.

He'd learned something that would add fuel to his fire. More leverage.

Madison Granger wasn't looking at the camera, but her profile was gorgeous. He could see her appeal, and no doubt Elise's brother had enjoyed hitting that, if they'd, "dated."

Had they reunited since she was back in town?

Gian totally would've, if he was Gio. Maybe he could implement a double, 'fuck you,' instead of just one. He grinned and spun around in the executive computer chair like a little kid.

When he faced the desk again, he woke his desktop PC up with a click of the mouse and went to Google. He pulled up the number he needed and reached for the phone next to his keyboard.

This was an official call, so there was no need to do it from his cell, or his burner phone.

"Las Vegas Metro Police Department, how may I help you?" A female asked after a couple of rings.

"Hi there, I need to speak to Detective Nico Giovanni's supervisor. I have to a report a serious conflict of interest."

The last few days had been like a dream. They'd worked together, come home together, and spent time together…like a family.

It was hard as hell not to get swept away, carried into the vortex of things Maddie was afraid to *want*. She'd tried her best, pinning her caution to the forefront of her brain, but it was getting harder to maintain.

Gio had unpacked Jake's room with him, and even helped her organize the kitchen. Working beside him in that capacity, in making their place *home*…well, it made her think.

Thinking, concerning Nico Giovanni, was…bad.
*Very* bad.

Their son and Jamie were only in town until Wednesday morning, and her sister had a few job leads she'd wanted to chase down before they moved there full time, in about a week. She'd even had an interview Monday.

Maddie wanted her to reenroll in college, and she was considering it. Her sister was somewhat of a free spirit, and had dropped out a few years ago in Chicago, with three or four semesters away from a bachelor's degree in business, but Jamie wasn't interested in that anymore.

Jake's school had been closed Monday, and she filled out paperwork for withdrawing him, and was sending them back with Jamie to hand in. He'd missed school on Tuesday, but it wasn't every day a kid met his dad for the first time, so she didn't care so much. He'd be in a Las Vegas school soon enough.

Jamie even took him to see his new school yesterday morning, and Maddie was relieved he was more excited than dreading the move. He'd made her promise he could Skype with his two best friends, Owen and Charlie. Her sister had told her she would coordinate with their moms, as she often handled Jake's playdates.

Nearly all the boxes were gone, and Gio had hauled them out to the dumpster without being asked.

The apartment finally looked lived-in, complete with the requisite kid stuff Jake left in his wake.

Vegas was starting to feel like home.

Something she'd never expected.

It was going to be hard to put them on a plane in the morning, but Gio had said he wanted to go to the airport, too. The flight was early enough, before they needed to head into the PD.

Work had gone okay Monday and Tuesday, and she'd been eager to get home to Jamie and Jake, and Gio had felt the same.

He hadn't really been back to his own place since Friday. He'd gone home to grab clothes, but Maddie was still scared shitless of his declaration, and didn't dare consider his things in her place a permanent fixture. He wasn't moving in.

It just *couldn't* happen.

He could see Jake daily if he wanted, but the sleepovers — in her bed — really should stop.

They hadn't talked about it; the declaration or the sex, other than admitting the weekend had meant something.

To both of them.

She was trying to convince herself it didn't matter. They could take things one day at a time, at home *and* work. Which was why she'd told him she didn't know what she wanted from him. *With* him.

Of course she *knew*. Just couldn't say it out loud.

*Everything* had been on the tip of her tongue that day.

Why she couldn't open her mouth and have a real conversation with him about their future was a mystery. She was usually really direct.

Maddie watched him with their son all day, and her heart pounded, but she couldn't ask him what any of it meant.

Maybe she was too afraid to believe him. Despite what he'd said, that he wanted to be in *her* life, too, she was afraid of a real answer.

Had that been real? Had he *really* meant what he'd said?

If he didn't…she'd be heartbroken.

Of course she'd be shattered. However, it wasn't the organ in *her* chest she was concerned with. She had to protect Jake.

If it all fell apart, and that was inevitable, wasn't it? *When* it all fell apart, where would their little boy be left?

She'd *kill* Gio if he hurt Jake.

It was difficult not to contemplate overwhelming love-like emotions when she saw him and their son interacting. Then even more so, when he kissed her, showed her open affection around her sister and Jake, and took her when he was in her bedroom.

She especially didn't want to think about when he was in her bed.

Maddie pushed the ideas away for later, and contemplated all she needed to get done in the morning, after the airport.

They didn't have arrest warrants yet. The judge wanted more concrete evidence, but since Elise was one of the parties they'd likely have to bring in, she wasn't in a hurry. Couldn't bear the idea of betrayal on her pretty face when she had to cuff her.

Her stomach churned.

*Just a matter of time.*

Gio's father was still in the hospital, and they could go talk to him there, but it wasn't on the agenda yet.

They still hadn't figured out the mystery of Marco Fratelli. Maddie had done more digging that afternoon, to no avail.

Gio had been correct that "Marco's" arrival coincided with when the money laundering had started, but other than that, they still didn't know his identity, and hadn't been back to the casino to question him.

Paul Allemand — *The Giovanni's* high powered ball buster — had collected the PC Affidavits and imparted veiled threats about coming onto casino grounds, using the words 'harassment' and 'slander,' so the team was treading carefully.

They couldn't leave it forever, despite what the attorney had said. "Marco" was the key to her case, no matter Gio's family's roles in the crime.

Her hopeful heart wished he was right for the first time since the FBI had looped the Marshal's Service into the case.

She didn't want to admit she was a little distracted with the personal stuff; even if the work stuff also included Gio. Maddie had never been bad with balancing before. Jake and her job, not to mention her sister, were equally important, and they would always stay that way.

Just because Gio was now a factor in her "family" changed nothing.

*Right?*

The team still pored over financials, and she still waited on a call back from Nash Grey to discover any progress with Cesare Fratelli. Grey was the FBI Special Agent in Charge out of Chicago, and her liaison for the case.

If the FBI had managed to get the CPA to talk, no one had told her. Maybe she should reach out in the morning.

"Why're you so quiet?" Gio whispered.

He was in her bed for fifth day in a row, and her

heart skipped.

"Just going over the plan of attack for tomorrow."

"Well, stop it." His warm hand cradled hers, then he dragged their joined fingers downward. "You can do that over your first cup of coffee."

Maddie smiled against his neck when he'd stopped his journey. He'd settled her grip on his cock, adequately distracting her.

"Trying to tell me something?" she asked, nibbling the stubble under his chin.

She felt his chuckle rumble against her breasts, she was tucked in so close.

"Maybe," he whispered and pressed a kiss to her temple.

"You're usually more direct." She lifted her head and met his eyes.

He was carefree and relaxed, and there was a twinkle in those glinting sapphires visible even in the nighttime dimness of her room.

"Putting your hand on my dick isn't direct?"

Maddie grinned. "Maybe. I guess I'll have to get to work then."

Just a few tugs and he was granite in her palm.

Gio tilted his head back, and his Adam's apple bobbed. He groaned when she pushed her thumb into the underside of his sensitive tip and rubbed.

"Damn, Mads. Don't stop."

"Wouldn't dream of it." She stroked and squeezed him with just the right amount of pressure, from root to tip.

When their gazes brushed, he dipped down and

took her mouth, dominating her lips and tongue like he always did.

She got swept away, despite the hand-job going on below, and moaned into the lip-lock. Desire smacked into her, settling low and hot, her burn slowly working its way into a searing char from the inside out as he continued to kiss her. Harder. Deeper. Her sex throbbed and she bumped her pelvis into his.

Gio growled, and shoved her shoulders into the bed.

Maddie kicked the sheets away when her feet got tangled and reached for him as he loomed above her. She lifted her hips to meet his, but he didn't take her.

"I want you," he panted.

"That's the point."

He grunted by way of answer and grabbed his erection.

She watched him guide himself to her center. It revved her up even more; the sight erotic, with the arch in his back, the strain in his chest, stomach and arm muscles, the intense determination in his handsome face.

He was incendiary.

The man oozed sex, and he didn't have to be naked for her to see it. She was going to combust before he even reached his goal.

Then he was there, filling her with a jarring thrust. Gio wasn't gentle, but Maddie didn't need soft lovemaking. She needed him to answer the call boiling her blood. She needed him hard and fast. Rough and raw.

Completely Gio.

He took her mouth again, pushing deep to rub his tongue against hers.

She kissed him back until she couldn't breathe, and lifted her hips over and over to meet his downward strokes.

Their pelvises slammed together, making skin-slapping sounds that betrayed his speed.

Maddie was covered in sweat, but didn't care. She was on fire.

Gio grabbed her hips and drove forward even harder, his fingers digging in, but she kept up with him until she exploded.

She threw her head back and called his name as her orgasm smashed into her, making all her muscles contract and tremor. Her vision went in and out, spinning in a chaos of ecstasy. She had to pant to get air down.

He said her name and stilled above her. His cock jerked inside her as he came, too, then Gio buried his face in her neck.

His way-past-five-o'clock shadow scratched against her skin, shooting tingles down her spine, making her want more.

She snuggled closer, wrapping herself around him even as his sex slipped from hers.

Her detective pulled her to him, nestling her into his side, and slipping his leg between hers. "That was hot," Gio whispered.

Maddie's belly fluttered. She caressed his rough face and dragged her thumb across his kiss-swollen bottom lip. She'd put the color in his cheeks, and the plumpness in his mouth. "I loved every minute of it."

*And I love you.*

She almost startled as the little revelation settled in her head and she couldn't shake it.

Wasn't she just trying to convince herself to take things one day at a time, and worrying about his new constant place in her bed?

She'd loved him eight years ago.

Not *now.*

*Right?*

Her heart sped up, as if it hadn't calmed from the frantic pace of Gio's lovemaking. Hard or soft, that was what they'd done together.

Making love.

*Love.*

The day Jake and Jamie had shown up, she'd worried her heart was already involved, after all the sex they'd had over the weekend. But Maddie had been able to talk herself out of it, hadn't she?

*Evidently not.*

She loved him.

Again.

Had she ever really stopped?

She fought the urge to close her eyes. Didn't want to know the answer.

Gio's stare didn't waver. His gaze darted all over her face as he studied her. Like he was a human lie detector.

She wanted to squirm. Maddie was a glutton for punishment. Or maybe just a glutton for Nico

Giovanni.

*Idiot.*

He cupped her face, his hold gentle but fierce as his eyes commanded hers. "I hope it wasn't too rough. I don't want to hurt you, Mads. Ever."

*Too late.*

That was her own fault, not his.

She shivered in his grip, but couldn't pull away. Couldn't lose the physical contact. She was starved, as if he hadn't just rocked her world.

Twice, because they'd had sex right when they'd come to bed, less than two hours before. Right after making Jake call it a night, around eight p.m.

Her core was already throbbing; an ache, not arousal, but she'd do it all again as soon as his body was ready for another round.

*You really are an idiot.*

What was it about this man that made her a giant hormone?

She'd always felt a connection with him. Of course, they shared a child, so there was always that sentimentality in the back of her mind, even before Gio had known about Jake, but…

He'd always had this magnetism Maddie hadn't been able to resist; even when he'd been more boy than man at twenty-three.

Maybe he scrambled her brains.

*Or maybe I'm just crazy.*

"It wasn't too rough, Gio. I promise."

He finally relaxed into the bed and tugged her close, like she had been before he'd played wandering-hands.

"You locked the door, right?" he asked after a few moments of silence.

Maddie lifted her head. "Yeah, why?"

"You were...loud." He smirked, and it was as delicious as he was.

Heat of embarrassment kissed the back of her neck and scorched her cheeks. "Jake and Jamie's rooms are on the other side of the apartment."

Gio chuckled. "But your place isn't that big."

She groaned. The last thing she needed was her sister giving her shit if she'd heard them. Nor questions from their son, who was often too smart for his own good.

"I'm sure couples have sex with their kids down the hall all the time. If not, there wouldn't be any siblings," Gio mused, tucking his arm behind his head and closing his eyes. "I mean, people have to make the babies." He gave a soft laugh.

She stilled, but tried not to show it. Their bodies were so close, he'd feel the slightest movement, and she didn't want him to sense how her heartrate had kicked back up.

Siblings...babies.

He probably hadn't meant anything by it, but it only made her think of when she'd been pregnant with Jake. Maddie had known then she didn't want children with more than one father, so her baby...his baby...would be an only child.

Could that change now? Did she want it to?

She'd always imagined a little girl with her golden

curls and big hazel eyes, like she and Jamie had had when they were little.

Jake had asked for a younger sibling, too, as kids were prone to do.

She really needed to stop this.

First, realizing she loved him, and now a second kid?

It blew the one-day-at-a-time thing out of the water.

*I am an idiot.*

"Mads? What's wrong?" Gio asked. He cupped her cheeks and caressed them with his thumbs.

"Nothing."

He paused, studying her. "Are you sure?"

"Oh yeah, how could something be wrong?" Maddie leaned up and brushed her lips against his mouth. "You're here with me and…" she gestured between their bodies.

He flashed a lopsided grin, then sobered. "Can I ask you something?"

Her heart skipped, but she nodded. "Absolutely."

K ♥

"Why'd you leave me, Mads?" Gio stroked her shoulder and down her back. "I thought what we had was good." He tried not to cringe at the emotion that made his voice shake.

He'd wanted to ask since she'd told him she'd answer any questions. He just hadn't worked up the balls until now. He should drop it, let it be. After all, it was in the past, and he himself had said to move forward. But damn, he burned for the truth regarding his broken heart…and his son.

She tried to sit up, but he held her fast. Maddie tugged, then shoved, and he let his hands fall to his sides. "You really want to talk about this now? While we're naked, after what we just did?" She averted her eyes and his heart sank a little.

"Yes. Don't I deserve to know?"

She nodded. Then those hazel orbs he loved so much swung around to pin him with a look that was almost a glare. "You don't remember *that* night?"

Maddie didn't need to specify. It'd been exactly three weeks after his mom had died, and two since her funeral. His father had picked a fight, pointing out all sorts of things that were correct about the path he'd been going down, and they'd had a huge blowout, less than an hour before he was supposed to meet her in the VIP bar at *The Giovanni*.

Gio had waited for her, but not alone. He'd had all the scotch he'd wanted, and had already downed a full bottle before she'd arrived.

She'd texted she was running late. He'd had plenty of time to mull over Big Tony's accusations, and how he wasn't good enough for much.

Including Madison Granger.

"I remember I was drunk and we had a fight. At the bar."

"A fight?" She scoffed and averted her eyes again.

Damn, if he made her cry, he'd want to shoot himself.

"That's all, Nico?"

He stilled when she said his name — something she *never* did.

"Hey," he whispered. Gio grabbed her wrist and tugged. "C'mere."

Maddie shook her head, making her honey locks dance. "No. I can't have you touch me if I'm going to say this." Her words wavered with a sob and a tear slipped down her cheek.

He tried to wipe them away, but she leaned out of reach. "Mads?"

"You told me you weren't good enough for me, Gio. You told me I was better off without you because you couldn't get your life together. You might've been drunk, but you didn't give me a chance to talk, to defend *us*. And damn, I wanted to. So I blurted I was pregnant, and you laughed. You *laughed*. You broke my heart, Nico Giovanni." She inhaled, and instinct told him she needed it in order to continue. "I ran out of there, because I couldn't take it, because...I *loved* you."

A cold flush oozed over his head — hell, maybe that was why things started spinning — and went down his chest, making him freeze, despite her thigh touching his in her bed. His limbs started to quiver, and even his teeth chattered.

Gio remembered the massive fight with his father; the *real* reason for twelve or thirteen too many shots in the private high-roller lounge in the casino. Where the bartender wouldn't dare cut him off.

He didn't remember more than a fight with Maddie, and she'd fled.

She'd told him she was pregnant?

He couldn't breathe. His chest burned and his limbs kicked up their tremors, like he was having a mini-seizure.

He'd *abandoned* her?

Because Gio had been so drunk he hadn't recalled she'd told him the most important news, *ever*?

"No." The denial came out as an agonized whisper, and when he had the balls to glance at her she had more tears streaming.

Maddie nodded.

Neither of them spoke for a long time.

Maybe he was going to puke before he got words out.

"I don't know what's worse, you never told me you loved me, or that I couldn't fucking remember being told I was going to have a kid. Jesus Christ, I'm the biggest asshole in the universe."

She stared, then one corner of her mouth shot up. Maddie laughed. It was small, but somehow as lovely as she was. "I've felt guilty enough for the both of us for not trying harder to tell you, so you don't have to feel like an asshole. I'm an asshole, too."

"I loved you, too," he blurted. "Back then, I mean." He stumbled over the clarification, because the truth wasn't something he was ready to admit.

*Still do.*

He *should* tell her, especially when she was looking at him like that, and they were having this moment of honesty, but the confession wouldn't form. He'd told her he wanted to be a part of her life, as well as their son's but Gio hadn't fathomed how that would work.

Maybe he didn't know. Maybe he was afraid to hope she'd agree. After what she'd just told him, it was no fucking wonder.

Her gaze sharpened on his face. "Why didn't *you* tell me?"

"I was a stupid kid that drank too much and had shitty family issues. That part hasn't changed." He didn't want to talk about the case or his dad's cancer.

"None of that mattered. Still doesn't. Jake's a Giovanni, too. I was never ashamed of that."

A wave of emotion hit his stomach, and warmth rose, chasing away the chill in his bones. He kind of wanted to cry like a pussy.

"Gio?"

He settled his hands on her upper arms, since he didn't have the guts to bare his heart. Tugged her into his chest and claimed her mouth.

If he couldn't tell her how he felt, he could sure as hell show her.

Gio let his hands wander, cupping her perfect breasts and thumbing her nipples until Maddie moaned into their kiss and the taut peaks pushed back.

She didn't fight him when he urged even closer.

"Ride me, Mads," he begged, pushing the plea into her mouth, and pulling her thigh across his waist.

Her sex hit his hardening cock, giving his body all the remaining encouragement it needed.

She broke their lip-lock, and arched upward, her delectable ass landing right where he needed it, but his dick wasn't in the right place as his lover started to rock her pelvis against his.

He groaned. "Don't tease me, baby. Take me."

When their eyes met, Maddie flashed a wicked grin. "Why not?"

"I'll get you back later," Gio growled.

"Promise?"

He chuckled and flicked her clit. "That's a preview."

She hissed and grabbed his wrist. "You better be glad I need you so bad."

He tilted his head back and smiled. Grabbed her hips and helped Maddie lift up.

She palmed his cock and stroked him a few times, squeezing his tip until he writhed beneath her and rocked his hips.

"Mads." His voice was half-demand and half-plea.

She put him out of his misery by lowering herself onto him, but she was in no hurry as he filled her inch by painfully-slow inch.

Gio grabbed her ass and yanked her down at the same time he thrust up.

Maddie gasped his name and braced herself on his chest.

He leaned up so he could kiss her as they started to rock together, finding a rhythm that teased more than satisfied. "Harder, Mads. I need more of you."

She whimpered in answer, but put her hands on his shoulders and started to ride in him earnest, revving him higher and higher with each slap of her ass on his thighs.

When she started to tire, Gio held her waist and helped her move up and down, until she started circling her pelvis as she undulated, and the sensation was too much.

"I'm gonna come," he groaned.

"Me too," Maddie moaned. She lifted up once more only to slam down on his lap and cry out. She threw her head back, closing her eyes as her sex clenched around his.

He exploded inside her, panting, as his vision danced and his head spun.

It was always so intense with his Mads.

Gio caught her as she collapsed on top of him. His mouth found hers, because he had to taste her again.

Their kiss melted into something languorous and meaningful, and emotion pricked behind his eyes. Damn, he wanted to tell her how he felt about her. Everything.

Eight years ago, they'd never admitted feelings for each other, but tonight they both revealed it'd been true.

Would it be such a stretch to tell her it was still true now?

Maddie had finally admitted they made love, not fucked.

Could she feel the same way about him as she had once? Or was there a reason she'd said it the way she did?

Because she *didn't* love him now?

Gio ended their kiss and gathered her closer, even as his softening dick slipped from her body.

Her closed eyes revealed pleasure and contentment, which made him lose his nerve.

Was it because he wasn't ready to say how he felt? Or because Maddie wasn't ready to hear it?

He gulped.

Those hazel orbs, still amber with passion, opened and zoned in on his face. "What's wrong?" she whispered.

"I had a massive fight with my dad that night," he croaked. He cringed internally. His father was the last thing he wanted to talk about while holding the woman he loved after she'd made him come hard.

Why had he blurted that?

Maddie's expression cleared of her post-coital haze and she settled against his chest, snuggling close. She maintained eye contact and cupped his cheek. "I know."

"You know?"

"I mean, I'd always guessed that was why you were doing all the '*I'm worthless*' bullshit talk."

Gio nodded and turned his head to press a kiss to her palm. "I don't ever want to make Jake feel like that."

"You won't."

"How can you be so sure?" He fought a wince at the obvious self-consciousness in the inquiry.

Her eyes were so serious. "You're *not* Big Tony, Gio. You're a great guy. You're already a great dad to Jake. Even after only a few days, he adores you."

"I adore him, too."

Maddie's face lit up and it took all he was made of not to tell her how much he adored *her*, too.

He loved her more than his own life.

G io had just climbed into the driver seat after shutting the car door for her, when their cellphones rang simultaneously.

They exchanged a glance and Maddie released her grip on the seatbelt.

The airport trip had sucked, especially since *she'd* been the only one with tears. She hated being the emotional freak of the family.

Jake had hugged them both, and kissed her cheek, but his concern wasn't about when he'd see his weepy mother again.

He was worried Gio would disappear.

Of course, the man had been a champ in reassuring their son, just like his term of endearment for the little boy.

Jake loved that, and loved Gio. The little guy had been all smiles and waves after he was sure his father would be there when they came back.

Jamie had rolled her eyes a lot. She'd whispered in Maddie's ear that she could be as loud as she wanted in the bedroom while they were gone, but she needed to get it together before they moved in permanently. Or get some sound absorbers, if there was such a thing. She'd even suggested padding the walls.

It wasn't like her sister to *wait* to give her shit about any given subject, but it did figure she'd do so when she could maximize Maddie's embarrassment.

No doubt her face was ripe tomato-red.

Jamie had made sure her whisper was more of the stage variety, and Gio had sported a shit-eating grin.

*They're both brats.*

For once she wasn't referring to her seven-year-old.

"Giovanni." Gio's deep voice was like a caress, as he put his cell to his ear.

She had to clear her throat to concentrate. "Granger," she said into her own.

"Granger." Her name, a gruff male bark in her ear.

Her new boss, Doug Randall, the head Marshal for Nevada's territory. Maddie hadn't talked to him much, as she'd been working out of LMVPD's conference room, but she recognized him.

"Morning, boss," she said.

"Report to Deputy Chief Patton's office at Metro, immediately."

She'd only met him a few times before her transfer, and he'd been friendly then, as well as when she'd checked into the office that day before heading to LMVPD for the first time. Randall hadn't seemed like the stoic stiff man his current tone implied.

Was he upset or irritated with her?

"I was headed in. I had to put my son on a plane

back to Chicago; sorry about the delay. Is there something wrong?"

"Just head into Metro, and I'll meet you in Chief Patton's office."

*Wait.*

He'd *meet* her?

Something was wrong.

Her boss wasn't overseeing the case. Of course, he was *her* supervisor, but the technical authority rested with her, and the lead FBI agent who'd first looped them in.

She hadn't spoken with Nash Grey since before she'd officially changed posts. He checked in when necessary, and vice versa, via phone or email.

"What's this concerning?"

"I'll see you when you get to Chief Patton's office. Step on it."

The line went dead and Maddie frowned. She looked at her phone's screen, which had gone dark.

"I understand, Captain. See you there." Gio ended his call too, which could've only been with Olinsky, if the title meant anything. He also wore a frown.

They exchanged another look.

"Chief Patton's office, ASAP?" she asked.

He gave a curt nod.

"Did he say what it was about?"

"Nope. Who called you?"

"My new boss."

"Shit," he spat. "Lemme guess, he didn't enlighten you, either?"

"Nope."

Gio cursed long and hard.

Trepidation twisted Maddie's stomach, and her heart tripped over the next few beats. "What d'you think it's about?" she managed.

"I dunno, but it can't be good." His kissable lips set in a hard line.

Her sense of dread spread up to her chest.

She, Jamie, Jake and Gio had eaten breakfast together before heading to the airport, and Maddie suddenly wished she hadn't downed eggs, bacon, and two pancakes.

The food was churning like a cyclone, and the ejection seemed eminent.

Gio's white knuckles gripped the steering wheel of his beloved classic GTO.

Yeah, this wasn't good.

K ♥

Maddie gnawed her plump bottom lip in his periphery for the whole too-fucking-short three-mile-drive into work.

Gio tried to convince his shoulders to loosen, and his gut to climb up his legs and settle where it belonged. It'd taken a dive for his toes the moment Olinsky had ordered him to come in.

Maybe if her boss hadn't called her at the same time, it wouldn't have freaked him out, but instinct told him the double call wasn't a coincidence.

He wasn't that lucky.

He knew what it was about.

There was only *one* reason his boss, *and* Maddie's

would call them in at the same time.

They'd discovered his tie to the casino.

*Fuck. Me.*

Gio wouldn't let her go down for what he'd kept from his supervisors for years. It wasn't Maddie's fault Olinsky never knew.

She might have to answer for keeping him on the taskforce, but even that, he could deny she knew.

Would she let him lie for her?

Madison Granger might be too good for that shit, but *he* wasn't.

*Son of a bitch.*

He wanted to slam his hand on the steering wheel. He gritted his teeth instead. It'd taken him more than four years to restore this car, and he barely drove it, because he had the Ducati. This vehicle was his pride and joy, besides Maddie and Jake.

The 1967 GTO had been his dream car as a kid, and he'd bought one that was barely a bucket of bolts when he'd turned twenty-five, as a birthday present to himself. Both his brothers had helped him with the restoration, so it'd been a brotherly bonding project, too. He could say what he wanted to about Dom, but the guy was a hell of a mechanic. He'd helped Gio with all the hard stuff he couldn't figure out on his own.

If only his brother would apply himself, he could have his own shop. Dom was equally good at suping them up, as getting them back on the road. But he was still too far up Big Tony's ass to want to branch out and be a real success.

He also needed to get off the constant pussy

carousel and out of the bottle before he could do anything meaningful.

Gio had kept to the original equipment as much as possible, except for seatbelts and the stereo system—even he needed USBs to charge his cell—but the body had been a bronze color, and he'd had it repainted a baby blue. He'd done research and made sure it was the same shade available in 1967, too.

Maddie had gushed when he'd pulled up to pick them up for the airport.

Jamie must not be into cars, because she hadn't said much, but his son had been excited.

His lover had always had a thing for classic muscle cars, and it was nice to see that Jake wasn't much different. He'd seemed genuinely impressed; well, enough for a seven-year-old.

Gio pulled into the same parking spot he always left the Ducati, and didn't want to even see the damn building. People came and went, both uniform cops checking out marked cruisers, and a few detectives running late like them.

"What're you thinking?" Maddie asked. Her voice was low and shaky, and he immediately wanted to comfort her.

Should he tell her what he thought this little meeting was about?

If he didn't, perhaps any shock she'd display would be genuine instead of rehearsed, so he held his tongue.

Why should they both feel like they were on the hot-seat?

Then again, she wasn't stupid. She'd probably done the math, too.

"No clue, Mads." The lie came out smooth, and for that he was grateful. He reached for her thigh and squeezed. "It'll be okay."

God, he hoped he wasn't lying.

She stared hard; he felt like he was under an X-ray. "I don't believe you."

His heart thumped from the area his gut was residing, but swallowing didn't fix either sensation.

"We both know what this is about," she whispered seriously. "What do you want to do about it?"

"Fuck." He shoved his hand through his hair. It was getting long, and he needed a cut. "What can we do?"

"I don't want to lose my job," Maddie admitted, her cheeks tinged pink, as if she was embarrassed about being honest.

"It won't come to that," Gio said. There was a hardness to his statement that made her eyes come back up.

"You can't know that."

Yes he could. He *did*. Because he'd take the fall for her.

Every. Damn. Time.

Because he fucking *loved* her.

Not that he could tell her that.

She maintained his gaze. "Gio—"

Maddie reached for his arm, but he pulled away, turned the car off and practically ripped his key from the ignition.

"Look, no use sitting here losing your shit. Let's go inside."

She glanced at the building then back at him. "To the firing squad."

Every step was heavier, like quicksand sucking Maddie down as she fought to move forward. She couldn't remember *not* wanting to do something more, despite Gio at her side.

He wasn't speaking, and that made it worse.

She'd been truthful in the car; Maddie didn't want to lose her job. Besides Jake and Jamie, this job was her life.

It couldn't be that bad, could it?

*Of course it is; Randall's here.*

She'd ask, *what the hell*, but she wasn't stupid. Randall's call had everything to do with Gio and the casino.

It couldn't be anything else.

She hadn't done anything to merit "getting in trouble."

Jesus, was she a kid?

*This* was way worse than getting called to the principal's office.

Captain Olinsky had called at the same time, so that really spoke to her instinct being spot-on.

They were screwed.

The conversation with Griggs floated into her memory. Had he shared his suspicions with Randall? Her boss wasn't *his* boss, so why would he?

Then again, the whole team had heard her yell at Gio about the little brown book, and seen his subsequent flight of the room.

Maybe there was a lot of adding up going on for task force members. They were cops; far from stupid. She'd like to think she could take Griggs at his word — or more accurately, that he'd taken her at *hers*, but did she know him well enough?

Trust was earned. Had she blown his?

What about April Bailey? Maddie didn't know her fellow marshals beyond *'acquaintance.'* She didn't know Gio's fellow detectives well, not even the smiley Hector Garcia. Maybe any welcome she'd been shown was all polite bullshit.

None of it mattered now. Building paranoia and microscoping every conversation wasn't going to help.

The stroll down the hallway was stressful. It seemed to stretch out, as if it was a literal mile long.

Gio remained silent as they walked with matching strides. Not fast or slow, just steady, until they turned the corner and Deputy Chief Patton's door was visible.

The glass-paned entry was open.

She studied Gio's profile.

His jaw was tight, like he was biting down, and his face muscles rippled. Still didn't speak, but paused in front of the doorway and gestured for her to enter in front of him.

They made brief eye contact, but she didn't offer any words. She didn't need chivalry to extend to an escort to the gallows.

*Oh, stop being dramatic.*

She rolled her eyes at herself.

Maddie visually swept the room. The requisite two chairs on the opposite side of the deputy chief's desk pretty much had a spotlight on them. She wanted to avoid them; as if snakes and spiders crawled all over them.

Patton sat behind her desk, her pen in hand like a weapon.

The two men—her boss, and Captain Olinsky—bookended her, standing.

The wall of intimidation might not have been intentional, but it was all Maddie could see. All she could feel. Air was harder to get out; an elephant was sitting on her chest.

The deputy chief's expression was implacable. She was stern by nature, with short brown hair and eyes to match, appearing younger than her fifty-odd years. No doubt her persona had been long-crafted by fighting to rise in a boy's club. Rise she had, to command two divisions at LMVPD.

Gio had told her she'd been a cop for almost thirty years. Patton didn't put up with any shit, either.

God, had it really been less than a week ago?

The room was large, lined with bookshelves and file cabinets. The deputy chief's desk was pretty much centered, making it the focus. To the right sat a medium-sized round table with four chairs.

There were two windows in the far left wall. She wished they were open. She wanted to tug at her collar. A collar that was nowhere near her neck.

Maddie tried to sit as tall as possible in the chair in front of the desk. The same chair she'd sat in the first day. The office was stuffy, with little movement to the air, contradicting the size of the space. It felt dismal, unused and uncomfortable.

None of that was true, but it didn't seem to matter, either.

Gio took a seat and leaned back, crossing one leg like a bridge over the other, his ankle on his opposite knee. He slapped his hand down, as if he couldn't feel the tension in the room.

Like this meeting was no BFD.

She needed to borrow some of his, *"I don't give a fuck."*

He was projecting pretty hard, so it was there for the taking.

Olinsky's almost comb-over was mussed, like he'd run his fingers through it a few times, and his expression exasperated, with a side of irritation.

If Maddie had to guess, Patton had probably chastised him for not knowing about Gio that should've been obvious.

She tried to avoid her boss' dark eyes, which were narrowed to slits. His ebony skin made him more intimidating for some reason. Not because of his race, but maybe because his expression was shadowed, foreboding, by his strong jaw line and trimmed goatee.

Doug Randall stood like a tree, his stocky arms

crossed over a beefy chest, as if he had better things to do with his time, and was disappointed with her.

That made the need to squirm tingle down her spine until she exhibited symptoms of Restless Leg Syndrome. She might not know him well, but Maddie sure as hell wasn't in the habit of letting down a superior, especially in *week one*.

His laser focus was on her, as he waited.

Chief Patton cleared her throat. "We've received a complaint, and wanted to give you both a chance to answer to it."

*Both?*

Weren't these things supposed to be handled one-on-one? There wasn't going to be even a hint of privacy?

*Great.*

"We need to make it quick, I'm on a plane to Virginia in less than two hours," Randall said. His eyes landed on hers.

Marshal Headquarters were in Arlington, Virginia.

Why was he looking at her like that? Was it because of *Maddie* that he had to go to Virginia? Assuming he was headed to Marshal Headquarters.

Instead of a suit, he wore black BDUs and black polo with the Marshal's Service star logo embroidered over his heart, so his clothes weren't a clue to his trip's purpose. His gun was duty-belted at his waist and his large form exuded threat and aggravation.

His presence was definitely not casual.

"What's the complaint?" Gio asked, meeting his deputy chief's eyes. His question was even, like nothing could bother him.

"A concern about a conflict of interest," Olinsky said.

Maddie wanted to wince, but pulled for the most placid expression. She could feel Randall's eyes on her, like he wasn't concerned with Gio at all. Made sense, since she was the one who worked for *him*.

"Regarding?" Gio prompted. His voice was that same low tone, as if he was mildly curious, but really didn't give a shit.

"You." Deputy Chief Patton pinned him with a serious stare.

He didn't so much as arch his eyebrow. "And?"

"Is your father Antonio Giovanni, the owner and president of the casino, *The Giovanni*, and the center of the taskforce's investigation?"

Maddie fought to keep her eyes open. She tried to stay still and not pant. She didn't need to give in to the alarm rising from her gut.

"Yes." His answer was unabashed, with a side of, *'no shit, you're in an idiot'* in his affirmative.

Captain Olinsky's fair complexion reddened to the ruddy color his hair likely once was, and he muttered curses, until the deputy chief shot him a look.

"Granger, were you aware—" Randall opened his mouth, but the rest of him didn't move. His arms were still locked iron bars across his chest.

"Senior Inspector Granger didn't know," Gio cut him off, and slammed his foot down, leaning forward in the chair.

Maddie bit her bottom lip to keep the gasp in. She

moved for the first time, turning her torso toward her lover. "Gio—"

He never looked at her, just kept his eyes on his captain and deputy chief. "She didn't know," he reasserted.

The reason Gio had been so silent on the walk down the hall hit hard.

He was going to lie.

For her.

He could lose *his* job.

Her heart skidded to an almost-stop. Everything inside her told her to shout *no*, to tell the truth.

"So there *is* a conflict of interest." Deputy Chief Patton's statement held a deadly edge.

"How so?" Gio's voice dropped an octave, which did nothing to disguise his demand. He was skating very close to being insubordinate, and he didn't need to add that to his list of offenses.

Maddie sat up and opened her mouth, but he kept talking, beating her to it.

"I want a union rep."

"Gio—" She tried again, but he shot her a silencing look, and readdressed their superiors.

"I haven't done anything wrong here."

The way his eyes had barked at her to shut up should've pissed her off, but her mind was still reeling to keep up with what he was doing.

Getting himself fired wasn't going to exonerate his sister and father. He needed to work the case, do what he'd declared, even if he did it, '*his way.*'

Maddie was on his side. She *wanted* them to be

innocent.

"You have. You owed full disclosure to your captain, not to mention the marshals running the taskforce. You should've never been involved."

"I'm an investigator. My personal ties have nothing to do with my abilities."

"I disagree." Olinsky made a cutting gesture. "This case has to do with your family; you can't be objective."

Gio pitched his body forward even more. In seconds, he'd either shoot to his feet or his ass would have to hover off the padded chair. "My work on this case hasn't been affected."

More lies.

He was too close to the case and he had been from the start, but Maddie sure as hell wasn't going to point that out. He *had* worked exceptionally, despite their arguments, and him going off on his own.

Gio *was* a hell of an investigator. She couldn't argue with that, but she also didn't want to bring his methods to light. Like the fact he'd removed evidence from the police department without permission.

If she did, they might both be out of a job, for real.

The ledger still hadn't been checked into evidence properly. The chain of custody could legitimately be called into question, and that could spiral, bringing other aspects of the case under the same scrutiny. Risks she wasn't willing to take, even if she didn't want Gio to cover for her.

"Hand over your badge and gun," Patton ordered, her dark eyes narrowed, and flashing with challenge.

"Like I said, I want a rep," Gio retorted.

"You'll need one. You're suspended."

He righted himself and flexed his jaw, but didn't say anything.

A few heartbeats passed and the tension shot up as silence hung heavy in the air.

No one moved or spoke.

Finally, Gio climbed to his feet. With stiff movements, he removed his badge from his belt, and his Sig soon followed. He placed them, reverently, on the desk directly in front of the deputy chief.

Maddie fought a flinch—she'd expected a slam.

Without sparing a further word or glance for anyone—not even her—he left.

K<br>♥

"Granger, a word." Doug Randall shook his head, and was the first to speak in the wake of Gio's departure. He gestured to the hallway outside the deputy chief's office.

Neither Olinsky, nor Patton, said anything.

*Now* her boss wanted privacy?

Maddie thought it better than to remark aloud, so she pushed on the arms of the chair to assist her rise to shaky legs.

They didn't go far, just a few feet away from Deputy Chief Patton's office. Gio wasn't anywhere in sight.

Not that she'd really expected him to hang out in the hallway, but he'd brought her to the PD that morning, so she was stranded.

"Is Griggs up to date on the investigation?"

Her boss' voice pulled her away from scanning the corridor.

"Yes, why?"

He sighed, and his barrel chest rose and fell before he met her eyes. "I'll be at Headquarters for a few days. Go home, and we'll talk when I get back."

"What?" Maddie blinked a few times.

Exasperation darted across his expression. "Obviously, you're off this case."

"No." She shook her head.

The deadliness seeping from his narrowed eyes earlier in the office was back. He also regarded her with a side of, *'you can't seriously be that naïve.'*

It made heat swirl at the back of her neck before it settled in her cheeks. She was back in high-schooler-being-chastised territory.

"You'll turn your command over to Griggs."

"This is my case."

Randall shook his head. "Look, I can give you the benefit of the doubt about the detective, but your command is over. You don't need to be anywhere near this case. There're too many implications."

He had *no* idea, and she needed to keep it that way.

At least her personal relationship with Gio hadn't come up. She'd never had to disclose the name of her child's father to the Marshal's Service, and she wasn't about to tell her boss now.

Talk about a conflict of interest.

They never should've worked together at all.

However, she still didn't want to let the case go, either. "At least let me work under Griggs—"

"Go home. I'm not suspending you, but if you push it, I will. When I get back, we'll talk, and I'll put you on something else."

A sense of defeat settled down on her shoulders, and Maddie fought the urge to crumple.

She cleared her throat. "This is my case," she repeated. "This investigation was the reason I transferred to Vegas. I've been working this for months."

Randall flattened his mouth. He was losing patience.

She stood taller and told herself to breathe.

"Do you want to transfer back to Chicago?"

Maddie blinked. Hadn't expected that. "No." As the denial left her lips, it hit home how true it was.

For the first time.

She wanted Jake and Jamie to join her. To make Vegas *home*.

Maddie wanted to make a real family.

*With Gio.*

Her heart skipped.

With all the unusual cardiac activity of the past hour or so, she was going to need to see a doctor—or get a pacemaker.

"Glad to hear that. You're an asset to my team. We have great things ahead of us. You won't lose anything by letting one go. Griggs and Bailey will finish this up. It's for the better. For your protection."

Again, her boss brought her head out of dangerous things she shouldn't want.

Maddie met his eyes.

The irritation was gone, at least for the moment, and his little speech seemed sincere.

"Fine," she whispered.

It would only hurt her pride to let go of this case. *Right?*

She could survive that.

Randall recognized her skills. That was something. It *should* make her feel better. It didn't.

"Make sure Griggs has everything he needs, and head home. We'll talk when I get back." Randall glanced at his watch. "I need to head to the airport. I'm cutting it close." He whirled away, leaving her standing in the corridor.

Maddie kind of felt like an abandoned puppy.

What the fuck was she supposed to do now?

G io peered into the fridge and made a face. Not a damn thing inside that was even halfway interesting. The half-gallon of milk was expired; there were a few old takeout containers, and maybe a half-empty box of dried-out pizza. Probably some things growing penicillin in the back.

Not like Maddie's refrigerator.

He fought the urge to close his eyes.

He wanted a fucking beer or three.

Or something harder.

*Whisky.*

He'd always been a Lagavulin man back in the day, but he'd walked away from it, same as anything else alcoholic.

Damn, he could use that burn in the back of his throat about now. The warmth in his belly. Lag was his favorite Scotch.

Gio could hit the liquor store. There was one around the corner from his place, but...

*Jake.*

He had a son now.

He already missed the little boy he'd only known for a few days. Putting him on a plane that morning, after the most perfect weekend of his life, had affected him in ways he hadn't seen coming.

They'd been a family. Him. Jake. Maddie, and even her little sister.

Those days felt like forever, and the place his son had taken up residence in his heart made up for all the years he'd missed. Or at least, it was a start.

He couldn't go back down the road of losing control. Gio hadn't had a drink in too many years to count. It was too dangerous. Too dark and tempting.

Now, there was more than himself to think of.

Besides, Maddie had told him she'd relieve him of his balls if he hurt their son. He believed her. Considering how fond she was of them, and their companion, that was saying a lot.

*Maddie. Shit.*

Today had been a serious clusterfuck.

He'd walked out of the deputy chief's office without so much as a glance in her direction. Hadn't looked back, either. He'd been too angry. Too afraid he'd say something he couldn't take back. Get his ass fired, instead of suspended.

She'd been collateral damage, really. His fury hadn't been pointed at Maddie.

*Suspended.*

Fuck Patton and Olinsky.

Sure, he'd been in hot water at work before. Gio was reckless, took too many risks, but it'd been a long time since he'd been called to the principal's office for a smack or two, and his work had always spoken for itself.

He got the job done, *no matter what.*

He hadn't been suspended in years.

Besides, he'd spoken the truth; his ties to this case hadn't affected his job. They'd just fucked with his head, and he wasn't about to go around announcing that.

Gio could handle it, right?

If he still had Maddie.

"Fuck," he spat.

He still had Maddie; wouldn't have it any other way.

Gio probably owed her an apology for leaving like that, but it wasn't like he was going to stick around to be *escorted* off the premises.

Fuck that.

He could play Patton and Olinsky's game for a bit; and he really did need to call his union rep. The guy was likely going to have his ass.

The last few times he'd needed a rep, he'd been assigned to Brian Flanagan. The older man was boisterous and of Irish descent, and even if he had his back, he had no qualms about expressing what an idiot Gio had been to require representation.

This time was no different.

He'd get a tongue lashing before any helpful suggestions for sure.

His phone buzzed from his pocket, but he sent the call to voicemail with the side button, without checking to see who it was.

He'd been doing that all day. His texts had been going crazy as well, and he'd ignored all of them, too.

Everyone could fuck off.

*Even Maddie?*

For now.

He wasn't ready to talk to her.

She would've never *let* him lie for her, so he expected her to tell him he was an idiot like Flanagan would, and he didn't need to hear it.

At least for a few hours.

Was she still on the case?

Hopefully he'd saved her ass in that regard. She was his sister's and Big Tony's only hope.

Pounding on his door made Gio honest-to-God jump. Not to mention, exercise his cursing muscle a little more creatively than, "fuck."

Maybe Maddie had come to kick his ass, assuming she was the one blowing up his phone. It'd been a few hours since he'd stormed out of the PD.

The knocking sounded angry, so it wouldn't be a shocker.

He strode to the door and braced himself as he opened it.

"I've been calling you all fucking day." Elise sported a scowl the size of Nevada, and her long blonde hair was in a messy ponytail, with more than a few locks slipped from the tie. Wisps framed her pretty face. She was…frazzled.

Her appearance was generally impeccable, even when dressed casually. That wasn't the case today. His sister wore an oversized pale blue T-shirt, cut-off jean shorts, and *flip-flops.*

He would've bet money—and lost, evidently—that his sister didn't own a shoe without at least a two inch heel.

Gio frowned, and not because she'd yelled at him by way of greeting. He hadn't seen Elise, the designer snob, dressed this *down* in years.

She had a white banker's box in her arms, with another at her feet. "Grab that box, and for God's sake, put on a damn shirt."

"Ummm…hello to you, too?" He ran a hand through his hair, but obeyed, bending at the waist to grab the white cardboard.

It was heavy, and he was curious as to how she'd hefted it all by herself. Maybe that was why she looked so out of sorts; she'd had to make two trips?

"Follow me to the table," she ordered and walked past him into his apartment, as if it was her domain.

"I thought you were too pissed to talk to me?" he drawled. However, he obeyed, setting his box next to hers on what passed for his kitchen table.

The thing was third or fourth hand. The light-colored wood had scars over most of the surface, and a broken leg he'd had to fix. The new leg was a different color, but he didn't mind.

He'd always liked it for the character it sported. It was durable and sturdy, and had been through some shit to come out still functional.

Kind of like him.

"I don't have time for that. I need your help."

When his sister met his eyes, there was more pain

there than anger, and his gut dipped like he'd been checked with a quick elbow.

"Shit, Lise, I'm sorry."

She looked away, probably because those big dark eyes went misty. When she met his gaze again, her chest rose and fell. "Do you think I'm guilty? Or Dad? Do you think we actually did this?"

"Hell no."

Relief danced across her face, and she swiped at the rogue tear making its way down her cheek. Elise didn't have much makeup on, and that too, was different than normal.

Gio liked her like this. Not that she was upset, of course, but in casual clothing and without the gunk on her face, she looked softer. Younger. More like his little sister.

He tugged her into his arms, half expecting her to fight him.

She didn't. Her arms slid around his middle, and she let him hold her for a few moments.

"You really need to put on some clothes." Elise pulled back and arched a finely shaped eyebrow.

"Why?" He looked down. He *had* clothes on. His favorite pair of dark jeans. He'd lost the socks and shitkickers when he'd got home, but he often went barefoot in his own place.

"It's kinda creepy to hug my half-naked brother."

"I'd rather have your snot on my bare shoulder than on one of my shirts. Washes off easier."

"Snot? Ewww. I didn't get *snot* on you."

Indignation overtook her expression, mixed with disgust.

It made Gio think of all the times she'd aimed that particular glare in his direction when they'd been kids. He smirked, and made a show of wiping his shoulder. "Hmm, not so sure about that. Fine, I'll grab a shirt, and you can tell me what you've brought."

She sobered, and her shoulders caved in, but she nodded. Her throat worked. His sister was fighting tears again, and Gio wanted to shoot something.

Or someone.

Armani-the-fucktard would be appropriate.

He went to his bedroom and pulled on the nearest shirt; it was plain gray and clean—probably. It'd passed the sniff test.

When he rejoined Elise at his table, one of the boxes was open, and she was thumbing through a thick stack of papers.

Gio grabbed a chair and took a seat beside her. "What's all this?"

"Casino financials, all printed out from the back-up hard drives, redundancies from what your people seized."

He wanted to wince when she said *'your people,'* but waited for her to continue.

"Since the day after the warrant was served, Paul Allemand has had his best forensic accountants combing through every line." Emotion darted across her countenance then, contradictory to her steady statement. She'd composed herself when he'd gone to his room, but his sister was far from okay.

"And?" Gio couldn't really discuss case specifics with her, and not only because he'd been kicked to the curb. Everything he knew of *The Giovanni's* financials from the taskforce's work was bad. It wouldn't make her feel better. It made her and their father look guilty of money laundering.

"There's something wrong." Elise's bottom lip wobbled.

"What've you found?" He forced an even tone out, hopefully devoid of any judgement or emotion that might upset her more.

"Not a whole lot." She whipped through the stack of papers with her thumb until it made a *thwack* sound. "That's the problem."

*No shit* wouldn't have helped, so he kept his mouth shut.

"Marco was gone all day when your team came to the casino with the warrant."

Gio tilted his head to one side. "Oh yeah?"

The cockstain had never called in, like Maddie had asked, and he'd been too caught up in her and their son over the weekend to process that until right now.

His sister nodded, then put her head down again.

"Did he happen to say where he was?" He kept his inquiry casual, because he didn't want her to fall apart again.

He needed every bit of knowledge she was about to impart.

"He said he went to LA, to consult an oncologist for Dad. He said he didn't tell me because he didn't want me to get my hopes up. He claims he lost his phone, and that's why he hadn't answered my calls." She stopped talking, but there was more.

Gio could tell from her posture, and how she avoided his gaze. "But…"

When Elise met his eyes, hers teared up again, and she bit her at tremulous mouth to stave off a sob. "I love him, Gio."

He sucked back a curse and reached for the bundle of financials. It wasn't difficult to free it from her shaky grip. He set it on the table and squeezed her hands. "I know, Lise." He didn't like it, but he could see the honesty of her feelings for the fucker all over her face. "You don't believe he was in LA, do you?"

Tears rolled down her cheeks and more of her hair floated up as she shook her head. "I want to. But…" The sob fell out then, and Gio sighed as he tugged her into his arms for the second time in less than an hour.

He didn't speak; just held her, because she hated showing vulnerability, and his sister would need time to gather herself. He needed her to get that composure because he needed to know *everything*.

Elise's big dark eyes were red-rimmed when she was done crying and backed away. She wiped her face and flashed a mock-glare. "Don't say a damn word about snot on your shirt."

Gio smirked. "Wouldn't dream of it." He darted into the kitchen and grabbed the roll of paper towels from the dispenser above the sink.

She accepted it, then wrinkled her pert little nose. "I suppose you're not grown up enough to have actual tissues." She balled up a paper towel and blotted under her eyes.

He let the jibe slide, and shrugged.

Allowing his sister to work things out in her head was always better than barging forward, so he let her have a few more seconds.

Elise inhaled. "Marco put himself in charge of helping the accountants investigate. He was the one who requested all the back-ups. He was the one who checked off all the manifests, to make sure we got everything. He was the one who printed all the reports, and he even delivered them himself. He helped go over the numbers."

"That's what made you suspicious." It was a statement, not a question.

His sister was a sharp cookie. Like him, she'd learned to follow her gut long ago.

She nodded. "At first, I thought it was because he was taking ownership, you know? Like he really wants to help, 'cause he loves me. He's good at numbers, too." Her voice broke, but she forged forward. "He promised to help prove I'm innocent. Dad's innocent."

"What exactly makes you doubt that?"

Elise sucked in a gulp of air, probably to push away more tears. "This." She leaned over and grabbed some papers from the box she'd opened, and shoved them at him.

Gio scanned the old-school style pale green and white striped paper, folded at a perforation in the middle, and complete with the little dotted rip-off strip at the top.

It appeared to be a manifest, and had a carbon copy

still attached to the back.

He studied the printed lines of text in front of him. Each had a reference or record number in the left column, with the original date it'd been sent to storage to the right.

It didn't escape his notice that all the dates were within in the last nine months.

"What am I looking at?"

"Missing records."

"Missing? What d'you mean?" He lifted his eyes from the manifest, and his heart slid to his gut.

His sister's expression was desolate. Desperate. Her slender hands were tight fists on her lap and her shoulders were shaking. Elise was fighting to hold herself together, and it shattered him.

"Marco…" She had to stop talking and try again. "Marco was the only one who checked the manifests against the materials we received from both data centers. I found that manifest at the bottom of an empty box. Only…" His sister sniffled. "There were no records to match the contents of the manifest. So I asked him if he had all the records in the conference room we were working in."

"And he said yes."

She nodded. "I checked everything twice. Those records weren't anywhere to be found."

"Then…?" Gio gestured to the two boxes she'd brought.

Fat tears rolled down her cheeks again, and it broke his heart.

He cursed in his head, then silently vowed he

would personally escort the fuckwad to Hell. Maybe he'd even relieve him of a few body parts.

Elise pulled away when he reached for her hand. "Dad's not tech-savvy, but he's not a stupid man."

He nodded, leaning back to adjust to the subject change. Gio let his sister get to the point on her own.

"We've always used two main back-up centers for all the important information, records, and software for *The Giovanni*. But when Marco and I finally convinced Dad to do the major overhaul on the accounting department, he would only agree on one condition."

Gio straightened his shoulders and pushed to the edge of the chair. "A third redundancy?"

His sister nodded.

"A third redundancy Armani didn't know about?" His pulse kicked up, his heart revving against his ribs before settling into overdrive. "Why?"

"Because he never trusts completely. Because some things should stay within the family, he said." Elise's answer was stronger, and she didn't acknowledge his most tame nickname for the cockstain.

"So those boxes are—"

"The records from the missing manifests. Proof me and Dad are innocent."

Gio's head spun. "We need to call Maddie."

"Thanks for the ride, Garcia, I appreciate it." Maddie flashed a smile she wasn't really feeling.

"Oh, my pleasure, Inspector. I'm just glad I could help. It's a shame you won't be running the team anymore," the detective said.

*Yeah, 'cause I need that reminder. Thanks, Garcia.*

Griggs had made the announcement after she'd pulled him to the side to relay Randall's orders. Her coworker didn't ask why, and for that she was grateful.

When he'd told the taskforce of the change, he'd only said Maddie had been pulled to another case. Another reason for her to be thankful.

She slid from the car so she wouldn't be rude; it wasn't the detective's fault. Besides, Garcia had agreed to give her a ride home without hesitation. "It's okay, I'm sure I'll see you around." She forced one more smile as she shut the passenger door of the unmarked LMVPD Ford Fusion. It was a copper color, and the only thing revealing it was a police vehicle was the spotlight on the driver side.

He smiled and offered a wave as he pulled onto the

road.

Maddie's stomach churned and she sighed. She glanced up at her apartment building. The place was home. It was starting to *feel* like home, too, but she didn't want to go inside.

She should be at work. Perusing over financials. Prepping reports and documenting information for arrest warrants. Conferencing with her taskforce. Calling Agent Grey from the FBI to touch base. Checking emails.

Any. Fucking. Thing.

She peeked at her phone's screen. It was black, inactive, just like she'd been relegated.

She touched it to wake it up, although her earlier text to Gio had gone unanswered. Maddie sent her thumbs to work on another one.

*Hope you're okay. Call me.*

Why was he ignoring her?

*He* was the one who'd chosen to lie.

She never would've asked that of him, and when she did get a hold of him, they were destined for an argument, because she was going to tell him so.

Although, Gio had changed so much.

The Nico Giovanni from this past weekend was not the hotheaded cop she'd known eight years ago. The tenderness, the humor, the gentleness and genuine interest in their son.

He'd finally grown the hell up.

What she'd always wanted. What she'd always

dreamed when she'd thought about what a *family* with him would look like.

The weekend had shown her what it would *be* like.

Tears stung Maddie's eyes.

She wanted more.

That was a very dangerous thing. Especially if he wasn't going to talk to her because of something *he'd* done on his own.

She shook her head and cursed him to hell and back.

Gio needed to get over himself and call her.

Maybe he wasn't so grown up, after all?

She smirked.

Something told Maddie to glance right, where a small parking lot sat next to the building. It only had about twenty coveted spots, but the high-rise also had a parking garage around the corner. Her neighbors seemed to prefer the surface lot, so the place was generally full.

She'd managed to snag a spot on Friday, and her car hadn't moved since, because Gio had done all the driving.

The silver Toyota Camry glinted in the desert sun.

She still hadn't been assigned her duty car, and likely wouldn't until Randall returned from Virginia. Good thing she didn't have to pay for the rental out of pocket.

There was something on her windshield, but she couldn't make it out from her distance. Had she gotten a parking ticket?

That would piss her off.

Maddie trotted over and lifted her wiper to retrieve the item. It was a goldenrod envelope, about half the size of a piece of paper.

She flipped it over. There was no writing on the front or back, nor was it sealed; the flap was just held in place by the attached brads. It was warm from the afternoon sun.

She looked around, as if she could magically discover who'd put it there.

There was no one in sight.

Maddie opened it, sliding its contents toward her palm.

A photo hit the cement before she could catch it.

"Shit." She bent to grab it, and when she flipped it over, her heart stuttered.

It was of her, crossing the street with Jake. They were holding hands, and their hair was windblown. They were in winter attire, too. On the busy street their apartment high-rise in downtown Chicago was on.

There were more.

Of Jake, of her, of Jamie.

*What the fuck?*

The last thing inside the envelope didn't make her heart skip; it made it stop.

It was a folded piece of paper with one typed line — not handwritten.


*Is Jake's life worth The Giovanni?*


Maddie's lungs constricted. She had to pant to move air. The world spun and she had to plant her hand on the car's hood to keep from falling over.

Who had…

Someone who…

*Knew* her son's name.

She kicked her ass from petrified mother into federal law enforcement agent.

Maddie reached for her phone and dialed Jamie. It didn't even ring.

*"Hi, you've reached Jamie. Leave me a message…"*

"Fuck!" She glanced at her Fitbit. It was about thirty minutes *after* their plane should've landed. Her heart wasn't beating; it was cantering. She needed to calm, before she passed out.

*Jesus. Breathe, Maddie. Just breathe.*

With shaking fingers, she pulled up the airline's app and punched in Jamie and Jake's flight number.

*'Delayed'* was in all-caps, red text next to the flight info, across from the three letter code for O'Hare.

She pushed out air as slowly as she could, and inhaled until her lungs stung.

*They're just late.*

They were fine, the plane was just late.

She called Jamie's phone again, waiting for the voicemail *beep* this time. "Hey, you need to call me the *second* that plane is on the ground." Maddie sent a text with the same message, then dialed another phone number. She exhaled another ragged breath so she could speak without fucking crying.

"Crosby," he answered on the first ring.

*Thank God.*

"Colt, it's Maddie. I…I need you to do something

for me."

"Granger? Hey! How're ya doin'? How's Vegas treating you?"

Her short pants ratcheted up with the small talk she didn't have time for. "Listen. I need you to meet my son and my sister at O'Hare. Their plane was delayed, but it should be landing in the next twenty minutes. Can you do that for me? Are you at the office?"

"Granger, what's wrong?" His pleasantness was gone. Colt must've plugged into her urgency.

"There's a threat to Jake's life, related to my case. He's headed back there with my sister, Jamie."

"Shit. Yes, of course. I'll grab Drew and Sid and go there now."

Maddie blew out more air. Three marshals were better than one. "Thank you. I'll text you the gate and flight info. Can you get through security?"

"With riot gear if I have to."

She was able to smile. She'd always been fond of her former teammate. He was an ex-Seal, and a hell of an investigator. He was huge, too, about six-six and just as wide. Full of muscles and scary as hell when he needed to be.

Being a marshal would afford them certain allowances at the terminal, and he and the guys should be able to get Jamie and Jake right off the plane.

"Thanks, Colt. You have no idea how much I appreciate this, and how much better I feel knowing they'll be with you."

"Anytime, Maddie."

She could hear his smile.

"I'll take them to your place and sit on them?" Colt asked.

"Yes. I'll hop on the first flight I can to get them."

"Sounds good, keep in touch."

They ended the call, and Maddie dialed her sister's number again. This time her message wasn't as frantic. "Colton Crosby is going to take you guys back to the apartment. I'll fill you in later, but I'm sure you remember him from work. Call me, please."

Jamie wouldn't like the cryptic message, but she wasn't about to freak her out via message — text or voice. Her sister would call her when they landed. Probably rudely demand to know what was going on.

Maddie dug her keys out of her pocket and slid behind the driver seat of her rental after slamming her thumb on the fob's *unlock* button. She called Gio's cell.

*"You've reached Detective Giovanni, from Las Vegas…"*

"Fuck, Gio. Answer your damn phone. Call me back." She cursed him some more, and dialed one more number. She really didn't have time for his pout-fest.

"Garcia," the detective said.

"Hey, I have an odd request."

"Oh, hey, Inspector. Everything okay?"

Hector Garcia was a genuinely nice guy, so Maddie shouldn't be irritated by his pleasantries, but for some reason she was.

"It will be. Do you happen to have Gio's address? He's not taking my calls."

"Ah. Word is, he's gotten himself suspended. It's pretty hush hush, so we don't know why."

She rolled her eyes, glad he couldn't see her. He might not be digging for information, but she wasn't about to give him shit anyway. "Do you have his address?"

"Oh, sure. I'll text it to you, okay?"

"Absolutely. Thanks."

"No problem. Tell him if he needs anything, let me know. Same goes for yourself. Take it easy, Inspector."

She ended the call without another word, and when her phone *dinged* with a message, Maddie felt a tiny bit guilty for being short with him.

Gio's apartment was only a nine minute drive, according to Waze.

She took a breath, and shifted the car into gear.

"**W**hy do we need *her*?" Elise demanded, crossing her arms over her chest and glaring. No more tears in sight, which was good, but the flip-flop to rage was about to make Gio's head spin.

"Because she's a shit-ton better at numbers than I am."

His sister shook her head. "I got that handled. No one's better than me."

If he wasn't busy defending the woman he loved, he might've taken time to give his sister shit about her egotism. "You're the one who said you needed *my* help, Lise."

"Yeah, because you're the cop. *You're* the one who has the power to help. I brought you the proof. You fix it."

Gio shoved his hand through his hair. "Yeah, about that…"

Elise straightened her shoulders. "What?"

"You'll really need Maddie now."

"Why?"

"At the moment, I'm not a cop."

Her fair eyebrows dipped down and she cocked her head to one side. "What happened?"

"I'm suspended."

"What the fuck, Gio?" Elise's frown deepened and she shook her head.

He couldn't remember the last time he'd heard his sister drop the f-bomb, but she'd done so more than once since coming to his place.

After he'd explained the whole sordid situation, she shook her head. Her arms were crossed even harder, but it was more like she was hugging her torso. Trying to squeeze any comfort for herself. Anger, desperation, defeat made up her form, and Gio wanted to slay all the dragons he could for her.

Armani the fucktard had gotten her into this situation, and she was going to come out scarred.

He'd keep her out of a prison cell, especially now, since they had the proof they needed. But she was rocking a broken heart that would take a long damn time to heal.

His sister didn't open up easily, and sure, there'd been guys, but no serious relationships. This asshole really had one over on her, *and* their father.

How had that happened so fast?

Big Tony didn't trust easily, either, but the tertiary redundancy proved their father didn't completely trust Armani.

Which was a good thing. The thing to save their asses.

Maybe he could cut his dad a break in that regard.

Maybe Big Tony had seen something Elise had

missed. Or, he was just a paranoid freak, like always.

"Fine, call her," his sister spat, an ugly scowl marring her beauty.

Gio sighed and grabbed one of her hands, tugging her arms free of her body. "Listen, don't be upset with Maddie. She was just doing her job. This all started when the FBI arrested an old friend of dad's. An accountant named Cesare Fratelli."

"Marco's dad?"

He winced. It wasn't a shocker he'd have to break it to her that Armani wasn't who he'd claimed to be. He just wasn't excited the "done" timer had popped up *now*. He didn't want to make her feel worse. "Might as well rip the Band-Aid off," he muttered.

"What?"

"The man you know as Marco Fratelli isn't who he says he is."

His sister blinked. "What?"

"Marco Fratelli was a very sick little boy who died a long time ago, before he reached age six. And he was the son of Cesare Fratelli, yes."

"And...you *knew* this?"

Gio nodded.

Before he could open his mouth to explain, Elise yanked her hand from his grip and reared back, landing a hard smack on his chest. Another followed, and another, until he had to grab both her wrists to protect himself.

She was crying again, and when their gazes brushed, his sister crumpled.

He closed his eyes and gathered her close for the

third time that day.

Gio was going to kill that fucking cockstain.

"No, Gio… No…" she sobbed against his shirt.

"I'm sorry, Lise. I'm so fucking sorry." He rubbed her back and held her until she got it together.

When she pulled back, Elise wouldn't look at him right away. She wiped her face on the bottom of her shirt, instead of grabbing a new paper towel.

The inelegance of it made him smirk.

"Call Maddie," she sniffled. "If she's who we need, she's who we need."

*She's who I need.*

Gio didn't realize he'd spoken aloud until Elise spoke again.

"Are you two back together?" His sister's mouth was hanging half-agape, and she had one eyebrow arched. She didn't appear angry, just curious.

"Something like that. We, um…I have a son."

Elise popped up in her seat, her eyes wide. "What?"

Maybe he was a coward, but he already had his cell to his ear, and the phone was ringing, so he wouldn't have to answer his sister.

"Gio!" Maddie barked. "I've been fucking calling and texting you for hours!"

He winced.

She sounded *pissed.*

Gio rammed his hand into his hair. "Yeah. Sorry about that."

"I'm around the corner from your place. We have to talk."

Relief and trepidation bounded off each other in his gut. As much as he didn't want his ass handed to him by Maddie; his sister—and his dad—needed her. "Text when you get here. I'll buzz you up."

K<br>♥

Maddie tumbled into his apartment, shoving a gold envelope into his hand, without so much as a hello. She was upset, just as frazzled his sister had when she'd arrived. "This was on my car."

He almost missed taking the thing from her shaking hands. "What is it?"

She didn't speak, and the question was answered when pictures slid into his waiting palm. There were a few shots, all had Maddie and Jake in them, and one included Jamie.

Gio's heart didn't pick up speed until he saw the white piece of paper. It was small, like an afterthought, until he read it.

*Is Jake's life worth The Giovanni?*

"Fuck," he spat.

"What is it?" Elise asked from the periphery. She seemed hesitant to come closer, but she joined them right inside the front door.

Gio cursed some more, trying to keep his panic in check, but it wasn't working.

Maddie was too quiet, and she'd paled out, like she was trying to mimic a ghost.

"This is him? My nephew?" his sister asked, but

her tone was a muse, as if she was talking to herself.

Maddie took a big breath and their eyes met. "I called someone to meet them at the plane."

A million questions went through his mind, but he needed to breathe through them so he could speak. "Good." He was about to follow up with, who, what, where, when why, but she beat him to the punch.

"Three marshals will take them to my place and sit on them. Jamie will want to know what's going on…"

"These pictures weren't taken in Vegas," he said. "Someone's been watching you."

"No shit." Maddie had an eyebrow arched when he swept over her pretty face again, but at least she had some color in her cheeks again. "Someone in Chicago."

He had to smirk. "Who do you think—"

A cellphone rang, and Elise dug her device out of her pocket. Her eyes widened and she flashed the screen before them. It displayed a photo of the cockstain's smiling face. "It's Marco, what do I do?" Panic dominated her expression, and she shifted in her flip-flops.

"Answer it," Gio ordered. "Put it on speaker, and act normal."

"Normal?" his sister squeaked even as her thumb hovered over the green circle.

He nodded as she said hello.

"Hey, *tesoro*."

He scowled.

Elise stumbled through a greeting, and inhaled audibly.

Gio shot a glimpse at Maddie.

Confusion, then anger shot across her eyes, and she flattened her lips.

"What?" he mouthed.

She shook her head and gestured to Elise. She was plugged into his sister's call.

"Where'd you go?" Armani asked.

"Uh, the hospital called. Dad…passed out." His sister sounded like the mess she was. It worked, since the asshole would believe she was emotional over Big Tony.

"Oh. I'm sorry. Is he okay now? I'll come right—"

"No!" She had to take another breath. "I mean, stay at the casino with Paul's team. That's the most important thing right now."

There was a pause on the other end of the line.

Gio shot his sister a look. "Normal," he mouthed.

Her chest heaved. She was struggling through pants.

Maddie had paled out again, and she wouldn't meet his eyes. Her hazel stare was on Elise's phone. Like it was a gun or a knife. Or a plague she wanted to avoid.

"Dad's okay, he's resting." Elise rushed her words. "His…electrolytes or something caused him to crash, but they're on top of it. I only came down 'cause it's been a few days since I've seen him, and I didn't want him to worry." Now his sister was rambling, and Gio whirled his index finger. She shrugged and he could feel her nerves.

"Are you sure?"

He sucked back a snort; like the cockstain was

really concerned. Their father being out of the picture was no doubt better for him.

"I am, but thanks for calling. I'll be home later, and I'll update Sam and Dom."

"Are you sure you're okay, *tesoro*?"

"Yeah, under the circumstances." His sister's shoulders went taut, and she tightened her grip on the phone.

"You sure? You don't sound that great."

"Would you be okay considering what we've been going through?" Elise snapped.

"Are we still on for lunch?" Armani asked, obviously changing tack so he didn't get yelled at.

Gio snorted again.

"Uh, I think I should stay with Dad…"

"Are you sure you don't want me to come? We could stay there, eat at the cafeteria."

Elise made eye contact with him. She was in panic-mode again, and she shook her head.

He squeezed her forearm.

"Dad just wants me to sit with him for a while. Dinner instead?"

"Oh, sure. *Maggiano's*?"

"My favorite, absolutely."

Gio flashed her a thumbs-up.

"Marco, the nurse needs me; call you later?"

"Keep me post—"

His sister hit the red *end* circle even before Armani had the word all the way out. She stared at her darkened phone's screen. "Do you think he bought it?" Her inquiry was just above a whisper.

"I think so. Good job, Lise."

Maddie cursed, and they both glanced her way.

Her expression was unreadable, which was odd; she was usually pretty transparent.

"I know who Marco is."

G ian. Fucking. Falcone.
How had she *not* known?

Maddie's head spun and she wandered forward, wobbling on very shaky legs. If she didn't find a chair, she was going to fall over.

She located a small dining area and a round table that'd seen better days. She clutched the back of a chair, then managed to round the front and plant her ass.

Gio and Elise had followed her from the front door, but they didn't crowd her; like they could both sense she needed a few.

"Maddie?" He finally breeched the silence. His Adam's apple bobbed.

She could read the demand on his lips and feel his urgency, but he didn't push her. Maybe he'd really grown up.

"Who is he, really?" Elise asked, beating her brother to the verbal punch.

"She knows?" Maddie looked at Gio.

"I told her everything."

"I'm so sorry, Elise."

Her former friend pursed her lips, but offered a small nod.

Maddie would take what she could get. "He's..." She had to clear her throat and try again. "Gian Falcone, heir to the Falcone Syndicate. A glorified name for old Chicago mobsters. The FBI has been after his father, Luciano, for years."

"The mob? That's still a thing?" Elise was incredulous, her surprise and disbelief equal.

Gio nodded. "*The Godfather* style, right, Mads?"

Maddie opened her mouth, but didn't get the chance to speak.

"Oh, shit. Jake."

She had to tamp her panic down her to gut, so she could function. So she could speak. She'd also done the math Gio had obviously had just figured.

"We need to get Jake back to Vegas, now." His voice was hard.

"Agreed." She dug her phone from her pocket. "I'll book a flight."

"No, you need to stay here—" Gio said.

She made a slicing gesture, cutting him off. "This is *my* kid we're talking about."

"*Our* kid." This was just as hard, but she didn't miss his challenge. "You're not doing this alone."

Maddie scoffed. "I've been '*doing this alone*' for eight years."

"Whose fucking fault is that?" He shot forward, intentionally towering over her in the chair, his eyes flashing like cut sapphires.

She glared and shot to her feet. "I knew you were

lying. I just fucking *knew* it. You haven't forgiven me. You're not okay—"

"You're calling me a fucking liar?" he barked. His eyes were narrowed to slits.

"Guys," Elise said.

"You lied this morning at work. So, I guess I am." She lifted her chin. "Which, by the way, I *never* asked you to do!"

"That was completely different, and you fucking know it." He took a breath, as if he was trying to get a hold on his temper, but his expression was still made of rage. "Mads, I'm a lot of things, but you don't get to—"

"Nico!" Elise yelled, probably because it was the only thing that would shut him up. She grabbed his wrist and tugged.

Gio looked at his sister. His chest heaved.

"That's it," she soothed. "Take a breather." She looked at Maddie. "You, too. Now's not the time for a pissing contest."

Maddie snorted. "I've always preferred calling it *'dick measuring'*."

Gio smirked. "If you had a dick, we'd be having a different conversation."

Elise smiled, and even though it was small, it was almost like her friend was back. "Piss or dicks, we need to focus on my nephew." The younger woman sobered.

Maddie nodded. "She's right." She dialed her cell and put it to her ear.

"His name is Jake?" Elise asked her brother in a whisper.

"Yeah, and he's great. Looks just like me."

She didn't let the joy in Gio's voice flip her stomach...too much.

"Maddie, who're you calling?"

She turned away, ignoring both siblings.

The phone only rang twice.

"Crosby."

"Hey, Colt."

"Granger, good. I was just about to call you. We've got them."

Jamie was talking—an obvious protest—in the background. She imagined her younger sister fighting even a gentle guiding touch of a helpful marshal, and almost rolled her eyes.

Maddie didn't hide her sigh of relief. "Good. Let me talk to my sister."

"You got it."

"Maddie, what the hell's going on?" Jamie demanded by way of greeting.

"Just listen to Colt. Go with him and the guys. It'll be okay."

"Bullshit. Tell me what's going on."

She paused. Jamie wouldn't be persuaded to cooperate without the truth. Maddie closed her eyes for a split-second. "There's been a threat, and you and Jake need to be protected. Just as a precaution."

Jamie's intake of breath was harsh and rocked her.

"Okay," she whispered.

If she'd had her wits truly about her, Maddie might've teased her about the one word acquiescence. It was un-Jamie-like. "It'll be okay. I promise. Colt and the guys will keep you both safe for now, until we can get you back down here."

Gio was eyeing her so hard, he was likely to bore a hole in her shoulder, but Maddie didn't want to face him.

"Lemme talk to Jake."

Jamie didn't say anything else, but she could hear the shuffling of the cellphone.

"Mom?"

"Hey, little man. You okay?" She forced herself to sound positive.

"Uh huh. Where's Dad?"

She rolled her eyes. "Right here, hold on." Maddie's fingers shook as she handed the phone over. Her adrenaline had finally dumped.

First the pictures, then rushing to Gio's and finding out who Marco Fratelli really was. The argument had carried her on. Now that she'd heard their voices, she could breathe.

Really breathe.

*They're okay.*

Colt would keep them safe. If she didn't trust him, she wouldn't have reached out.

Her chest ached, and she needed to sit again. Maddie thumped back down—she didn't even have to back up.

Elise squeezed her shoulder.

She met her dark eyes and was able to give a small smile.

There were so many questions in the younger woman's gaze, but they would all have to be for later.

Elise nodded, as if she'd picked up the mental put-off and understood.

Maddie nodded back, and plugged back into Gio's conversation with their son.

"Glad to hear that, champ. Hey, can I talk to Colt?"

She narrowed her eyes. What an eavesdropper. She should've known he was sharp enough to catch her friend's name.

Gio quickly introduced himself to her old teammate.

Then he did what Gio did best; took over the damn situation.

Maddie didn't have the energy to protest. Her rollercoaster ride needed to come back to the bottom of the hill and stay put for a while.

He put the call on speaker, and the two men quickly coordinated a plan, but she appreciated his attempt to include her.

The three marshals would take Jamie and Jake to a safe location, not Maddie's Chicago apartment, and remain there until everyone felt the coast was clear enough to return them to Vegas.

"Now what?" Elise asked when Gio had hung up, and Maddie had tucked her phone back into her pocket.

"Now, show me what you've got." She gestured to the two banker's boxes.

K<br>♥

Gian's gut told him something was up. Wrong. Off.

*But what?*

Elise was stressed. Ever since the afternoon the warrant had been served, so that wasn't a shocker. But something about her today was off.

He twirled his cellphone like a fidget spinner on his desk. He didn't want to risk odd looks from his casino coworkers, or he'd play with his knife; it'd always calmed him.

The investigation was going well. For *him,* anyway.

Paul's team was hard at work with the financials he'd given them, and Gian was still in the clear. If the accountants were frustrated about the slim pickins', they hid it well, but then again, they probably got off on this line-by-line numbers kind of thing, so maybe they were more orgasmic than disappointed over the challenge.

Uncle Dino was still checking with his sources to see if his *'conflict of interest'* call had reaped results, and only time would tell if the ol' pictures-and-threat had been a success.

The easy thing would be to ask Elise if she'd heard anything regarding her brother's work situation, but that wasn't really something he could drop into normal conversation—especially if she was mad at him.

Was she?

His fiancée had been shrill, something she rarely was in his direction. Sure, she'd always been fiery when irritated, but she hardly ever yelled at *him.*

Gian sighed.

A phone rang, but it wasn't his normal cell, or the casino direct line on the desk in front of him.

His heart skipped as he dug the burner from his pocket.

Hopefully Uncle Dino would have good news.

"What did you find out?" he asked as soon as he'd placed the device to his ear.

"That you haven't changed a bit."

The deep voice made him sit forward in his chair and his breath dissolved.

"D-d-dad?" He winced. He'd actually stuttered, something only the man who'd raised him could bring out of him.

There was a pause, and his father made a throaty growl. "You are a bigger fool than I ever could've imagined."

"Dad, let me explain—"

"Dino told me everything," Luciano Falcone barked. "Get back to Chicago. You've put everything I've ever worked for in jeopardy, and if the FBI comes knocking, *you* will answer."

Gian's gut dipped.

*Does that mean death or prison?*

He didn't want to know. He'd never manage the balls to ask.

Why had Uncle Dino betrayed him?

Was his youngest uncle still breathing?

"Tony Giovanni stole money from our family! The ledger proves it! He's made millions off our backs, and he needs to pay!"

His father didn't need to know the little relic he'd sought was in police custody.

A bark of laughter sounded in his ear...the *last*

thing Gian had ever expected.

"Boy, you have no idea what you're talking about. Leave the skeletons in the desert, where they belong."

"But—"

"Get back to Chicago."

He frowned.

His father hadn't said, *'come home,'* which meant he wasn't welcome in the house he'd grown up in—or any residence owned by the Falcones. If something had happened to his uncle, he wouldn't be able to house Gian, either.

"I'm not done here." He was proud his retort hadn't shaken.

"You. Are."

"I'm doing this for you. I'll marry Elise Giovanni, and everything will be mine."

Again, his father laughed, but there was no humor in it. "*Every* word you speak shows how much of a child you are. You've done enough damage for a lifetime."

"Damage?" he barked.

"A flight has been booked in your name for this evening. Be on it," Dear-ol'-Dad said, as if Gian hadn't yelled.

Then the line went dead.

"Fuck you!" he screamed and threw the little burner phone to the hardwood of his office. He jumped up from his chair and stomped the phone.

He kept driving his Ferragamo loafer down until the *cracking* and *crushing* was satisfying.

It was staring them right in the face.

The proof that would exonerate his sister and their father.

Now that his son was safe, they were going over the records Elise had brought.

Gio didn't like leaving the protection of his child to a man he didn't know, but Maddie had sworn the marshal, Colt Crosby, could be trusted. She said the other two guys were equally good, so he had too cool his jets. Even if he didn't like it.

Talking to the man had made him feel better. Crosby seemed to know what he was doing.

They debated whether or not it would be safer for Jake and Jamie to be in Chi-town or Sin City. Since the mob thought he was in Vegas, as far as they knew, Chicago was the winner, but somewhere *other* than Maddie's old apartment.

Crosby said he would handle it, and picked a hotel outside of downtown.

"Holy shit!" Maddie said for about the fifth time as she studied each line of each report. "This is exactly what we needed."

"Now you can go arrest the fucker, right?" Elise asked. She was now driving the "fuck the cockstain" train instead of laying on the tracks.

Gio approved. Admired her for it.

He was also reintroduced to why he'd always been a little bit afraid of his sister. She'd always been ruthless when wronged. Or when one of her family members was wronged.

It was a good thing to have her on one's side. On the wrong side of her, she was scary.

*Good luck, Armani.*

Elise was likely to have his head — or his cock — on a platter.

"Well, not exactly," he said.

"Why?" his sister demanded, crossing her arms over her chest.

"It's all circumstantial," Maddie finished, still poring over the latest set of financials.

"Why?" Elise repeated.

"This," Gio gestured to both boxes, "is the what, when, where."

"Not the who," Maddie finished again.

"Why?" his sister demanded for the third time.

Maddie smirked. "The why really doesn't matter."

Elise frowned. "You know what I meant. The *who* is what matters the most, and it's Gian Falcone." She spat the name, like a curse.

She'd transitioned pretty quickly into accepting that Marco Fratelli wasn't a real person; at least not anymore, and every time she said the twatwaffle's real name, she spat it, in true disgruntled Italian fashion.

"Right. We know that," Maddie explained patiently. "But we have to prove it."

Elise reclined in the chair at his kitchen table, but didn't ease her posture. If anything, the bars across her chest tightened. "Gian started working at *The Giovanni* nine months ago. The money laundering started nine months ago." She stuck her bottom lip out in a half-pout.

"Right," Maddie and Gio said at the same time.

His sister drew her brows tight, cocking her head to one side. "What do you need?"

"Confession would be nice," Gio said, mirroring her posture, as Maddie still pored over reports.

Elise's frown deepened. "But you said this stuff was all you needed." She'd already gone over the financials herself, highlighting each line from the hidden hard drives that mattered.

"Not *all* we need. This is the missing piece from the financials we already have. The proof, like direct records, of the money laundering activity…it totals at a startling four mil, by the way, but this right here," Maddie gestured to the books. "Doesn't have Falcone's name on it. Not literally."

His sister let her arms fall to her lap and stood, leaning over one of the boxes. "What about this?" She presented the manifest to Maddie, then passed it to him. "See where that yellow highlight is? It says 'M. *Fratelli*' originated the record in the accounting software. Isn't that definitive proof? *He* created it. He was logged in."

"It's certainly helpful," Gio said. "But it's not

foolproof. He could claim someone—*you*—used his login to frame him."

"He could make the argument that you started laundering money when he arrived, just to make him into a scapegoat," Maddie added.

Elise honest-to-God growled low in her throat. "Fuck him!" She sat down in a huff.

"I know it sucks, Lise, but he'll get a good lawyer, and all these things are Law School 101. We need to have him dead to rights."

"Then what do we have to do?"

Maddie set her current stack of papers down and reached for the next group.

They'd been at his place for hours that felt like days, and she'd already looked at everything a dozen times, attacking the poor dead trees with three colors of highlighters to differentiate her work from his sister's.

"Why don't we get some grub?" Gio asked. "We've been at this forever."

"No." His sister's mouth was set in a stubborn line. "Not until we work this out."

Maddie exchanged a glance with him.

He knew what she was going to say before she opened her mouth. It didn't make him like it anymore.

"You could get him to tell you."

"She's not wearing a wire," Gio barked.

"I would *totally* wear a wire," Elise retorted.

"It's too dangerous," he said.

"He's my fiancé," his sister said. "He has no clue I know."

"It could work," Maddie said, perking up.

"No," he growled.

"You don't get to pick. You're suspended." His sister looked at Maddie, completely dismissing him. "We can make this work, right? I'll do it. I want to do it."

"Mads…"

His lover shrugged and maintained eye contact with Elise. She didn't acknowledge him, either. "Are you sure?"

"Absolutely. I'm not afraid of him. I've been living with him for six months. He'll be there when I get home. The biggest challenge will be *not* giving in to the urge to smash his balls the minute I walk in the door."

"Six months?" Gio grumbled. "You moved him into your penthouse after knowing him only *three* months?"

Maddie ignored him. "Elise, try to be nice for one more night."

"Six months?" he repeated, but neither Maddie, nor his sister said a word about his protest.

Jesus, was he invisible?

The two females he cared most about in the world were not only ignoring him, but were doing a champion job of ganging up on him.

*What kinda shit is this?*

"I think it's time to call Griggs," Maddie said.

K<br>♥

Roger Griggs wanted to see the proof before he agreed to a damn thing, and he wanted to do it alone, in case involving the team turned out to be a moot point.

Maddie had always liked the guy, and she had to give him some grudging respect, even if he was being a pain in the ass. He could've hung up in her face, instead of giving her the courtesy of listening to their revelation.

It was a start.

Gio remained not completely on board, but only where his sister was concerned. He was all about slapping cuffs on Falcone's wrists.

Or maybe shooting him for what he'd done to Elise.

The only Giovanni daughter had grown up a lot, too, and Maddie could only admire the woman. She wasn't convinced the firecracker had completely forgiven her, but they were well on their way of reviving the closeness they'd shared eight years ago.

Working on the case as a team helped, and it was fun as hell to gang up against Gio. Not that Maddie would ever admit *that* out loud.

Elise was certainly whip-smart when it came to the numbers, and she'd spotted the issues at first glance, without much digging.

She admired that. Had no doubt Gio's sister was running the casino with efficiency and good leadership.

Elise was excited to meet Jake, and hadn't really butted into the whys of Maddie keeping him from his father over the years. Maybe she felt it wasn't her business, or maybe it would be for later, but Maddie would roll with the punches.

She'd always adored Gio's siblings, and the guilt

about keeping her baby from his dad had already been insurmountable at times. She hadn't spent a ton of time contemplating how her actions had also kept him from the other Giovannis.

"You're sure you want to do this, Miss Giovanni?" Griggs pinned Elise with his very green gaze. He hovered over scattered financials at Gio's kitchen table. He had a piece of paper in his hand. It was the manifest, with Falcone's alias printed on it.

"Fuck yes," Gio's sister said. Her dark eyes said so much more.

Maddie felt a pang of regret. Not because of Falcone, but because this beautiful woman she cared about had been hurt because of her case. The mobster scum had weaseled his way into Elise's life, and her heart. Only to frame her for his crimes. She'd hurt her, too, although unintentionally.

Like Gio, Maddie suddenly kinda wanted to gut the fucker.

The Giovannis were her son's family, but weren't they hers, too?

She wanted them to be.

The idea wasn't for now, so she pushed it away. She needed to focus on wrapping up this case—finally.

Griggs squared eyes with Maddie. "Okay then, let's do it."

Gio grumbled something under his breath, but it wasn't intelligible.

"I'll make sure your sister's safe, Detective. You can bet on that." Her colleague stood with his arms on his utility belt, so confident with what was about to happen.

Maddie wanted to reach for Gio's hand, but kept hers on her lap, and her eyes on the table. She wanted to be included in this operation; maybe selfishly so. She hadn't broached the subject with Griggs yet, but *he* was running things, since Randall had removed her from the case.

Someone was going to have to disobey orders for her to participate, and her confidence that Roger Griggs would do so for her was a tossup. Trying to add Gio in, something he'd insist upon, might be the deciding, *hell no.*

They'd worked together many times in Chicago, but she didn't *really* consider him a friend. He was a colleague.

"Oh, don't worry about that." Gio crossed his arms. "I'll be there to do that, myself."

*Oh, here we go.*

Griggs frowned. "Granger, you on board with that?"

Surprise washed over her and she straightened. "I am, but LMVPD sure as hell won't be."

Gio snorted, but his mouth set in a hard line. He was projecting, '*I don't give a fuck,*' just like this morning.

Holy shit, was it only *that* morning?

Hours felt like days ago. An eternity.

Her Fitbit told her it was just past seven p.m. She'd wanted to check in with Jamie and Jake before her son's bedtime. She'd missed the window.

"She's not doing it if I'm not there." Gio grunted.

Elise's immediate protest died when Griggs raised a palm.

"I don't have issues with your presence. Just stay out of it, if only to save your job. Can you be an observer?"

Disagreement darted across his blue eyes, but Gio didn't speak. He lifted his chin, as if nodding would be giving in too much.

Maddie shook her head.

"Granger, you in?" Griggs asked.

Her eyes shot to his. "Randall's not gonna be down with that."

The marshal smiled; it took years off his stern expression, and his mustache twitched. "Randall's not *my* boss now, is he?"

She laughed.

Griggs was on loan from the Chicago office, so he was correct. He might be in charge of the taskforce in Maddie's stead, but his immediate supervisor was definitely *not* in Nevada.

"Forgiveness permission sitch?" she asked.

"Something like that." He nodded. "Besides, *you* did most of the legwork."

"Thanks, Griggs. I really appreciate it." Maddie smiled, and her body warmed to the guy. Maybe he was more friend than associate, after all.

"When are we doing this?" Elise asked.

"Tomorrow morning." Griggs gave a definitive nod. "We'll fit you with the wire in the morning, and go over what's next."

"Brief the team at seven?" Maddie asked.

"You got it. Meet you at *The Giovanni* at eight?"
"Sounds like showtime to me," Gio said.

None of Maddie and Gio's former teammates batted an eye when they showed up at the casino the next morning, and climbed right into the surveillance box truck parked outside the back entrance that lead right to the executive offices.

Garcia had even waved from his seat in front of the bank of monitors.

Half the team was posted in the truck; the other half were in nearby places, some in vehicles, and some outside. All watched, and all with earphones listening in.

Elise had already been briefed and was wired up, inside the building and ready to go. The test-talking she'd done to her receptionist had come to the truck loud and clear.

Before she'd gone inside, she'd slipped Griggs a keycard for the back door.

They were prepped and ready.

Maddie's heartrate was already faster than a patter, and she donned a Kevlar vest before trying to take a seat, but she only managed to be perched on the edge, her knee bobbed a-mile-a-minute while they waited.

Elise had told them her soon-to-be former fiancé usually graced the office with his presence about nine a.m., and he'd still been sleeping when she'd left their apartment.

Last night had been a long one, despite Gio by Maddie's side. She'd spent it in his arms at his place, after a call to Chicago. Stared at the ceiling more than slept, even though they'd burned off some energy christening his bed.

Jake had indeed been cajoled to sleep at the hotel Colt had taken them to, but she'd talked to her sister, promising Jamie the situation would soon be over.

Damn, she hoped she'd told her the truth; Falcone would go down quietly today and no one would be hurt.

Gio had come armed, of course, despite having given his duty weapon and badge to his boss. He wore his own vest, too.

She'd rolled her eyes when he'd told her not to ask any questions—plausible deniability and all that. "Yeah, right," Maddie whispered.

Randall could fire her for her involvement. But if this endeavor led to catching their man, he'd have to forgive her, right?

She blew out a breath. Sure as hell hoped so.

Since when had her job become nothing but hopes and prayers?

"Falcone's headed down the hallway," Inspector April Bailey said.

The small wall of monitors in the truck displayed cameras in and outside of the casino's executive suites. Evidently, they'd tapped into *The Giovanni's* security system.

Gio muscled his way to the microphone, but Garcia let him have control. "Lise, he's headed your way."

"*Thank you,*" Elise replied. Her voice came out of the speakers, strong and confident. "*I'm leaving my office for the conference room, then I'll go to his office. I hope people don't think I'm talking to myself.*"

Maddie smirked. "Tell her to put her phone to her ear, if she's worried about it."

"Or one of the in-house radios," Garcia said.

Gio rolled his eyes and grabbed the mic. "Remember, if the cockstain goes too far, just say '*big brother.*'"

Elise snickered. Maddie smiled.

She had a feeling if his sister appeared to be in distress, Gio would rush in, and the team would follow no matter what.

He wouldn't wait for any signal.

The exchange she had with Paul Allemand's forensic team was also transmitted with no issues; they could even hear the other people Elise interacted with in the conference room.

All good news.

The system would have no issues recording her conversation with Falcone.

She needed to get him to confess.

"He's in his office. She's headed there, now"

Garcia announced, but it wasn't necessary. Maddie's eyes were glued to the monitors in the truck.

"Showtime, Lise," Gio said into the microphone. "Be strong."

Elise nodded almost imperceptibly, from the screen.

"Kick his ass," she whispered.

Falcone was at his desk, sipping coffee and typing on his keyboard when Gio's sister opened the glass door.

The view of his office wasn't awesome, because the camera was in a high corner, showing most of the room, but not the whole thing, and there was a few seconds of transmission delay, so movement didn't necessarily match what they could hear through the wire.

However, seeing something was better than going in blind. They weren't always lucky to have visuals on a sting.

Falcone greeted Elise with a smile, from what Maddie could make out.

"What a skeeze," she whispered, and Garcia nodded his agreement.

"*Good morning, Marco,*" Elise said, with a slight emphasis on Falcone's alias.

"Relax, sis, don't blow it," Gio said, but he didn't transmit.

"*Is something wrong?*" Falcone leaned back in his chair, as if genuinely concerned and completely innocent.

Maddie rolled her eyes.

"*We need to talk about something I found.*"

Maddie admired that Elise made no move to sit. She was lording over the asshole and it was awesome.

"*What's that,* tesoro?"

"*Oh, you can cut the* 'tesoro' *crap.*"

"Good girl," Maddie said.

"Tone it down," Gio said into the microphone.

Falcone made no moves to stand, but his posture stiffened; it was visible even at their angle.

Alarm bells sounded in her head, and Maddie stood, shifting closer to Gio and Garcia in front of the monitors.

Elise was as hotheaded as her brother, so maybe the caution wasn't misplaced.

"*What's wrong?*" Falcone asked.

Elise slapped the manifest for the two hidden hard drives in front of him on the desk, then stepped back and perched her hands on her hips. "*Can you explain this?*"

Maddie wished she would've moved back one more step, so she could turn and flee the office with ease. She'd left the door open when she'd come in, so that was a good thing. Hopefully Elise was thinking of her escape route, if necessary.

"*These are my private records.*"

Maddie had to give it to him; Falcone had delivered the statement without a flinch or delay.

"*Private records?*"

"*Yes, some documents I needed to keep safe, but they have nothing to do with casino. I'm sorry I didn't tell you. I shouldn't have used Giovanni servers without permission. I should've let you know.*"

"Damn, the fucker even sounds sincere," Garcia muttered.

*"You have got to be kidding me,"* Elise spat.

Falcone froze. He still didn't stand, but his shoulders were tense and he didn't speak, either. As if he was waiting for the other shoe to drop, just like the watching taskforce.

*"I cannot believe I fell for this shit for nine months. You're one smooth son of a bitch, you know that?"* she demanded.

"Shit, this is going south," Garcia said. "We should get ready to go in."

"Not yet," Griggs ordered.

"Let's see what he says," Bailey agreed.

Gio was on edge.

He'd backed away from the microphone, and moved toward the closed double doors. He was going to storm the castle in a few seconds.

He wasn't even official law enforcement, so he couldn't go in alone.

Maddie moved behind him, grabbing his arm. "Wait, Gio."

"That fucking temper of hers is going to get her killed. I knew this was a horrible idea. I'm going in." He paused. More talking came from the speaker.

It was louder, so someone must've turned the volume up.

*"Tesoro, calm down. What're you talking about?"* For the first time, Falcone's voice had gone up an octave, revealing his alarm.

*"They have nothing to do with the casino all right,*

*because they're records of all the money you laundered, Gian Falcone."*

Maddie opened her mouth to retort, but when Gio was right, he was right.

"Son of a bitch!" he hollered.

Gio was already running toward the back door, when Griggs yelled, "Go, go, go!"

K<br>♥

Gio had his gun drawn and was through the door before he even heard footfalls behind him.

His sister had better hope the cockstain didn't kill her, because he wanted to do it himself.

People screeched and scattered when they made entry, and rushed down the hallway to the executive suites. All the walls and doors were glass, so they had an audience regardless.

He didn't know who was with him, save Maddie, but he didn't care, either. He needed to get to his sister before she got hurt—or worse.

Just one more corner to round, and they were there.

Alarm rolled over Gio before he skidded to a halt; the glass walls allowed *him* a view, too.

Maddie was at his side, and they stopped in tandem on either side of the office doorway, both their weapons up at-the-ready.

His sister, dressed in one of her typical rides-the-line of businesses-appropriate attire was plastered to Falcone's torso behind the desk, and the bastard had a knife to her throat.

What the hell had happened to make him go from passive arguer to *this*?

When had he grabbed his sister up?

*Fuck.*

"Let me go, you asshole!" Elise struggled. She continued raising her voice, cursing him to hell and back.

"Be still, *tesoro*," Falcone taunted. "Or I'll cut that delectate throat of yours." He proved he meant business, and nicked the tender flesh under her chin with the tip of the blade.

Blood dripped down her pale skin.

His sister gasped, and went stalk-still in his grip.

"Give me another excuse to put a bullet in your brainless skull," Gio growled.

The problem was he couldn't get a clean shot; the fucker kept shifting behind Elise.

Falcone knew the game they played.

"Let her go," Maddie ordered. "And you don't have to die today."

Falcone chuckled. "Oh, I won't be the one dying today."

Their teammates all filed in behind them, in formation and waiting.

Watching.

Guns cleared holsters and were aimed.

From his peripheral vision, he caught the nod Griggs threw him.

Looked like the lead marshal was going to let him do his thing, despite the caution last night of him staying out of the way to save his job. Not like Gio would back off now anyway. He'd deal with Patton and Olinsky consequences later.

This was his sister. In danger.

"Cuffs are better than a bullet," Maddie said. "Less permanent."

Falcone shook his fat head.

Too bad it wasn't fat enough for Gio to get a damn clean shot. He wouldn't risk hitting his sister.

"This didn't have to go like this," Cockstain started. "I would've really married you, you know. You had to be a fucking nosy bitch, didn't you?" Falcone ranted and raved, sticking his sister a little bit with every word. "Too smart for your own fucking good. Why couldn't you have just believed me? It could've been good. You're a great fuck. We're compatible. It would've worked out."

Elise didn't move a muscle. She had several bleeding cuts on her neck now.

"Mads, you got a shot?" Gio asked as low as he could manage.

"Nope. You?"

"Shit."

"If you get one, take it," Maddie said in the same low tone.

*With pleasure.*

Falcone was still yelling, and cutting his sister, spittle gathering at the corners of his mouth and flying. "We could've run this place together. Run it, and *owned* it. The whole thing should've been mine. It's supposed to be mine. Mine! Just like you!"

"The only thing that's yours is my next bullet," Gio

said.

"Elise, duck!"

His sister obeyed Maddie's order, at the same time the *bang* reverberated in his ears.

Falcone didn't go down, but he did drop the knife, only to clutch his left shoulder.

Elise came running toward them, but the cockstain was on her heels.

"You bitch!" he yelled, but this time his anger was aimed at Maddie. "Your son is dead, now. You hear me?"

Gio stepped in front of Falcone and rammed the butt of his Glock in the fucker's face. The little backup gun was smaller than his duty weapon, but it did the trick just fine.

The asshole went down like a sack of bricks, sprawled spread-eagle in the hallway, on his back.

He leaned down, staring into fluttering dark eyes.

Blood ran from Falcone's nose like a faucet.

"Don't fuck with my sister or my son."

"I don't need to get checked out," Elise complained. Gio tilted her chin up to examine her neck. The cuts were all superficial and had stopped bleeding.

"Maddie, talk some sense into him."

They made eye contact.

"I'm fine," she insisted.

Maddie smiled as she approached. "I'm so glad you're fine. Gio, leave her alone. She's a tough girl."

He growled, but took a step back so his sister could throw her arms around Maddie.

"You saved my life!" Elise settled her hands on her upper arms and squeezed, when she pulled back. "Thank you so much."

"If you hadn't run your damn mouth, it wouldn't have gone down like that," Gio grumbled.

Elise cast her eyes down, and bit her bottom lip. When she glanced up, she had the decency to appear sheepish.

Maddie bit back a laugh. "She was just exercising her Giovanni-ness."

"Yeah, you know, apple, tree and all that. Sibling peas in a pod?" Elise beamed.

He shot both of them visual daggers.

Griggs approached then, concern and exhaustion in his expression. "Has the dust settled over here?"

"Just about," Maddie said.

"Are you okay, Miss Giovanni?"

"Yes, sir. Thank you."

"Thank you for today, and I'm glad you're okay," the marshal said. He smiled, and didn't seem so tired.

"Falcone make it to the hospital yet?" Gio asked.

Griggs rolled his eyes and Maddie smirked.

She wouldn't have thought her colleague capable.

"Whined all the way. 'Do you know who I am? You're all in for a serious law suit,' blah, blah. Wish you would've knocked him out, Detective."

Gio chuckled. "Detective? Nah, not today. Just concerned big brother."

"I can't imagine what that report is gonna have to look like," Maddie said.

"What d'you mean, Granger? You're in charge here." Griggs winked and laughed. His mustache twitched with his amusement. Then he walked away.

"Perfect." Maddie shrugged.

Gio offered a soft smile and slid his arms around her shoulders. "Don't worry, Mads, I'll help you clean up the mess."

"What help is a suspended cop gonna be?"

"Hopefully, Randall's not a yeller, like Olinsky and Patton."

Maddie sighed. "Elise, are you really okay?"

She nodded and offered a small smile. "I'm glad I could get revenge on that fucker. Does this mean it's all put to bed? Dad and I are free and clear?"

"There'll be some red tape, but we'll get it figured out."

"Promise," Gio said.

"When do I get to meet my nephew?"

Maddie looked at Gio; he was looking right back at her. "Soon. I'll let the marshals protecting them know it's safe for them to come back to Vegas."

"So, you're sticking around?" Elise asked.

"Planning on it, if today didn't get my ass fired." She grimaced.

Gio tugged her tighter to his side. "You'd better not; we both can't be unemployed badasses." He winked.

Maddie cringed. "Don't even joke about that."

"C'mon, Randall has to recognize your prowess. You got the bad guy, and I'm sure Griggs will help."

She was back to hoping and praying.

"Let's go get our kid, then you can worry about the 'splainin' you gotta do."

"Hey, Dad?"

"Yeah, champ?"

"How come you don't live with us?"

Maddie paused with her hand on her bedroom doorknob. She could hear their voices, but they wouldn't be able to see her where she was—down the hallway and around the corner. Her pulse quickened.

How was Gio going to answer?

When she'd left them moments before to get dressed, Jake had been eating breakfast and Gio had been sitting across from him sipping coffee. Since the apartment had an open floor plan, sound carried.

"C'mere, buddy."

There was a screech, probably her son scooting his chair back. Then the hurried pattering of bare feet, so he must've rounded the small breakfast table.

She crept forward, chiding herself.

Maddie should make her presence known, but she wanted to see how her lover would handle a serious conversation with their seven-year-old.

Jake was Gio's as much as he was hers, and the

man *wanted* to be in the little boy's life.

Too bad she wasn't clear on where *she* fit into that.

Their case might be over, but they hadn't put...perimeters on their relationship.

Her chest burned.

She needed more than sex, as much as she was a fan of him rocking her world.

Maddie loved him; as much as she loved his son.

Over the last week, Gio had retreated a little bit, and she was torn between respecting him and demanding why.

Randall hadn't fired her, or even suspended her, but Maddie had had to endure the disappointment in his dark serious gaze, a lecture about following orders, as well as *all* the red tape that'd been associated with her case.

She had been put back 'in charge.' Griggs hadn't just been giving her shit.

He'd covered for Gio, though, so as far as LMVPD was concerned, he hadn't been at the casino that day in any law enforcement capacity. His name would be in the report as a witness, and he'd been there to see his sister.

The Giovannis were officially cleared of money laundering, and the federal prosecutor was going to indict Falcone.

Everything was going to work itself out. She was staying in Vegas, Jake and Jamie were settled, and he'd told her he wanted to be a part of their lives, not just Jake's.

*So what gives?*

Gio had stopped sleeping over about a week ago. Last night, he'd kissed the crap out of her, then promised he'd be back the next morning to spend the day with them.

He'd shown up at eight with gourmet coffee and donuts when she'd been making scrambled eggs and bacon.

She inched as far as she could go to remain unseen.

Maddie could hear the hum of them speaking, and didn't want to miss a word.

Jake talked about his friend from his new school, and how the kid's dad was his baseball coach. Gio said something, then they fell silent for a second.

"How come, Dad? I want you to live with us."

Leave it to her son to not fall for a subject change — and it seemed Gio had tried.

"It's complicated, champ." He sounded breathless, like he'd sighed.

She pictured Jake in Gio's arms and her heart skipped. She'd seen the like since they'd met, of course, but it always made her melt inside. Their son had become attached to Gio at light-speed. She'd kill the man herself if he broke his heart. Hers was already destined to be shattered, wasn't it?

Maddie couldn't fix both of them.

But...was that her fear talking?

Was she afraid to give *them* a real chance?

Hadn't Gio been awesome all this time? With her *and* Jake. Individually, as much as together.

"What does that mean?" Jake asked.

"Uh..."

*Gio, don't blow it.*

God, he was probably about to call her to save him from an answer. She closed her eyes and waited for her name.

It didn't happen.

"Me and Mommy…need to work some things out before that can happen."

Maddie pictured Jake's innocent face and those big blue eyes widening and trying to comprehend what his father was trying to explain.

"Is it my fault?"

Her eavesdropping resolve cracked; she needed to go out there.

Her man was there to save the day.

"No way, champ! Never."

Jake giggled, and she didn't know what Gio had done, maybe a tickle, or ruffled his hair.

She still hadn't found time for a haircut for him, and he needed one. They'd been back in Vegas for almost two weeks, and case wrap-up had kept her in the office late almost every day.

"I love Mommy."

"I love her, too, big guy. And I love you."

Jake's voice sounded far away as he enthusiastically returned the love Gio had just declared.

Her head spun. Her tightening chest churned her heart into overdrive until it rebounded off her ribs.

*Holy. Shit.*

Had Gio said that for Jake's benefit?

*It can't…be true?*

Maddie had fallen for him hard and fast eight years ago, but then, he'd never told her he felt anything other than lust, or how hot she was, how desperate he was to have her.

The now-sex was just as intense, but for Gio, feeling words were never present. She, on the other hand, had struggled *not* to tell him she loved him.

God help her, she *did*.

The stupid man told their son how he felt about her *before* he told her?

She crushed her eyes shut and ordered her breathing to normalize.

He must've said it for Jake's benefit.

It couldn't be true.

Could it?

Maddie clenched her jaw to keep the agony at bay. She didn't *want* to be right.

She wanted Gio's words to be true.

The night she'd told him he'd been too drunk to remember hearing she was pregnant, they'd both admitted there *had* been love there eight years ago. On both sides.

Was his confession now simply an echo of that?

She inhaled and held it until her lungs burned, then hurried back to her room and slipped inside silently.

Maddie panted as if she'd climbed a mountain, and dashed into the bathroom. Needed to get ahold of herself before she could face the two males that meant the most to her in the world.

Her eyes were puffy, so she splashed water on her

face and patted dry with a hand towel. It was Saturday, so she hadn't bothered with makeup, but she almost wanted to grab some to disguise the emotion printed all over her face.

When Maddie left the bedroom again, she intentionally shut the door loudly so they'd hear her coming. "Jake, are you done eating? Wash your plate, please," she projected on purpose.

Two sets of very blue eyes landed on her as she hit the end of the hallway, and they both smiled.

*Damn, they even have the same smile.*

God really must be testing her.

Her heart stuttered all over again. Jake was indeed on Gio's lap, tucked against his chest, and her man's arms were around their son. They were so comfortable with each other, as if they hadn't met less than a month before.

*Why do I feel like the odd man out?*

She almost wished Jamie hadn't had to catch the early shift at that ridiculous job of hers. There was a show at eleven, and she'd had to be in by nine, but she headed out before eight, saying she was meeting new friends for coffee.

*Lucky brat.*

Maddie told herself to stop freaking out. This was what she'd dreamed of—Gio and Jake together and *happy*.

No, she'd dreamed of the *three* of them together, being a family. Four of them, really, since her sister was a fixture in her household.

The dream was before her now, wasn't it?

"Mads, somethin' wrong?" Gio asked as Jake scrambled off his lap and went to put his plate in the sink.

"Can I have a donut now? Daddy said they were for me!"

She ignored the man she loved. "Uh, did you eat all your eggs and bacon?"

The little boy nodded.

"Just one, okay? Brush your teeth when you're done."

"Yes!" He jumped up and down, then ran to the kitchen counter.

Gio leaned forward and grabbed her hand.

That was funny, she didn't remember entering the living room.

"Mads, what's wrong?" He kept his voice low, probably for their son's benefit, but Jake was stuffing a cake donut with blue frosting into his mouth.

"Nothing." She shook her head for effect.

Gio's brow furrowed, but he didn't contradict her.

"That was yummy!" their son announced, with blue stains all around his mouth.

"Ugh, you look like you ate a smurf!" Maddie ruffled his hair when he giggled. "We have got to get you a haircut, bud."

"I'll take him," Gio said.

Jake pin-balled from her to his dad and back. "I wanna go with Dad!"

"Oh, that's okay, I can take him."

"I want to. I bet my barber has time this morning."

"I want a haircut just like my dad!"

Maddie sighed. "Of course you do."

Gio smirked, and Jake echoed his expression, blue mouth and all. They looked so much alike, even then.

"Well, before you take one step out of this house, you need to wash your face, brush your teeth and get dressed."

"Now?" Jake asked.

"Now," Gio said.

The little boy's eyes lit up and he scooted down the hallway.

His chuckle brought her attention back to his face, but Maddie didn't want meet his eyes.

"Thanks, but you really don't have to take him."

"He's *my* kid, too, so I do." Gio stood and naturally, her eyes followed until she was peering up at him. He took her hands, bringing one to his mouth and pressing a kiss into her knuckles. "I don't know why you don't want to tell me, and I won't push you, but something *is* bothering you."

She cleared her throat and tried not to show her surprise. Her rebuttal about Jake's haircut dissolved. "I'm good."

He stared, but didn't call her on her bullshit. "I thought we were good."

"We are."

Gio's gaze burned until Maddie *had* to avert her eyes.

"Mads."

When she didn't respond, he tugged her into his arms.

Her palms landed on his pecs and she didn't push

away.

Maybe she couldn't.

Gio dipped down, pausing for a second, but she made no move to escape.

Maddie met his mouth and opened for him, even as he was shoving his tongue against her lips, demanding entry.

Moving into the kiss and letting him deepen it felt natural. Pressing her body closer, and letting the physical—his feel, his taste—take over filled her fuzzy mind with a temporary peace. The flavors of sugar from a glazed donut and coffee, as well as his normal, just-Gio appeal swept her away.

She didn't need to think. Didn't want to, either.

Desire simmered below the surface when Gio broke the kiss. Maddie whimpered a protest.

"Easy." One corner of his mouth shot up as he rested his forehead against hers. "Always so hot. So responsive. But I don't need a boner when I'm about to take my kid out in public."

Her brain was foggy, and took a moment to catch up. "Sorry," she blurted.

He chuckled, and she liked how it vibrated against her breasts.

"Don't be sorry. It just shows me how much you're mine."

That instantly sobered her, and Maddie blinked. She wanted to look anywhere but *at* him. However, her gaze was glued to his against her will.

"There's that worried look again."

"Worried?"

"Yeah, you're freaked out." Gio brushed a sweet kiss to her mouth, and cupped her cheek. "I can't guess what's going on in that head of yours, but if you want to talk, I'm here. That's the thing I want you to remember."

"What?"

He dragged his thumb down her cheek and across her lips. "I'm *here*, Mads. I'm not going anywhere."

"I'm ready!" Jake announced.

Maddie jumped.

Gio kissed her forehead and gently released her. "All right, champ. Let's go on our men-only outing."

"Yes!" Her son pumped his little arm.

"Say goodbye to your mom."

"Bye, Mom!" Jake waved, only a few feet from the front door.

For some reason, it snapped her back into her own skin. "I don't think so, bud. Come hug me, and I want to inspect your cleanup job."

With an overdramatic sigh only a seven-year-old boy and a teenage girl could perfect, Jake's little shoulders caved in and he lumbered to her as if she'd asked him to bury a body.

Maddie let it slide and cupped his cheeks. "Teeth."

He rolled his eyes — *thanks, Jamie* — but obeyed.

"No smurf in sight." She made a loud smacking kiss on his cheek, but her son grinned instead of making the face she'd expected.

"Love you, Mom."

"Love you, too, buddy. Behave for your dad."

Gio winked on their way out the door, promising

to take them out for lunch when the mission-haircut was accomplished.

Maddie stared at the door, rubbing her arm.

He'd said he wasn't going anywhere.

He *kept* saying it.

How long would it last?

Maddie paced. Gnawed her thumbnail. She should use the unexpected alone time to go over her official statement one last time, but she was blowing the time on obsessing over the eavesdropped conversation.

Not to mention Gio's vow.

The federal prosecutor on the case, as well as the team working on the Cesare Fratelli trial wanted full disclosure, so they could compare notes, and she still had tons of work to do. She probably owed Special Agent Grey another call, too.

Funny, how easily Griggs had relinquished her command. The jerk had gotten out of a lot of the paperwork.

Her mind spun in a chaos of foolish hope, back to calling herself an idiot.

Gio had been so great that weekend they'd spent as a family, before the chaos of getting removed from the case, the threat to her son's life, and Elise showing up with the hard drives.

Then the takedown, and now…they were settled in Vegas, she was starting a new investigation on

Monday.

Gio had pulled back.

He'd been inching away little by little, and it'd been driving her crazy; not to mention left her with blue balls.

They'd had sex a few times, but not like when she'd first arrived, and him not spending the night was confusing the hell out of her.

Gio was still great with their son, of course, but what about her?

Hadn't he declared he wanted to be a part of *her* life, too? What if he didn't mean *permanently*?

The confusion only sky-rocketed when he'd kiss her like he had before they'd left—and last night, too—then said he was there for good.

If he was there for good, why had he been so…distant?

The push and pull spun her into havoc.

What the fuck did it all mean?

She believed he'd always be Team-Jake, but what about Team-Maddie?

Maddie sighed and yanked her ponytail. First thing this morning, Gio had chided her for the up hairstyle; said he loved her natural waves free and flowing.

What did she want? Expect?

*Gio.*

In her life. In her bed.

Forever.

His ring on her finger, his last name behind hers. Behind Jake's.

She closed her eyes and told herself to breathe as her vision spun all over again. Refused to cry.

Things were good with them; who cared if he'd backed away, slowed things down without talking to her about it?

It didn't mean things were off track, did it?

Tears cascaded and she called herself an even bigger fool.

Her cellphone rang and she jolted. Answering was rote, and she didn't check to see who was calling. "Granger."

Silence greeted her for a split-second.

"Mads?"

"Yeah?" The word came out choked, so she subtly cleared her throat.

"Are you…crying?" Gio all but demanded.

She forced a laugh. "Yeah, silly me. Watching a sad movie. Wasting my time, really, since I should be doing more case wrap-up."

Again, he was quiet.

Nico Giovanni could see right through her, even over the phone. Would he call her on her BS?

He cleared his throat. "Well, I just wanted to give you a heads up we're about done. Wanted a feel about lunch…grab food and come back or did you want to go out?"

"We can go out." The sentence was rushed, and Maddie winced. She was effing up this call, for sure. Dreaded looking into his sapphire eyes when they got back. If he could tell she was lying over the phone, looking at him would *doom* her.

"Maddie."

Her name was all warning.

"Gio." She returned, going for the same tone. Failing miserably.

"You know, eventually you'll blurt it out. You always do."

"What?"

"Whatever the hell crawled up your ass." This was half-irritated, half-exasperated, and *all* Gio.

"Hey, watch your mouth around Jake. Jamie already has him saying '*dammit*'."

"You never could keep a secret from me," he continued as if she hadn't spoken.

*Except Jake.*

Maddie wouldn't say that, even joking.

She wouldn't keep secrets from him. Really didn't need to.

*He doesn't know I love him.*

She was doing okay with *that* secret, right?

"Maddie?"

She jolted and rolled her eyes. "I'm here. Just contemplating...you." She cursed that bit of truth.

He laughed. "I don't know if that's good or bad."

*Neither do I.*

"Anyways, let's go out to lunch. Jake said he wanted burgers last night." Maddie prayed she sounded normal, even. *And* that Gio would leave off the inquisition.

"All right."

"Good, see you guys when you get back." Her thumb hovered over the red *end* circle.

"Mads."

The nickname made her pause and put the phone back to her ear. "Yeah?"

"We're not done with whatever you're not telling me."

She didn't bother outright denying it. "I didn't think you'd leave me alone. But you're being silly. I'm good."

"Right. Well, just so you know, we'll never be done."

Gio beat her to ending the call.

Maddie cursed like she never could when Jake was around.

K<br>♥

Gio wrapped Jake's small hand in his, and his son grinned up at him. He couldn't help the upturn of his mouth, too.

Last week, he'd finally got his hair cut, returning to the neatness of a trimmed back and sides, just a little on top, and now the seven-year-old was truly his miniature.

Maddie was going to be blown away with how much they looked alike.

His Mads…

Something was upsetting her, and he'd get her to tell him; hopefully before the diamond ring he'd had with him every day for over a week — since the day after they'd slapped metal bracelets on Gian Falcone's wrists — burned a hole in his pocket.

He'd been trying to find the right time.

Gio hadn't planned on waiting, and the conversation that morning with Jake had spurred him on. The kid wanted them to live together as much as he wanted it.

He would've asked her the night Elise had given him their mom's ring, but since the conclusion of the case, Maddie had been...weird.

She'd withdrawn. Had been stiff with him, and he'd lost his nerve.

She wouldn't say no, right?

Before Jake and Jamie had come back to Vegas, Gio had made the decision to do things right. Stop the sleepovers until he and Maddie had a serious "them" talk, but then the chaos of the case had happened. Not to mention the threat on Jake's life. Time had never manifested for it.

He was trying to respect her, until she was his wife, but her behaviors weren't encouraging.

They hadn't had enough sex, either. Not nearly enough. It killed him to keep his hands to himself.

Elise kept asking him if he'd proposed yet. His sister had been hounding him, really. It was good to see she still adored Maddie and wanted them to be together. His sister's blessing meant the world to him.

"Dad, when will I see Aunt Elise and my uncles again?" Jake asked, tugging him free of his hand as they got to the GTO.

"Soon, champ. Aunt Elise wants you to come over tomorrow."

"I wanna see Uncle Dom, too. He's cool!"

Gio wanted to roll his eyes. Of course, his kid

would be intrigued with the black sheep.

His brothers had been stunned to learn he had a son, but both had accepted Jake with hugs and huge welcomes. Considering their dad's degrading condition, maybe they all needed something family-related to cheer on.

The kid had warmed to all three of them, but Elise had taken to the boy more than the guys. Or in a different way, perhaps. Jake was just as entranced with his aunt, and no doubt she was going to spoil the shit out of him to no end.

"I'm sure you will, soon."

Dom was still leery of him, and they had a little mending left to fully repair their relationship.

He wouldn't push the guy. His gut told him Dom needed to come to him, but Gio was glad his brother hadn't taken his ire out on Jake.

"I can see Uncle Sam at Aunt Jamie's work, huh?"

His youngest brother was in his last semester at the University of Arizona, and he did the majority of his classes online. He'd already been working at the casino part time, but Elise had just promoted him. Sam was now the Entertainment Manager, or some shit, and he was running all the show schedules and whatever came with it. It was out of Gio's wheelhouse, so who the hell knew. No matter what was involved, Sam would excel; he always did.

Damn good thing their sister hadn't given that job to Dom; the middle child would've tried to screw all the dancers.

"Yeah, I guess so, bud. Not that your mom would

want you running around with showgirls." He winked.

Jake wrinkled his little nose. "What's a showgirl?"

Gio smirked. "Your Aunt Jamie's new job." Much to Maddie's chagrin.

"But she's a dancer."

"Yup, that too."

"Mommy doesn't like it. Said she needs to make something more of her life. Is being a dancer bad?"

"You know what, champ? That's something you should ask your mom."

Jake nodded seriously, and Gio had a hard time not groaning. Although, overhearing Maddie try to explain it might be entertaining, too.

He could hear her calling him a coward in his head.

"Are we picking Mom up for lunch?"

"You bet."

"Yay!"

He chuckled at the kid's fist-pump.

# Chapter
## THIRTY TWO

Maddie had mostly pulled herself together by the time her boys got back to the apartment and she met them in the parking lot to go to lunch.

When they were done, after the ice cream dessert upon Jake's insistence, she couldn't really take Gio's soulful silence and questioning eyes anymore.

"What?" she demanded in a loud whisper.

Their son had run to his room for something he wanted to show his dad, and God knew the kid wouldn't be gone long enough for an argument.

"What?" Gio parroted, arching a one dark eyebrow.

She growled in her throat and narrowed her eyes. "You've been staring at me all day. What's your problem?"

He smirked, and she cursed the fact it was so damn sexy.

"I told you before we left; *you're* the one that seems to have a problem with me. Just waiting for you to out it, is all."

Maddie prayed for patience not to throttle him.

She needed to breathe through her irritation, because she just might blurt the overheard confession.

That would be a bad thing, wouldn't it?

"Come sit with me. Let's have a real conversation." He slid onto the couch, and patted the cushion next to him.

She crossed her arms over her breasts and stayed in the kitchen.

Gio had to crane his neck to make eye contact over his shoulder. "At least I know he comes by it naturally."

"What?"

"You're too stubborn for your own good, just like your kid."

Maddie tried not to smile. "So, now he's just *my* kid?"

His mouth—so damn kissable—curved in a lazy, sexy smile. "Will you just freaking come here, already?"

"You're getting better at not cussing."

Gio's smile slid into a grin. "It's hard as hell."

"Heck," Maddie supplied, but she inched over to the sofa.

His big hand swallowed her wrist, and he pulled her down.

She landed half on him, half beside him, and it took all she was made of to pin to her brain their son was down the hallway, and she *could not* climb on Gio's lap and have her way with him.

Besides, she was mad at him, right?

He helped her straighten, and slung his arm around her shoulders. Plastered her to his side.

His warmth seeped into her, and her tummy

wobbled at the same time her heart skipped. Maddie bit her bottom lip.

"Wanna tell me what's bothering you?" he whispered.

She shook her head.

"Why not?"

"Because..."

"Mads..."

"I heard you, okay?" Her cheeks heated, half from embarrassment, half from her libido.

"Heard me?"

Why did his eyes have to be so damn blue?

She sniffled and tried to avert her eyes, but something wouldn't let her.

"Heard me what?" Gio prompted.

"You told Jake you love me." Her vision blurred and she *really* wanted look away.

"I do." Confusion crossed his expression. "Why're you crying?"

Maddie shook her head, then closed her eyes when he brushed his mouth lightly over hers. Shivers danced down her spine. "You're a big jerk."

"I am?" He reared back, arching an eyebrow again, like he had minutes before.

"You're so damn confusing! You pull away from me. Stop sleeping over. Barely touch me. I thought...I thought... Then you tell our son you love me, but..." She had to pant to breathe, and her tears spilled over. "But you've never said those words to me."

Gio thumbed them away, then closed his eyes. "I'm a fucking idiot, is what I am."

Maddie gave a half-laugh. "I certainly won't disagree."

"I'm so sorry, Mads. There was a method to my madness, really."

"What?"

"I wanted to do things right."

"Meaning?"

"I want to be with you and Jake, but I didn't want to confuse him with the back-and-forth, with the sleepovers, so I thought..." He sighed and shook his head.

"You being here is doing things right." Her bottom lip wobbled, but Maddie sucked in a relieved breath. What he'd said made sense. "I wish you would've said something. It would've saved me tons of turmoil."

"Turmoil?"

She nodded. "I've been a mess inside since you've been so distant."

Gio shook his head. "You've been really weird."

Their gazes locked and held, then they both laughed.

"Can I start over?" he whispered.

Maddie nodded again, because she didn't think she could speak.

"I love you, Madison Granger. I fell for you when I was a hotheaded little shit, eight long years ago and I never stopped loving you. You gave me a son I couldn't love more than I do. I'm going to love you both for the rest of my life." He gently pushed off the couch, and knelt in front of her, digging something out of his pocket.

"Gio…" she sputtered. "What're…what're you doing?"

Gio flipped open a little black box, and Maddie hiccupped.

"Mads, will you marry me?"

Her vision wouldn't clear. She swiped at her cheeks but more tears came. "How…how can you ask me that?"

"What?" He blinked, and licked his bottom lip, as if he was nervous.

"I haven't even told you I love you, yet."

Gio's shock melted away, and he grinned. "You just did. Besides, I already I know."

"You do?" She cocked her head to one side.

"Jake said he heard you tell Jamie."

Maddie's own bark of laughter shocked her, and she shook her head. "I'm gonna kill that kid!"

"Mom, will you tell him yes already, so I can come out of my room?" Jake's voice was filled with exasperation.

Her gaze locked with Gio's. "Did you tell him?"

He shook his head; the surprise on his face was genuine.

The moment might've been broken, but somehow it was still perfect.

Maddie laughed again, despite the tears still wetting her cheeks. "Yes, Nico Giovanni, I'll marry you. And, yes, I do love you. I've loved you for as long as you've loved me."

Gio pushed off the floor and crushed her against his chest. He covered her mouth with his and kissed her until her whole body was jelly, and she wished like hell they were alone.

"I love you so damn much," he whispered against her lips.

"I love you, too."

His hand shook as he pushed the gorgeous cluster of diamonds on her left hand's ring finger. "This was my mom's, and I think she would've loved you to have it."

"Oh, Gio."

Jake hopped down the hallway, a silly grin on his face. He threw himself at them, and they laughed as they caught him up together. "We're gonna get married?"

Maddie laughed again, wiping her tears away for the last time — she hoped. "Yes, buddy, we're gonna get married." Joy filled her heart, pushing into every inch of her body. She hugged Jake and Gio as tight as she could.

"Champ, how did you know I was going to ask Mom to marry me?"

"Aunt Elise told me she gave you Grandma's ring."

Gio and Maddie exchanged a glance and laughed again.

Jake was either going to be a therapist or a detective when he grew up. People seemed to volunteer information, as much as he successfully eavesdropped it.

"I'll be damned," Gio whispered, shaking his head.

Maddie threw him a death look for the cuss word,

even if it was minor.

"Hey, Mommy."

"What, bud?"

"What's a showgirl?"

She tossed her fiancé another black glare, but he just threw his head back and laughed.

Gio had to tell himself he wasn't really a pussy. Over and over he had to chant it, and it wasn't doing shit.

Maddie squeezed his hand and he shot her a grateful look.

He had to take a breath.

Then another.

He counted, and when he got to ten, his chest loosened, but only a little.

Jake had his other hand and was smiling up at him.

He told himself to nut up.

"It'll be okay," the love of his life whispered.

*No, it really won't be.*

He couldn't say it out loud. His voice had packed bags and moved the fuck out.

"Do you want us to go in with you?" Maddie asked.

Gio nodded.

"Dad, it'll be okay," Jake echoed. "Aunt Elise said Grandpa want to see us."

He had to close his eyes.

*Fuck. Me.*

His freaking seven-year-old was reassuring him.

How could he face guys with AK-47s and mobsters with a knife to his sister's throat, but he couldn't walk down the hallway of a hospital to see a sick old man?

Maybe he really was a pussy.

"What the hell—heck—am I supposed to say to him?" he croaked.

Maddie's smile was soft. Sweet. Loving.

Damn, he needed it.

"Start with hello."

Such a simple suggestion. Could he even do that?

They headed down the wide corridor, people passing; nurses, patient techs, family members of other patients, and even an older man clutching an IV pole. He was dressed in a johnny and hobbling along.

Muttering voices and calls for doctors on loudspeakers tuned out along the walk of fear. The closer they got, the more Gio saw a glow of light around the doorframe of the room at the end of the hallway. Like a spotlight, calling to him.

Or was it repelling him?

He halted when they were about five feet away. "I can't do this."

Maddie slipped her hand from his and came around to face him. Her soft warm palms cupped his cheeks.

Gio couldn't peer anywhere but into her beautiful hazel eyes.

"You can."

Jake tugged on his hand. "It's okay, Daddy."

He met the eyes so like his own, then hauled the

kid into his arms as if he was a baby. Hell, the kid was stronger than him already.

He drew Maddie against his chest with his other arm.

None of them spoke through their group hug moment. An odd peace settled over him as he held his wife and son. The rhinoceros lifted off his chest and he inhaled a big breath that stretched his lungs.

The astringent hospital smells permeated his senses and he set his son to his feet.

"Thanks," he whispered.

"That's what family's for," Maddie whispered back.

Jake retook his hand and they entered room 305 together.

Elise and Sam had left a few minutes before, so they could have privacy with Big Tony, but Gio wished all three of his siblings were there right now.

He didn't feel alone, since he had Maddie and Jake by his side, but he felt…incomplete. And so damn guilty. It swirled in his gut and made him want to puke.

He blinked when his vision wavered, but he told himself there was just something in his eyes.

It was so fucking hard, seeing his father in that bed.

Big Tony sat up and smiled.

The bastard had the nerve to smile at him? Gio didn't know whether to scream or run.

"Hi, Grandpa!" Jake tugged free of his hold and rushed to the old man's bedside.

It wasn't their first meeting; his sister had been the first to introduce the two, because Gio hadn't been able to, even after he'd married Maddie in a small ceremony at the casino's chapel.

All his siblings had been present that day two weeks ago, even Dom.

Jamie had been Maddie's Maid of Honor, and Sam had been Gio's Best Man. His brother had walked her sister down the aisle.

Maddie hadn't worn a traditional dress, but it'd been short, tight and off white, and he'd wanted to strip it off her right then and there. She'd been so hot. So *his*.

Dom had walked her to him, even though he was still irked at Gio. But walking his bride down the aisle proved that at least to Gio, his brother was open to repairing their relationship.

Jake, of course, had been their little ring bearer, but he'd been so ecstatic his parents were getting married, he'd darted like a bullet, and everyone had laughed.

Hell, Gio had even invited Hector Garcia. The guy had been all grins, and *I-told-you-so's*.

Despite his beef with his father, he'd regretted that the man hadn't been able to be there. Of course, Elise had used the casino's best cinematographer to record it all, so Big Tony could watch it.

His sister had told him their father had praised Maddie's beauty and grace.

What about *him*?

Big Tony looked up from his grandson, and their gazes collided.

His father's dark eyes—so like Elise and Dom's— were clear and pain-free, something that was a bit of an oddity lately. The doctors had told them the bad news just the day before.

Dad was stage four, and it wouldn't be long now. Chemo and radiation wouldn't fix it, even if he'd agree; which he still wouldn't.

Pancreatic cancer had a high mortality rate even when caught early, and his father had ignored it for months, so his sister had said.

Gio had to bite his bottom lip.

Maybe he *was* a pussy.

He cleared his throat so he wouldn't lose it.

Maddie still clung to his right hand, and her body heat at his side gave him strength.

His feet froze just inside the door. He was fucking afraid to approach the bed. Yup, he might as well pack his shit and move to Pussyville.

"C'mon," Maddie whispered. She tugged his arm, and somehow his feet obeyed.

"Hi, Dad." The words breeched his lips and Gio fought and honest-to-God sob.

His father had always been a mountain.

To see him so small…fragile between the rails of the adjustable hospital bed hit him like a dagger to the gut, spreading regret and guilt all over him.

Gio needed to sit, before he slid to the floor on his ass.

His kid must've been a Grade-A mind-reader, because Jake dragged a chair from the periphery and put it right beside his grandfather's bed.

Instead of sitting, he glanced up at Gio. A silent invitation he would've rather fled.

"Nico, it's good to see you." Big Tony reached for

him with both hands.

Gio stared at hands he'd always seen as unbreakable.

Hands that were lined, wrinkled. Creased with years he'd wasted — they'd both wasted — with their estrangement.

Callouses that were no shocker, his father had always been a hard worker, but now they stood stark against skin that'd once been lush and olive-toned, dotted with liver spots that weren't there before.

Was it from the cancer?

Hands that'd once been so strong were now as brittle as butterfly wings.

When had Big Tony aged so much?

Gio sat hard on the edge of the chair, but he immediately leaned forward and did his father's bidding, putting both his hands in the pair that'd beckoned for his touch.

He tore his gaze away so he wouldn't compare the differences and met his father's eyes again.

"It's so very good to see you, Nico," Big Tony repeated on a sigh.

"It's good to see you too, Dad," he managed, but his voice shook harder with every word.

They sat there like that, with his father still holding his hands in a firm-yet-gentle grip. At least his father's hold belied the delicate appearance of his skin.

They didn't speak for a long time.

That was all well and good for Gio, because he didn't know what the fuck to say.

Jake climbed on his lap, and Maddie came to his

side, quietly reacquainting herself with his father.

They'd met years ago a few times, but nothing more than a passing hello.

"I cannot change the past," Big Tony said after minutes that felt like hours.

"Dad, don't—"

His father lifted a much-too-slender palm and demanded silence. "I have many regrets in my life, but now that's its nearing the end, I owe apologies to many. You are one that deserves more than I can say."

Gio took a stuttering breath and shook his head.

Somehow, he couldn't hear it.

Didn't *need* to hear it, for the first time in his life.

He squeezed the hand he still held. "I don't want you to, Dad."

Big Tony's mouth set in a thin line and he shook his head. "I don't care." The declaration was strong and even.

He smirked. "There's my dad. You haven't changed a bit."

"But you have." This was a whisper.

Gio's heart dipped to his gut.

"You are a good man. I'm proud of you."

He blinked because his eyes teared, and this time he couldn't fight it. Relief washed over him that Big Tony hadn't used the words, *"I'm sorry."*

That, Gio couldn't have taken.

*I'm proud of you* was something he hadn't known he'd needed to hear from his father. Funny, things he'd always thought he'd wanted had dissipated before the old man had even opened his mouth.

"Thanks, Dad. You're a good man, too."

His father's smile was shallow, and sad. "I wasn't always."

He looked away from the old man's sunken cheeks and grayish pallor. His brown eyes were huge in his face, and cheekbones that'd always been high and regal stood out with a skeletal sharpness that made them blunt instead of attractive.

Elise had delivered the bad news with sobs, but he hadn't really believed it. Their dad was a stubborn prick who couldn't die.

*Seeing* how sick he really was jarred Gio to his soul. Things hadn't been right between them for years, but he wasn't ready for him to die.

"I always wanted the best for my family."

His father's voice brought his attention back to his face.

"Your mother was the love of my life. She was the heart of our family, and I'm relieved to be able to see her again soon." This time, Big Tony's was wistful.

Gio averted his gaze, and met Maddie's eyes.

His wife smiled and squeezed his shoulder.

Jake nestled closer, tucking his head under Gio's chin. His son's soft hair tickled but he ignored it and smiled for his father.

Words weren't really going to happen, so he just listened to his father talk about his mother in a way he'd never heard before.

Big Tony told the story of when they'd met, a beautiful blonde girl he'd claimed was too good for him. He said the first time he'd seen her in a Chicago nightclub, he'd known his fate was sealed.

Gio sat up, sliding his arm around Jake's waist so the movement wouldn't knock the kid off the chair. "Dad, Mom never lived in Chicago, you met her in Vegas."

His dad shook his head, a smile still firmly in place. "No, your mother grew up in Chicago. It was her idea to start the casino. She was the one who gave me the initial investment. *The Giovanni* was really all hers."

He looked up, exchanging a glance with Maddie.

"She kept all the records in a little brown book. I still have it, in my office."

Gio shook his head and Maddie's eyes went wide. "I'll be damned," he whispered. "Mom hated the casino."

Big Tony shook his head. "She didn't. It was *her* legacy. Your mother was behind it all; it was all her idea to get out of Chicago." Fatigue asserted itself; his voice was heavier, the words slower.

The older man leaned back into the bed, and Gio helped him adjust it so it reclined, and he could lie back on his pillows.

"Dad, the money wasn't from the Falcones?" He pitched forward again, still clinging to his son. He didn't want to yell at his dad, but he wanted an answer.

Big Tony shook his head. "No. Your mother won it at the races."

"Races?" Maddie asked.

His father focused on her and smiled. A tiny thing, as though he relished the small secret he'd kept for decades. "Yes, she liked to bet on horses. She was so good at it."

Gio smiled. He couldn't help it.

"She picked me. Not Luciano. She picked *me*." His father's repetition came out on a soft breath, and he closed his eyes.

Panic tickled, but only for a second. He watched his father's thin chest move up and down in repose, not something...worse.

Maddie shook her head. "I can't believe it."

Gio snorted. "Me, either. Man, was I wrong. And Luciano Falcone had a thing for my mom? Jesus, wouldn't life have been different?" He shook his head.

His father hadn't started the casino with mob money, after all.

"Let's let your dad sleep," Maddie whispered.

They quietly slipped from the room.

"It's not always a bad thing to be wrong, you know," his wife said, as she weaved her fingers in his again.

"Oh yeah?"

"I was wrong about you." She flashed a mischievous grin.

Gio snatched her to him and claimed her mouth.

"Ewww!" Jake yelled, interrupting before he could get lost in the kiss.

Probably not a bad thing.

"Get a room!" the little boy added with a grin.

Maddie pulled away and mock-glared. "You have got to stop hanging out with your Aunt Jamie!"

Gio laughed and shook his head. He grabbed Jake's hand, then Maddie's with his other one. "I'm glad you were wrong about me. I'm glad you came back to me. Both of you."

"I love you," she whispered.

"I love you, too."

"I love you, three!" Jake yelled loud enough to make his mother wince.

Losing his father was going to be hard, but as long as Gio had Maddie and Jake at his side, he could get through anything.

The whole deck of cards was his.

## ♥ The End ♥

*USA TODAY* Bestselling, award winning author of historical and epic fantasy romance, as well as romantic suspense, C.A. loves to dabble in different genres. If it's a good story, she'll write it, no matter where it seems to fit!

She's a hopeless romantic and always will be.

Risking it all for Happily Ever After is what she lives by!

C.A. is originally from Ohio, but got to Texas as soon as she could. She's happily married and has a bachelor's degree in Criminal Justice.

She works with kids when she's not writing.

WEBSITE: www.caszarek.com
BLOG: www.caszarekwriter.blogspot.com
TWITTER: twitter.com/caszarek
FACEBOOK: www.facebook.com/caszarek
INSTAGRAM: www.instagram.com/caszarek
GOODREADS:
www.goodreads.com/author/show/5815085.C_A_Sz
arek
BOOKBUB: www.bookbub.com/profile/c-a-szarek
AMAZON AUTHOR PAGE:
www.amazon.com/C.A.Szarek/e/B00BJY74BY
NEWSLETTER SIGNUP: https://bit.ly/2m4wT3l
EMAIL: ca@caszarek.com

www.ingramcontent.com/pod-product-compliance
Lightning Source LLC
Chambersburg PA
CBHW061039190726
48286CB00006B/1527